Dressed in Levi's and loafers, with a stethoscope hanging over his open-collared polo shirt, he looked the perfect yuppie doctor. "I just want to talk to you for a few minutes."

"Sure." She gestured toward the two chairs facing her desk. "Anytime."

He settled into one and gave her a weary smile. "This is...a personal situation."

Oh, God. Erin's mouth went dry.

"And apparently it's no good." He studied her for a long moment. "I ran into your kids again on Saturday, Erin. I'd like to know what's going on."

Lily. Had he noticed anything? Had he caught that dimple in her chin—or the pale gray shade of her eyes? Taking a deep, steadying breath, Erin recalled the promises she'd once made to her cousin Stephanie, and gave a vague wave of her hand. "I–I'm not sure what you mean."

"They were way up in the wood."

"Oh." Closing her eyes, she leaned back, pinching the bridge of her nose.

"I've seen more than just tracks–I saw a large black wolf on Saturday morning, just north of my house."

"I'll talk to them right away."

"While you're at it, I get the feeling that they've got the wrong impression of me. I'm not the monster who lives up on the hill."

Dear Reader,

Blackberry Hill is a small town nestled in a heavily forested lake area of northern Wisconsin. It's a town where most people have known each other all their lives, but there are a few newcomers, as well. Like Erin Lang, the new administrator at Blackberry Hill Memorial Hospital.

Six months ago Erin Lang's life seemed perfect—until her husband abruptly walked out, leaving her with the three troubled children they'd recently adopted. She hopes to create a warm and secure home for her young family in Blackberry Hill. She doesn't expect to run into her late cousin's husband, Dr. Connor Reynolds, or to discover that all is not what it seems at the cheerful little hospital. Patients are unexpectedly dying...Connor could be involved...and if she doesn't uncover the truth in time, someone in her own family will be next.

I hope you enjoy the story of Erin and Connor, and come back to town in 2006 for the next two books of my BLACKBERRY HILL MEMORIAL trilogy.

I also invite you to join me for *Back in Texas* in October 2005. It's the first of five books in the ranch series, HOME TO LOVELESS COUNTY. Each book, written by a different Superromance author, is set in a dying town in the beautiful Hill Country of central Texas and involves the unique people who move there as part of a modern-day homesteading program. They're all in search of new beginnings...and some of them find far more than they expected!

I love hearing from readers. There are contests, articles, photos, a free downloadable cookbook and previews of upcoming books at www.roxannerustand.com and www.booksbyrustand.com. Or you can write me at P.O. Box 2550, Cedar Rapids, Iowa 52406-2550. Send a business-size SASE and I'll send you bookmarks and other goodies!

Wishing you peace, prosperity and love,

Roxanne Rustand

ALMOST A FAMILY
Roxanne Rustand

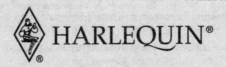

HARLEQUIN®

TORONTO • NEW YORK • LONDON
AMSTERDAM • PARIS • SYDNEY • HAMBURG
STOCKHOLM • ATHENS • TOKYO • MILAN • MADRID
PRAGUE • WARSAW • BUDAPEST • AUCKLAND

ISBN 0-373-71284-7

ALMOST A FAMILY

Copyright © 2005 by Roxanne Rustand.

This edition published by arrangement with Harlequin Books S.A.

® and TM are trademarks of the publisher. Trademarks indicated with ® are registered in the United States Patent and Trademark Office, the Canadian Trade Marks Office and in other countries.

www.eHarlequin.com

Printed in U.S.A.

Many thanks to the wonderful people who so graciously provided their expertise: Adrian P. Wydeven, mammalian ecologist, Wisconsin Department of Natural Resources, for his information on the wolves of northern Wisconsin; and Michelle Klosterman, RN, CEN (Certified in Emergency Nursing), whose experience in the operation of small-town hospitals was invaluable. Any errors in this book are mine alone. As always, best wishes and thanks to Diane, Jacquie, Nancy, Pamela and Muriel, who are continuing sources of encouragement and support.

To author Lyn Cote, with many thanks for our friendship, and for the wonderful "writers' getaway" weekends spent at your lovely lake home in northern Wisconsin. You are a treasure. Also, to my mother, Arline, whose gracious spirit, energy and humor have always been an inspiration.

CHAPTER ONE

ERIN LANG HAD EXPECTED challenges when she moved to Blackberry Hill.

She hadn't expected to run into Connor Reynolds the moment she stepped out of her minivan.

Tall, broad-shouldered and self-assured, he'd been strikingly handsome in college, but now his dark hair was longer, the lean planes and angles of his face far stronger and more interesting. Impassive, he sauntered down the sidewalk past her bumper, clearly lost in thought.

And then he caught sight of her.

He snagged his sunglasses off. The crinkles at the corners of his silver-gray eyes deepened as his startled gaze swept from her to the kids piling out of the minivan.

That glimmer of a smile faded to a grim line as he gave her a polite nod and continued on without another word.

He was, she noticed with a shake of her head, just as cool and distant as ever—not that it was any surprise.

She and her cousin had attended the same college as freshmen. Stephanie had skillfully pursued this guy, apparently choosing flash over substance, but from all accounts, their troubled marriage had been a mistake from day one.

If the family rumors were true, she'd paid for that mistake with her life.

Connor had apparently ignored his wife and immersed himself in his career, while Stephanie spiraled into deepening loneliness and depression. Two years ago, she'd lost her life driving too fast on a curving mountain road. Maybe it had been ruled an accident, but Erin still had her doubts.

Drew jostled her elbow. "Who was *that?*" he demanded.

Erin smiled down at her ten-year-old adopted son and tousled his curly black hair. "Someone from the past."

Righteous indignation flashed in Drew's deep brown eyes. "He knows you, and he didn't even say nothin'!"

"Yes, well…" She chose her words carefully. "We were never close friends."

Since her college days, she'd seen Connor just once—at Stephanie's funeral. It was one of the most difficult services she'd ever attended. All of Stephanie's friends and relatives had been grieving the loss of such a young, vibrant woman, but from her parents there'd also been a palpable undercurrent of hostility toward Connor.

In return, he'd been stony-faced and silent, holding in whatever emotions he might have felt. When Erin offered him her condolences at the grave site, the flat, cold expression in his eyes had chilled her blood.

Drew's seven-year-old brother, Tyler, tentatively edged closer to her, thumbed up his thick glasses and peered down the sidewalk, a worried frown wrinkling his forehead.

Erin rested a reassuring hand on his thin shoulders, wishing for the thousandth time that she could erase everything the boys and Lily had gone through in their young lives before they'd come to live with her. She'd adopted the boys ten months ago and Lily five months later, and they were all still struggling with the adjustment.

"Maybe that man doesn't remember my name. It's no big deal." Forcing a cheery smile, she shifted her gaze to the minivan and beckoned to Lily. "Come on, let's get the key from the Realtor so we can settle into our new place, okay? The mover's truck should be meeting us out there in an hour."

Lily climbed awkwardly out of the vehicle, her Harry Potter book still clutched in her hand, a page marked with her thumb. The trip north from Wausau had taken just a couple hours, and every mile of the way she'd been immersed in the story.

A good distraction, Erin mused as she herded her troops into the small, brick Dolby Realty building. When she'd told the kids about their move to a small town in the far north of Wisconsin, Drew had masked his worries with his usual belligerent bravado. Tyler had become even more withdrawn. But Lily—

Lily had cried over leaving her beloved fourth-grade teacher. She'd been even more distraught over leaving the little house in Wausau and her newly painted pink bedroom. The apple tree in the back-yard. The flower beds they'd all planted in a riot of colors. And no wonder—it was the first real home she'd ever had, even if the illusion of permanence hadn't lasted very long.

When Erin's husband, Sam, had abruptly an-nounced he was leaving her for another woman, he did more than simply end a six-year marriage. He brought even greater insecurity into the lives of three children who'd already endured too much.

And for that, Erin would never, ever forgive him.

Squinting at them through her bifocals, the Real-tor behind the single desk in the office patted at wisps of gray hair escaping the loose bun at the top of her head. "You must be the…:um…"

"The Langs, Mrs. Dolby. I called you last week to let you know we'd be coming this afternoon." Two months ago, the woman had taken her for a tour of four rentals in the area. "We're here to pick up the keys for the house out on Aspen Road."

The woman pursed her lips as she shuffled through a stack of files, withdrew one with a gusty sigh and spread it open on the desk. "Of course, the Hadley cabin. Six-month lease. Gas and electricity not included. Option to renew for a one-year period." She shook two silver keys out of the envelope and handed them to Erin. "Looks like everything's already signed and in order. If you have any problems, call me."

"Thanks." Erin gestured for the kids, who were riffling through the bass-fishing magazines stacked on a low coffee table under the front window. "Let's head out."

"You got that job as the new hospital administrator, right?" The older woman's voice stopped her at the door.

"Yes." Erin turned back to her and smiled. "I start on Tuesday."

"I never use the local hospital." Though Mrs. Dolby had appeared a tad absentminded, she'd been pleasant company during Erin's house-hunting expedition. There was no trace of that friendliness now.

Surprised, Erin sent the kids on out the door, then she lowered her voice. "Why not?"

"Because I'm no fool."

"Did you have a bad experience there?"

The woman gave a derisive snort as she picked up her phone and dialed a number, then launched into a rambling conversation with someone about housing inspections and septic tanks.

Erin watched her for a moment before heading back outside to join the children.

She'd worked as a nurse for years before going back to college, and knew situations could be misconstrued by the public. Rumors could start over nothing. Grieving relatives sometimes figured that modern medicine should have been able to save their loved one, no matter how hopeless the case, so they blamed the staff, the hospital, the attending physicians for their loss.

But as Erin stepped out into the early September sunshine, the stark reality of her situation hit her. She was alone now, with three children to support. She had no friends here, no relatives within several hundred miles.

Maybe this move had been a mistake.

THE KIDS WERE SILENT as Erin drove down Main Street. Lily pressed her face to the front passenger-side window, her heavy book clutched to her chest like a security blanket. In the back, each boy huddled at a window.

Three blocks of small businesses—mostly gift shops, upscale clothing stores and the sort of arts-and-crafts stores that appealed to the tourist trade—soon gave way to pine trees and a scattering of coffee shops and bars. Beyond the downtown area, a string of sporting goods stores, geared to outdoorsmen who needed anything from fishing rods to snowmobiles to mountain bikes, rimmed the shore of Sapphire Lake.

The sparkling, dark blue waves crested in the Saturday morning sunlight, jostling the array of brightly colored boats docked at a marina near the highway.

The smart, white facilities and sprawling supper club overlooking the lake spoke of money. Lots of it, if the largest boats were any clue.

Past the marina, a pretty county park followed the shore for a good half mile, then a haphazard network of tumbledown docks and aging fishing boats. A shack with a hand-painted sign promised Fishing Guide—Good Rates.

"Wow," Tyler whispered as a glittering red boat swept close to shore, sending a high spray of water arcing like diamonds. "Can we—"

"Yeah, *cool*," Drew broke in, leaning across the backseat to give his brother's shoulder a bump. "Are we getting a boat like that one?"

Erin thought about the debts she still had to pay and the shaky financial situation at the hospital, and smiled at Drew through the rearview mirror. "Probably not for a long while. I'll bet we can rent one, though. Wouldn't that be fun?"

He flopped back in his seat. "Yeah, right. Like that's gonna happen. You'll think it's too dangerous, or say it costs too much money. Like with the horses."

Erin shifted her attention back to the road, knowing that explanations would just provoke an angry response.

Back in Wausau, there'd been an old man with horses who lived just a mile away. She had no doubt that Drew had badgered the poor guy until he finally agreed to let Drew clean the stalls in exchange for riding privileges.

The next day, a woman at the local saddle shop had rolled her eyes when Erin asked her opinion. The two geldings had been used for barrel racing and had been hot as pistols, she'd said, so who knew what they might be like after not being ridden for ages?

It had been clear to Erin that a boy from the inner city would be no match for twelve hundred pounds of barely leashed energy, but Drew still hadn't forgiven her for refusing to let him ride.

A mile farther out of town, she slowed down after passing a ramshackle shed emblazoned with a faded Smoked Fish! sign. She turned up a narrow gravel road leading through a stand of aspens, then into a dark pine forest that crowded the road on either side.

"Almost there, guys," she called out.

Lily twisted in her seat, her eyes wide. "Here? All *alone?*"

"Just wait," Erin assured her. At a *Y* in the road she bore to the right, the van's suspension creaking as the road grew rougher. "I think you'll like it."

A moment later, the narrow lane ended at a small, one-and-a-half-story log home shaded by a trio of towering pines, and beyond, a meadow strewn with a late summer rainbow of rosy fireweed, blue vervain and goldenrod. Only the distant rat-a-tat of a woodpecker broke the silence.

"So, guys—what do you think?" Erin pulled to a stop in front of the little house and held her breath, hoping for a positive reaction.

The past few months had been hectic, thanks to

Sam's insistence that their house be sold as soon as possible. Perhaps he'd been right in wanting to list it before the winter slowdown in real estate, but the abrupt change had been just one more painful chapter in a fast divorce she hadn't expected.

Luckily, she'd finished her degree in hospital administration the semester before, and had found the job in Blackberry Hill. The interview and house hunt had involved a quick trip north—this place had been the only decent rental in her price range. There hadn't been a single weekend free to bring the kids to see their new home.

She'd expected them to launch out of the van like missiles, excited about seeing the place. Instead, all three remained still and silent, their expressions wary.

Erin unbuckled her seat belt and twisted around to look at them. "Just a couple of rules, okay? No fighting over bedrooms, because we'll get it all figured out. And *everyone* helps until we're done today. Any questions?"

"How far are we from town?" Drew asked, his voice heavy with suspicion. "Like, can I bike there?"

Erin shook her head. "It's almost a mile down to the road, and after that there's another couple miles of busy highway into town. I don't think that would be safe."

His eyes widened in horror. "I'm going to be *stuck* out here?"

"Monday's the Labor Day holiday, but after that

you'll be in town five days a week for school," Erin said firmly. "I'm sure we'll also be running lots of errands while we're settling in, so you aren't going to be 'stuck' out here. What do you two think? Lily? Tyler?"

Lily stared out of the front window of the car, her hands knotted in her lap. "A-are there any other kids out here?"

"I'm not sure, sweetheart. We'll find out."

"What about a dog? Can we get a dog?" Tyler piped up after a long silence. "We'd have room for a dog!"

"Yeah—what about a dog? Something big," Drew suggested with obvious relish. "Like Angelo's dog that knew how to *attack*. Not some sissy dog."

Erin could well imagine the sort of guard dog Drew meant. Their mother and her last boyfriend, Angelo, had lived in a rough inner-city area, and both of them were now serving twenty-five years of federal time for multiple drug offenses.

"I'd never buy a dog that might be dangerous," Erin warned them. "It's not worth the risk to us, or anyone who visits."

"But you'd get a nice one?" Tyler whooped with joy. "Really?" He bounced on the seat. "When? Can we go today?"

Back in Wausau, she'd never been able to get them a dog or cat because Sam had been allergic to both. "Look, guys," she said. "I know it sounds like a great idea. But first, we're going to give this town a try. If things work out—if my job goes well and if the school system is good—then we'll look into buying a house of our own. Until then, a dog just isn't possible."

"Why not?" Drew demanded. "We'd take care of it."

"This is a rental. I didn't check the lease, but I'm sure the landlord wouldn't let us."

"Please," Lily pleaded. "Can you ask? Please?"

"Well…" Erin found herself confronted by three desperately hopeful faces. "Okay. Once we get moved in, I'll ask the Realtor, but if she says no, then we have to abide by that. And if—*if*—we can have a dog here, I'll expect you all to help look after it. Deal?"

All three kids nodded, their eyes sparkling with excitement, and she knew she had to do everything in her power to make it happen.

They'd each faced the loss of one home after another, and they'd learned to avoid attachments to people and places. Maybe they weren't excited about this cabin, but having a dog to love would be wonderful therapy for them all.

From behind her car she heard the rumble of a truck creeping up the steep, rocky lane, and minutes later a small moving van lumbered into view.

"Okay, so here's the plan. The guys I hired will help us get everything into the house and put the big pieces where they belong. The rest of it is up to us." She grinned at them, her own excitement rising, as she handed Drew one of the house keys. "The sooner we get settled, the sooner we can have some fun. Let's go inside and figure out who gets which bedroom."

At that, the van doors flew open and the kids ran for the house, with Lily lagging behind as always, because of her weak left foot. At the porch, though, the boys waited for her to catch up.

Watching them, Erin's heart filled with such deep love and pride that her eyes burned.

Sam had betrayed their family, but he'd thrown away something very precious and he'd been too self-centered to even realize it.

A good job, a good town, and these children were all she needed from now on. And if a puppy could help with this latest upheaval in their lives, then so be it.

After conferring with the two men she'd hired to move her furniture, she jogged up to the house while they backed the truck to the front door.

The wide porch, with its log posts and railing, looked out over a small meadow rimmed by a narrow stream on the northern boundary. Stepping inside the double screen doors, she sighed with pleasure. The entryway opened onto a great room with a stone fireplace dominating one wall, an exposed staircase to the loft another. On the left, an archway led into the kitchen.

Lily appeared in the doorway straight ahead, which led to a hallway, two bedrooms and the bathroom. "We figure you should have the big bedroom back here," she said shyly. "I really like the other one, if that's okay. It's real pretty."

"Of course it's okay." Erin cocked her head, listening to the footsteps thundering overhead. "Sounds like the boys found the loft—did you see it?"

Lily shuddered. "Yeah, but I wouldn't want to stay up there if they did."

"This is cool!" Drew shouted.

Erin looked up at the balcony, relieved to see the broad smile on his face.

She'd figured the boys would like the loft, with its built-in bunk beds and steeply slanted ceiling. There was a little cupola on the roof, too—a steep ladder on one wall led up into a small lookout tower, glass on all sides, and she could well imagine them up there, play-ing all sorts of games involving adventure and fantasy.

"Drew!" Tyler shouted. "Quick!"

At the hint of panic in his voice, Erin rushed up the stairs and into the loft bedroom.

She could see just his Nikes and the hem of his jeans up in the cupola, then Drew scurried up the lad-der and crowded him to one side. "What is it?" she called out.

The boys were silent for a long moment, then they scrambled down the ladder, Tyler's face pale and Drew's alight with excitement. "We saw a wolf," he exclaimed. "It was huge! Right out there next to the trees."

One of the movers knocked sharply at the front, then the screen door squealed open. "Ma'am— where do you want this couch?"

"I've got to get back downstairs," Erin said. "I don't think you could've seen a wolf, though. Not here. But just in case, I want you kids to stay within sight of the cabin, hear? Don't go wandering off. And keep a close eye on Lily."

"It *was* a wolf," Drew insisted, his voice following her down the stairs. "And it had something dead in its mouth, like a big rabbit. Tyler saw it, too."

On the main floor, Lily stood by the stairs, her eyes darting toward the large casement windows of the great room. "The men say it's true," she whispered. "There are wolves here…and you can't shoot 'em, 'cause they're pro—pro—"

"Protected, unless you can prove that one of them is killing livestock," one of the men said as he backed into the living room holding one end of a sofa. "They were reintroduced in the north country ten years ago, and they've been ranging farther and farther south."

Erin thought about the half-mile lane to this cabin, and the fact that there were no close neighbors…and no friends nearby to call in an emergency.

The idea of a dog—a very *big* dog—suddenly held far more appeal.

CHAPTER TWO

BEING A NEW KID SUCKED. Being a new kid who showed up a week after school started was ten times worse.

Drew scowled at the tips of his sneakers as he waited with Tyler outside the elementary school. Lily sat on a bench behind them, her face glum.

A cabin in the woods was pretty cool, but not enough to make this any easier. Back in Milwaukee, he and Tyler had lived in a tough neighborhood where there were sirens and drug busts night and day, but at least he'd had friends. In Wausau with Erin, they'd finally started to feel at home.

But here the local kids had known each other all their lives and were already settled into the school routine.

Lily, with her white-blond hair and shy smiles, had a better chance of fitting in with kids anywhere, though the meaner ones usually made fun of her weak leg. Tyler got sick a lot and was small for his age, so classmates tried to pick on him. And Drew had never been good at sports or schoolwork, because just surviving had been tough enough.

He gazed at his brother, and thought about the nasty glances in the lunchroom. The snickers out on the playground.

Fed up, he'd shouldered one kid aside as they lined up to go back inside after recess, just as a warning.

He hoped the kids here learned quick. Anyone who thought it cool to hassle his brother or taunt Lily about her limp would have to deal with him. And then he'd end up in trouble himself, like always—with the usual lectures and detentions that had dogged him at every school.

"It's Erin," Tyler announced, his voice filled with relief at the sight of her navy Windstar pulling up in front of the school. He hopped off the bench and stood next to Drew. "Don't say nothing 'bout school."

Oh, I won't, Drew thought grimly. To Tyler, he just nodded.

Erin smiled at them as they climbed into the van and buckled their seat belts. "So how did your first day go?"

"Okay," Lily murmured.

In the backseat, Tyler and Drew exchanged glances.

"Boys?"

Drew caught her looking at them in the rearview mirror, her brow furrowed. She seemed tired and worried, and he wondered if she'd had a bad day, too. Only where she worked, she was the boss—so she could fire anybody who gave her any crap. The thought of that kind of power made Drew clench his fist, thinking of a few guys at school.

When she didn't pull away from the curb, he finally mumbled, "It was okay. I guess."

"Good." She drummed her fingers lightly on the top of the steering wheel. "You know, I was thinking…we worked so hard this weekend, getting moved in. Maybe we could do something fun. Unless, of course," she added somberly, "you have too much homework."

Lily beamed at her. "Nope!"

"It isn't really the first day, though—the other kids have been at it a week now. What sort of make-up assignments do you have so far?"

"Just some reading…and a math assignment. Not much," she said earnestly. "It won't take long."

"Tyler?"

"Just some work sheets."

"Drew?"

He couldn't hold back his snort of disgust. "Another one of those 'what did you do last summer?' papers. And a bunch of work sheets, but they aren't due till Friday."

"Hmm."

"So, what did you want to do, huh?" Lily tugged at Erin's sleeve. "We got time."

Smiling mysteriously, Erin drove slowly down Main and pulled up in front of the Realtor's building. "Just wait a minute."

She locked their doors and disappeared inside the building, but was back in only a few seconds. "No luck," she said as she slid behind the wheel. "I don't have a phone number for the owner of our cabin and I'd hoped the Realtor might have heard from him by now."

"About a dog?"

Erin nodded. "I'm sorry, guys. I'd hoped we could go looking today. Anyone up for getting some pizza before we head out of town?"

Scowling, Drew slumped down in his seat. Promises. They never meant much—he'd learned that a long time ago.

"DO YOU NEED ANYTHING else?" The slender young woman shot a surreptitious glance at her wristwatch as she hesitated at the door of Erin's office. Eager, Erin knew, to race out the front door of Blackberry Hill Memorial to meet her boyfriend, who lingered at the curb in his red Mustang every day at noon.

"I think I've got enough for now, Beth," Erin said dryly, waving a hand over the stack of files on her desk. "Check in with me when you get back."

"Madge is back from lunch, so I'll let her know what you've been doing, just in case you need anything." Beth waggled her fingers and hurried down the hallway, her heels clicking against the polished terrazzo floor.

Sighing, Erin rounded her desk and shut the door, then continued looking through the files. She'd known that the hospital was in trouble before accepting the job. Now, on her fourth day here, she was learning just how much. The picture was bleak.

With operating losses exceeding twelve percent of patient revenue, and fewer than eight hundred admissions per year, there were definite challenges ahead. And on the second Thursday of October, she'd be standing before the board to explain what was wrong and how she planned to fix it.

No small task, she thought grimly, flipping through another file.

This was her first time at the helm, and success here would mean she could move upward if this town didn't suit. Failure would dog her forever and limit her chances at making a good, secure living for her children.

At a soft rap on the door, she glanced up. "Come in," she called out, "it's open."

Madge Wheeler bustled in, her bulky frame encased in a heavy, hand-knit red sweater and plaid skirt. Sparkly crystal earrings dangled beneath a cloud of curly gray hair. "Beth told me to drop in."

"Thanks. I do have a few questions." Erin tipped her head toward the stack of employee files. "How long have you been here?"

Madge pulled a chair up to the front edge of Erin's desk. "It's all there. I started here as a teenager, helping in the kitchen. Worked my way into the front office, from receptionist to clerk, and after thirty years, I became the office manager."

"And Grace Fisher?"

"Director of nursing for thirty-five years. Retiring this year, she says, though she's been saying that for a while now and she never gets around to it." Madge's voice was filled with pride. "This hospital has continuity. None of those fly-by-night employees here today, gone tomorrow. We have good people and they stay. Newest one on the payroll is the Baxter girl, just out of high school, but the average employee has been here for seventeen years. I know, because I wrote up a report for the hospital's fiftieth anniversary last year."

Erin frowned. "I need to meet with you and Grace soon—tomorrow, if possible. I also need to have a meeting with the medical staff. Can you set up a date?"

Madge pursed her lips. "Something wrong?"

Nothing that more patients and fewer employees couldn't cure, but given the small town and the longevity of the staff, change wasn't going to be easy.

"I know you and Grace have been here a long time—you two are the true experts on the hospital and what makes it tick. I'm sure you're both aware that we've got to look for ways to turn this place around, or it could go under."

Madge's expression grew wary. "A town this size isn't ever going to have a big city hospital. No one expects that here."

"But the board does expect it to break even. If it folds, and the entire patient load goes to Henderson

Regional, this town will lose a very important public service for young and old alike."

"True…"

"I'm counting on you and Grace to work with me as a team. I want this place to succeed just as much as you do." Erin picked up a pile of papers and tapped them into a neat stack. "I want to find effective solutions. Ones that will protect jobs here and provide better service to the community."

The older woman drew herself up. "Mr. Randall ran a tight ship," she huffed. "We never had a penny missing, and he was well liked in this town."

But that didn't make him a good manager. From what Erin had found so far, it appeared that her predecessor had spent more time socializing on the golf course than tending to business. She'd called a number of times to ask questions before taking this job, and quickly realized that he came in late and left early, and also seemed to have a lot of "business lunches."

"I'm sure he did well," Erin said carefully. "But sometimes a little change is a good thing, don't you think?"

"I'll continue to do my best," Madge said stiffly as she rose to her feet. "Grace has the day off tomorrow, but I'm sure she can meet with us Monday."

"Sounds good."

"The doctors have a weekly breakfast at Ollie's Diner on Thursday mornings, so that might be a good place to meet them. Otherwise, trying to find a time when they could all be at the hospital together would likely set back your meeting a good three weeks."

"Isn't a diner a little too public?"

Madge waved away her concern. "They always use the booth at the back, past the ice machine and the bathrooms. No one could listen in even if they wanted to." She tapped her pencil against her front teeth. "I'll go do some calling and make sure they all plan to meet next week."

"That would be fine. Thanks." Erin watched the woman leave, then flipped open another file and began poring over the names and numbers before her.

Of the seven board members, Hadley had been the most supportive of her, Dr. Olson had been rather cool and Dr. Anderson had been openly dubious about her qualifications. The mayor and the others had been more enthusiastic.

Erin would succeed at revitalizing the Blackberry Hill hospital whether or not she had full cooperation from everyone involved, but so far, it wasn't looking like an easy job.

And with a family to support, she couldn't afford to fail.

STARING OUT AT THE BRIGHT Saturday morning sunshine, Connor Reynolds whistled to his old yellow lab, Maisie, and waited until he heard her toenails click across the kitchen flooring before he opened the door wide for her to join him on the porch.

He took a deep breath, smelling pine and damp earth. Peace. Quiet. Here, he had complete solitude, except for the dog and a few larks trilling from the tops of the pine trees surrounding his house.

The days were long. The nights…longer. But despite everything that had happened, at least he had this, and life was good. *At last.*

The sudden jolt from the past—seeing Stephanie's studious little cousin a week ago—had startled him, bringing back too many unwanted memories, and the irony of seeing Erin with three beautiful, healthy children had reopened old wounds. He hadn't even trusted himself to speak.

After graduating from medical school, he'd worked tirelessly to establish a successful practice. Tried so hard to make his marriage work. Imagined a home bustling with children and a wife who loved him. Who would have guessed quiet little Erin would end up with the richer life?

Or that she would have changed so much. He remembered her as a petite little thing with glasses and her brown hair pulled back into a severe ponytail. Now, her hair was very short, accenting her big brown eyes and delicate features—like a young Audrey Hepburn in blue jeans. She couldn't be more different from Stephanie's blond, hard-edged sophistication.

With luck Erin was just passing through town. He didn't need a constant reminder of how he'd failed.

Reaching down to stroke the dog's soft coat, he

stepped off the porch and started toward his favorite trail at a jog, Maisie at his side.

Already the leaves were turning, the dark pines a perfect foil for the splashes of crimson and orange of the maples, the bright yellow of the aspens. The bowed grass was slick with first frost; the damp earth and fallen pine needles released their heady perfume as he ran.

The crisp, early September air burned in his lungs as he continued up the track, dodging rough-edged boulders and fallen trees.

At the top of the rugged, rocky slope above his property he stopped briefly to let the old dog catch her breath.

It was his favorite place, this craggy peak. An hour or so to the east lay the Upper Peninsula of Michigan. To the north, Canada. There was almost a holy atmosphere here, with a view of thousands of acres of pine forest and lakes in every direction. The vast reaches of northern Wisconsin made him feel small. Inconsequential. Made his past seem like nothing more than a minor flaw in the cosmos. Here, he—

From behind him came a loud whoop and a holler, and the sound of what had to be a hundred kids racing up the trail. Branches cracked. Pebbles skittered down the rocky precipice behind him.

The interlopers—two vaguely familiar, bedraggled and dirt-smudged boys—skidded to a stop when they caught sight of Connor and the dog.

Maisie, never much of a guard dog to begin with, promptly flopped over on her back and thumped her tail, her tongue lolling in a blatant appeal for attention.

The kids glanced uncertainly at each other, then took a step back.

"Who are you?" Connor asked sharply. A keen awareness of the dangers in this rough terrain, coupled with the surprise at seeing two children—alone—gave his voice an edge that sent the boys back another step. He softened his tone. "Are your parents with you?"

The two exchanged glances again—probably sensing the danger of telling *that* to a stranger—and the taller one leveled a defiant glare at Connor.

"Boys, you can't—"

But they both spun and raced down the trail, the sound of them skidding and crashing through the brush gradually fading away until the silence was almost too great.

Obviously disappointed, Maisie lumbered to her feet and gave Connor a reproachful look.

"I didn't mean to scare them, girl." He stared pensively in the direction they'd gone, remembering the family he'd almost had. That younger boy was probably about the same age as his own would have been....

After Stephanie's death he'd immersed himself in his career. He'd worked out every day until he was aching and exhausted. Ran until his lungs burned, then he'd traveled for months. Nothing helped. His grief and guilt had haunted him for over a year after he lost her.

It was clear he wasn't cut out for parenthood. He'd failed his wife, his unborn son, and even now his dog was better with kids than he was.

Cursing under his breath—knowing that the nightmares would be back tonight—he whistled sharply to Maisie and headed farther up the trail at a faster pace.

CHAPTER THREE

AT THE SOUND OF FOOTSTEPS coming up the front steps, Erin froze.

The dead-end lane leading to her house meant no one ever simply drove by. It was dark and quiet out here—even now, at eight o'clock in the evening. What had possessed her to choose such an isolated location?

Lily and Tyler, playing with their newest LEGO set in a corner of the dining area, looked up at Erin, then exchanged worried glances when the caller knocked on the door.

She gave them a reassuring smile and, moving to the entryway, pulled back the lacy curtain from the window in the door and flipped on the porch light.

Connor?

A stranger might have been preferable to finding him standing there, his expression cold and distant. What on earth was he doing here?

Taking a deep breath, she unlocked the door and released the safety chain. "Yes?"

His eyes widened. *"Erin?"*

The awkward moment lengthened as they stared at each other.

"*This* is the guy." Drew came to stand next to her, his chin lifted at a belligerent angle. "The one we saw in town that first day, and then yesterday, in the woods. I told you!"

Erin rested a hand on Drew's tense shoulder. "Kids, I'd like you to meet Dr. Connor Reynolds." She introduced each of the children, then frowned at Connor. "The boys said you seemed angry at them and that you looked 'really mean.'"

"I sure didn't intend to frighten them." Connor gave a low laugh. "And I'm not sure how 'mean' I could have seemed, with Maisie begging them to pet her." He snapped his fingers, and a huge yellow lab appeared in the doorway at his side, her eyes warm and friendly and her tail wagging. "They were a long ways from here, in a fairly rugged area. I only asked them if their parents were close by, and they took off running." He lowered his voice. "You may have heard about the wolves around here. I've seen fresh tracks several times since last weekend, and I was worried about the boys being alone."

Frowning, Erin studied Drew. "You were supposed to stay within sight of the house."

"We didn't go far," Drew retorted, a dark flush rising in his cheeks.

His gaze dropped, and she knew he was hedging. "You didn't follow the rules, then. We'll talk about this later."

Drew glared at Connor. "Yeah, right—like we did anything wrong. Big deal."

"Why don't you boys go on upstairs while I talk to Dr. Reynolds," she said firmly. She turned back to Connor as his words registered. "When I saw you in town, I assumed you were just vacationing. You *live* around here?"

"I moved into my uncle Ed's place on the hill a week ago." Connor cleared his throat. "He owns all of the surrounding property, including this cabin, and Hazel down at Dolby Realty said you had some questions. I'm not sure if I can help, but…"

"Ed Hadley is your *uncle?* I knew you were from northern Wisconsin, but…" Her thoughts spinning, Erin stared at him before finally finding her voice again. "I—I'm sorry. Please, come in."

He hesitated, then stepped inside the hallway.

There'd never been much love lost between Stephanie's wealthy family and Erin's. Though they'd been related, the social chasm between them had been far too great, and the families barely knew one another. After college graduation, Erin had only seen her second cousin at a few rare reunions, and with the exception of the brief encounter at Stephanie's funeral, she hadn't run into Connor at all.

When had he grown so tall, so broad through his chest and shoulders? She hadn't noticed at the funeral, but maturity had added layers of muscle and an air of confident masculinity, and the years had sculpted his face into rugged, intriguing angles.

His silver-blue eyes, framed with thick black lashes and sweeping brows, had changed most of all. The careless sensuality of youth was now shadowed with experience and hints of hidden pain. Intriguing.

He was far more polite today than when she'd seen him last, but she knew what lurked beneath the handsome surface of this man. Flustered, she asked, "Are…you're planning to practice in Blackberry Hill?"

"I start covering Ed's clinic tomorrow, but just for the next three months or so, while he considers retirement."

"Retirement?" The dapper old skunk had never once mentioned that he was planning to take off before she ever arrived, leaving a nephew in his place.

A nephew, Erin thought grimly, whom she could have happily avoided for the rest of her life without a moment of regret. "Dr. Hadley and I met when I interviewed here. He convinced me to take my job at the hospital, and then offered me his rental house. I looked forward to working with him."

Something akin to wariness flashed across Connor's face. "You're working at the hospital?"

"Right. I guess we'll run into each other, if you admit any patients." She gave him a forced smile. "I'm the new administrator."

"I didn't recognize your married name. Congratulations." His handshake was warm and strong, though he didn't appear delighted over the news.

"Thanks."

"Ask him," Lily stage-whispered into the growing silence. "Please?"

Shaking off her odd reaction to Connor's touch, Erin tipped her head toward Lily. "The kids have been begging for a dog. I'd feel safer with one around, but the Realtor found a clause in the fine print of my contract stating no pets. Can you ask Ed for me?"

Probably without conscious thought, Connor's fingers had been rubbing Maisie behind her ears and under her collar. Now, he looked down at the dog with open affection, and she lifted her nose to return that obvious adoration in full measure. "Go ahead. I'm sure it'll be okay."

"But the contract." Erin had to raise her voice to be heard over Lily's whoops of excitement. "Should we—"

"I'm sure you and the kids will take care of any problems a dog might cause. Ed gave me free rein here, because he's so confident I'll decide to buy him out." Connor laughed. "I guess he doesn't know me that well."

And I don't, either. Not anymore. "So you'll be leaving this winter?"

He shrugged. "I might find some rural area out West…or head back to the bright lights and big city. I have no desire to settle in one place."

A city—exactly what she planned to avoid. After Erin's small-town childhood, the bustle and crime and anonymity of city life made her feel dehuman-

ized and alone no matter how many people jostled
her at a bus stop or shoved past her on a busy sidewalk.

This town already felt like home, and knowing
Connor Reynolds would soon be on his way out of
Blackberry Hill should have given her a sense of peace.

So how could she possibly feel regret?

FACING MADGE WHEELER and Grace Fisher across
a conference table on Monday morning made Erin
feel as if she was taking a stand against two elderly
but determined bulldogs. Both of them were a good
two hundred pounds of solid experience and steely
determination.

And both of them were looking back at her with
narrowed eyes and pursed lips, clearly suspicious of
her intentions.

"This hospital has provided good service to our
town for over fifty years," Madge said stubbornly. "I
don't see how changing everything is a good idea."

Grace, the less defensive of the two, merely gave
Erin a patient smile. "Maybe it's a good idea, trying
to get more specialists out here. But they aren't
going to come. George tried that years ago."

"We need more admissions. We need more revenue. In a town that hasn't grown more than five percent during the past three years, we can't count on
a population increase to make it happen." Erin
tapped a forefinger on the table. "This is a resort
area. A place where people buy cabins on water and

spend long weekends away from the city. I've seen some incredible homes along the lake. Who lives in those places?"

"Weekenders from Chicago or Milwaukee or Minneapolis." Madge gave an airy wave of her hand. "Some fly private planes and land out at the municipal airport just east of town."

Grace chuckled. "Such as it is. It's a grass strip out on the Lindstrom farm, and there's just one approach. You get a crosswind there and landing is enough to scare you right out of your girdle."

Erin looked out the windows at a wall of pine trees. "It's a beautiful area. There are bound to be some specialists who already vacation here—or who'd be interested in a tax write-off. They could work a day or so, a couple times a month, then have a weekend place on the lake to relax. Not to mention physicians from the Green Bay area who could come hold specialty clinics."

"Why, when there's not enough patients here now?" Madge snorted. "What good would that do?"

"Where do people go for an oncologist, cardiologist or allergist? How far do they need to drive?"

"An hour or more," Grace said slowly. "But they're already established patients in other clinics by now."

Erin ran a finger down a column of figures on the paper in front of her. "We've got just five thousand residents in this town, but I figure there must be another ten thousand or more in our market area. People who could become loyal to this hospital. Who could use doctors who'd admit them here for in-patient care."

Madge and Grace exchanged uncomfortable glances.

"What?" Erin urged, when neither of them spoke. "We're here to discuss possibilities. Adding specialty clinics would certainly help."

"But it probably won't happen," Grace said with a long, drawn-out sigh. "There's some bad history here, over this same sort of thing."

An oppressive weight settled into Erin's chest as she studied the grim faces across the table. "Tell me."

Grace fiddled with a pencil. "Ten years back, the neighboring town had a hospital like this one—both of them struggling, both competing for patients. Neither was big enough for a full-time physician on staff, so the doctors all rotated through scheduled times to be there—just like we handle things here now. Everyone wanted something better for their own community."

"Our old administrator—the guy before George—made big promises," Madge added. "Talked about a new lab and radiology unit, and state-of-the-art equipment. Said he was going to have a beautiful new medical clinic built next door, and talked some of the doctors into investing heavily."

"He said he had big grants coming, too," she scoffed. "He spent thousands and thousands of dollars on feasibility studies and planning, and even contracted some expensive remodeling projects. Most of it fell through, leaving the hospital in debt."

"Everyone must have been upset," Erin murmured.

"More than that. When the other hospital folded, those doctors didn't transfer their patients here. Instead, they started referring clear over to Henderson Regional, and even some of our own doctors jumped ship. Henderson is more than fifty miles away, so our town lost trade, as well. There's still a lot of hostility over it."

"And George—how did he handle the situation?"

Madge's expression softened. "He did his best. He and his wife were wonderful assets to this community."

"He *didn't* handle it," Grace said shortly. "Not well. George was good with the staff. He was honest and caring. But he didn't like controversy and preferred smoothing ruffled feathers to taking an assertive stance."

Erin stifled a sigh. "So you don't think it's possible to lure specialists here."

"You know what it's like at state nursing or medical conventions. People talk, word spreads. I'd say it would take a miracle."

Erin shuffled through her papers, withdrew a summary of the financial status of the hospital that had been presented to the board last year, and pushed it across the table. "I know you've both seen this before, but this is the past. The future has to bring change, or we're looking at significant layoffs within the next six months."

Madge stiffened. "George never—"

"The hospital has been running at *eight* full-time equivalents per occupied bed." At the look of confusion in the woman's eyes, Erin added, "That's like saying we have eight full-time employees per patient, when you add full- and part-time staff. That's almost twice what the ratio should be, and we also have a high number of empty beds."

"But the patient care we give is excellent!"

"Maybe so, but that level of revenue per employee just isn't feasible if we're to operate in the black," Erin said firmly. "Still, if we can offer more services, build our market share and reduce staffing through attrition rather than layoffs, I know we can turn this place around."

At the word *layoffs,* Madge blanched.

"I need support—from the doctors, the community and especially the staff. Anyone not willing to change will need to think about whether or not they still belong here."

After a long pause, Grace's eyes twinkled. "I do believe you can do it." She gave Madge a nudge. "Right?"

Madge swallowed hard. "I *need* my job. So do my niece and my brother-in-law, and all the other people who work here. I...guess we'll have to do what it takes."

Erin stood and shook Grace's hand, then Madge's.
She watched pensively as they left her office.

It was a lukewarm response, but it was a start.

CHAPTER FOUR

BY THE TIME SHE GOT the kids ready for school and dropped them off at George Washington Elementary, Erin was ready for a strong cup of coffee and a few minutes' peace.

Lily had burst into tears over a missing homework assignment. Tyler hadn't been able to find his shoes or his baseball mitt. And Drew had announced that his teacher was dumb, school was a waste of time and he wasn't going back.

Not for the first time, she thought grimly about her ex-husband, who'd chosen to cavort with some pretty thing half his age rather than face the responsibilities he'd chosen when he and Erin had decided to adopt.

Single parenting was a challenge she hadn't expected, though given the choice of being married to Sam or having these children, she knew she'd gotten the far better deal.

At the single-story brick hospital, Erin walked through the wide front doors and greeted Beth, the receptionist, who was sitting at the desk in the lobby.

Past the open double doors to the left, the west wing housed a nurses' station, thirty long-term care beds and five beds designated for skilled care. The recreation and dining rooms were at the far end.

She waved to several patients in wheelchairs who were out in the hall, then continued straight ahead to the north wing, which housed her office, the other administrative areas, the main pharmacy and several infrequently used surgical suites.

From the first moment she'd stepped inside, she'd loved this place, with its big, old-fashioned windows and small-town atmosphere. It was a microcosm of a big city hospital, really—offering many of the same services, but on a much smaller scale.

At the sound of a shrill alarm, she spun around and hurried through the lobby to the east-wing nurses' station, which served the single, long corridor of hospital in-patient rooms. A few patients peered into the empty hallway from their doorways, then disappeared. At the end of the corridor, the double doors into the emergency department remained closed.

Surprised, Erin watched the lone nurse at the east desk reach across a stack of patient charts and flip a button to silence the alarm, then pick up a phone and dial a number.

"I think Frieda is dusting again," she whispered to Erin, her hand over the receiver. "This happens every Tuesday, the day she cleans her—" She suddenly held up a hand and talked into the phone.

"Frieda, this is Marcia at the hospital. Are you all right?" The nurse rolled her eyes. "I know, I know. Just don't worry about it, okay?"

After another few minutes of conversation, Marcia cradled the receiver and grinned up at Erin. "There's a base receiver in her living room, and she carries an emergency alarm on a cord around her neck. I'm not sure if she really worries that much about the dust or if it's an excuse to talk to us, but she sets off that alarm every Tuesday morning, and almost at the same time. If we ever *didn't* hear from her, we'd worry."

"Sounds like you know her well."

Marcia smiled. "In this town, we know everyone well. Frieda's ninety-six, still does her own housework and she's sharp as a tack. We should all be so lucky."

Erin glanced at the chart rack along the back of the station. This morning, eight of the charts bore name labels. Not many, given the number of available beds. "How is everything going down here?"

"Three patients in the E.R. last night—one asthma, a broken wrist and a chest pain. Dr. Olson was on call."

"Anyone admitted?"

Marcia chuckled. "Not on his watch—unless you're about dead." She ran a finger down a clipboard in front of her. "The Paulson boy has been discharged and will be going home this afternoon. Frank Willoughby will probably be going back to the nursing home after the radiologist reads his chest X-rays tomorrow."

"He had pneumonia, right?"

"Yep. A double, but he's doing really well." The blonde smiled. "He's the first patient the new doctor has admitted since he took over for Hadley on Monday. Nice guy."

"Oh?"

"Definitely the strong and silent type—and man, those gorgeous eyes…" Her voice drifted off in pure appreciation. "Like a guy would ever need those lashes, you know? It just isn't fair."

"Really," Erin said dryly.

The nurse's eyes flew open and she blushed. "Um…sorry."

"No problem. Have you seen Grace this morning?"

"On Wednesdays she usually comes around ten and stays until seven. Should I leave her a message?"

"I'll just catch her later, but thanks."

Erin moved on down the hallway, inspecting the terrazzo for dust and the door frames for paint chips and scratches. At the far end, she pushed through the double doors marked E.R.—Staff Only and found the hospital's third-shift housekeeper industriously attacking the gleaming floor with long swipes of her mop.

From her employee file, Erin knew Mrs. Banks was a widow of nearly seventy, but from all reports she still considered the hospital's cleanliness her mission in life, and had no intention of slowing down. According to Madge, she often talked to people who weren't there, and rarely deigned to speak to people who *were,* but that disconcerting tendency had never affected her efficiency.

"You're doing a fine job," Erin called out to her.

The woman glanced over her shoulder and nodded as she mopped her way past the admissions desk.

Carl Miller, the hospital's only male nurse, glanced up from the chart he was working on at the desk and smiled.

"Did you have a busy night?" Erin asked.

He peered at her over his glasses. "Yes, but that makes the time go faster…or so they say."

"What do you do when it's slow?"

"With all the regulations these days, there's never enough time to catch up on documentation. *Believe* me."

"Is the staffing adequate?"

"No, but what place can afford that? We all pitch in, and Grace does call in an extra nurse if the census goes high enough."

Erin moved past the desk and peered into the exam rooms, one by one. "Tell me—if you could write up a wish list, what would it be?" she called out to him.

"New state-of-the-art crash carts, fully stocked," he replied without hesitation, his voice edged in sarcasm. "A new cardiac monitoring system for the

E.R. and hospital side. New beds and new mattresses for every room. A new PACS system, for digitalized X-rays. But of course, I'm dreaming."

At the sound of footsteps behind her, she turned. Connor Reynolds was coming down the aisle. "Good list," he said. "Personally, I'd add a larger MRI, a dialysis unit and a wellness program. That's just for starters."

Erin ignored the heightened awareness she felt at the sound of his voice. *Awareness? How about hunger, just simple hunger.* With the ruckus at home, she hadn't had time for breakfast, and after her morning walk-through, she really needed to grab something from one of the snack machines in the staff lounge. "I couldn't agree more. If money wasn't an issue, those items would all be part of a very long list."

"There are ways," he countered. "Rental programs. Grants. Building a bequest program." A faint smile played across his sensual mouth. "Bake sales."

"I'll keep all that in mind."

When he walked past her, his dry glance suggested he didn't believe change was possible at Blackberry Hill Memorial.

Feeling a flash of irritation, she watched him disappear into a patient room. *Just wait,* she said under her breath, wishing not for the first time that she was five inches taller and had a far more imposing demeanor.

Like her three sisters, she'd been gifted with her family's genetic heritage for fine bones, which apparently made men think she was helpless, and she had the pixie sort of face that made them assume she couldn't think for herself. That she'd been a tomboy, ran on the track team in high school and had taken more self-defense classes than she could count had never given her the aura of strength she'd like to project.

Nodding at Carl, she turned to go.

"Carl—come in here, stat." Connor's sharp voice cut through the silence.

Surprised, she looked over her shoulder and saw Carl hurry into room 22. A split second later he darted back out, grabbed the electronic blood pressure unit sitting in the hallway, and pushed it into the room.

Frank Willoughby's room, she remembered. A sweet old guy and a favorite with the nurses, from what she'd heard. *Please, Lord, let him be all right.*

But one minute stretched to three, then five. No code blue, no rush for equipment or race to surgery.

Walking over to the nurses' station, she looked at the shelves of patient charts. On the spine of Willoughby's there was a bright orange DNR—Do Not Resuscitate—sticker, so there hadn't been an option to call a code blue.

She knew, even before Carl came out and shook his head, that Frank was gone.

His expression grim, Carl settled down at the phone to make the usual calls to family members, the nursing home and the mortuary designated on the face sheet of the chart.

Erin moved to the doorway of the old man's room and found Connor in a chair by the bed, his head bowed and his hands clasped loosely between his knees.

He glanced up at her. "Lost him. His last X-ray showed a lot of improvement, and he was on the verge of being discharged. But with his overall health and age, he'd signed the Do Not Resuscitate forms."

"I'm sorry." Erin stepped inside the room. "Was it his pneumonia, do you think?"

"That, or his heart, or any number of other things. He had a diagnosis list a mile long. But dammit, he was doing well last night. If I could have coded him…" Connor shook his head as he stood and smoothed back the old man's wispy hair. "He swore he planned to beat me at a round of golf the day he was discharged, and I bet he would have, if either of us actually knew how to play." Connor straightened the man's gown, then pulled the blanket up. "He teased me about that, too. Said he didn't think it was natural that a doctor didn't play golf."

The emotion in Connor's voice touched her. "Will there be an autopsy?"

"Doubt it. He was ninety-three, he had chronic health problems. He was hospitalized for pneumonia. In cases like this one, the coroner usually just goes ahead and releases the body to the funeral home."

She knew that was true. "Sorry—I hear he's your first admission to this hospital."

With a heavy sigh, Connor settled back in his chair. "You never get used to this."

"Are you staying here awhile?"

"As long as I can—hopefully, until his family arrives. I don't need to be at the clinic until nine. I asked Carl to call the chaplain, so he'll be here, as well."

Surprised, Erin stepped out of the room and headed down the hall toward the main lobby and her office.

Death was a given in a hospital setting. Healthy people weren't admitted, and despite the very best of care and technology, not everyone made it. Most doctors and nurses eventually developed a level of professional distance, trying to protect themselves from the pain of losing a patient, and Connor's reaction was unusual.

She recalled the man she'd known during her college days. His cool, sophisticated manner. His bored indifference.

So who would've guessed he actually did have a heart?

DREW KICKED A ROCK into the ditch as the big yellow school bus pulled away. "This sucks. Two whole days until the weekend!"

"At least we get to ride a real school bus home now. That's cool." Tyler hurried to catch up, tugging on his sleeve as a reminder that Lily was lagging behind. They both turned to see her bent over something in the ditch.

"Come on," Drew shouted impatiently. "You can pick some stupid flowers at home."

"Isn't flowers. Come here, quick!"

Drew rolled his eyes at Tyler. "Like I'm gonna care about this." But he headed back anyway, through the chest-high weeds in the ditch, with Tyler at his heels.

His heart flopped like a fish on a hook when he saw what she was looking at.

A black-and-white-spotted *dog.*

More of a half-grown puppy, really, with huge dark eyes, silky ears and soft wavy hair. Its ribs and hip bones stuck out and its long pink tongue lolled from its panting mouth. Clumps of dried mud covered its legs.

"Ooh," he breathed as he sank to his knees next to the cowering animal. "How'd it get here?"

Tyler hovered over his shoulder. "Is he hurt? Maybe he got hit by a car."

Lily shook her head. "I touched him and he didn't whimper. I think he's just lost and scared. I think we should take him home."

The three looked at each other.

"Erin did say we could get a dog," Tyler murmured.

Drew fought a smile. "And that man said it was okay."

"Maybe he belongs to someone, though. Someone who misses him a lot," Lily said sadly. "Wouldn't be fair."

"What if we put up a notice?" Imagining a very *small* notice, maybe just one of them, tacked to that telephone pole across the street, Drew stroked the dog. He felt knots of brambles tangled in its coat. "But I don't think the owner cares much—just look at how bad his fur is. No one has brushed this poor guy in a long time."

Lily sighed with joy. "We could name him… Buttercup!"

Drew shuddered. "Or *Bruno*."

"Or Scout, because he was looking for a new home," Tyler ventured.

"C'mon—maybe he'll follow us."

They scrambled out of the ditch, all calling to him, but the puppy hung back, whimpering, then crept farther into the weeds.

"He's too scared," Lily whispered. "We need a leash."

Drew surveyed all three of their backpacks for any straps that could be detached, then scanned the ground. "Maybe we can take turns carrying him. If he'll let us."

Drew struggled back through the tall weeds and knelt by the shivering pup. "Come on, Bruno."

The puppy had such fear in his eyes that a lump grew in Drew's throat and hot tears prickled beneath his eyelids.

"I know, buddy," he said softly, remembering his mother's belt and explosive temper. He never let anyone see the scars on his back from the lash of that belt buckle, but even now he could feel the pain and the terror. Her boyfriend's fists had been worse. "I've been real scared sometimes, too."

He held out a hand, palm up, until the puppy belly-crawled forward a few inches. "Would you rather be Scout?" He laughed a little as the pup nuzzled his fingers. "That must be a yes."

Gathering the puppy in his arms, he scrambled back to his feet and made his way up onto the road through the treacherous underbrush, stumbling under the weight of the dog.

Breathless, he grinned at Tyler and Lily. "He's happy, I think. Let's go."

After a few hundred feet, Drew handed him over to Tyler, then Lily took a turn. By the time they reached the turnoff for their cabin, Drew's feet hurt and his throat felt dry as sandpaper. He'd ended up carrying the dog most of the way, and now it felt twice as heavy as it had at first. At the sound of a car coming up the road, he turned eagerly to flag Erin down.

It wasn't her minivan, darn it—it was Dr. Reynolds's black Tahoe. Disappointed, Drew turned back toward home, but the vehicle pulled up beside them, and Reynolds rolled down his window. "I see you three got your dog."

"Sorta," Tyler said. "We kinda found h—"

"Yeah, we got a dog," Drew interrupted, elbowing Tyler in the ribs. "Come *on,* Ty. Let's go."

But Lily was too far away to silence.

"We found him in the ditch by the highway," she piped up. "We named him Scout."

Reynolds frowned. "He's probably just lost. Does he have tags?"

"He doesn't have no collar," Drew said quickly. "And he's skinny, like he's been starving. He doesn't have a home."

"And he's full of brambles," Lily added.

"Just don't get your hopes up too high." The man had sunglasses on, but a corner of his mouth sort of curved up, as if he was almost going to smile. "You kids know you shouldn't ever go with strangers, but can I give you a ride up to your house? You've had a long walk up here with that dog."

Lily nodded and started to speak, but Drew gave a sharp jerk of his head and cut her short. "No. We can almost see our house from here."

"I understand. You're a good big brother, kid." He twisted in the front seat to reach for something in the back, then stepped out of his car with a leather leash. "You can keep this—it might help a little."

"Thanks," Drew mumbled as the man fashioned a loop at one end and slipped it over Scout's neck.

"I'm no vet, but I think this guy needs a thorough exam, his vaccinations and a good worming." Reynolds ran a practiced hand over the dog's thin body. "If he has a home, it sure isn't a good one. What do you think your mom is going to say about this?"

"She *said* we could get a dog," Lily said shyly.

"And now we have one that's free!" Tyler added with an exuberant victory punch in the air.

"Good luck." Reynolds paused at the open door of his vehicle and gave Drew a level look that said, *Don't get your hopes up, kid.*

"Jeez," Drew muttered irritably after the black SUV headed on up the hill. "Why don't you guys tell the whole world that we found a stray?"

Tyler's wide grin faded. "He's our neighbor."

"But did you hear what he said? I bet he's gonna ask everyone he sees in town, and then for sure someone will come after Scout!"

He curved his arms a little tighter around the dog, and immediately Scout gave him a slurpy kiss up the side of his face.

There was no way anyone was going to take this dog away, he vowed silently. No way at all.

CHAPTER FIVE

"PLEASE, PLEASE, *PLEASE,*" Lily begged. "We gotta keep him. Someone prob'ly just dumped him out on the road and left him to starve!"

Erin surveyed the three children standing on the porch above her, and adjusted the shoulder strap of her purse. "Let's talk about this inside, okay?"

They parted like the Red Sea for her to pass, Drew clutching the puppy to his chest, his mouth curled mutinously, Lily's face a mask of desperate hope and Tyler... His expression alone would have melted the coldest heart. Clearly, he'd already decided that the situation was hopeless, and the sadness in his eyes made her own burn.

"I'm not an ogre, you know." She smiled as she hoisted her sack of groceries and her purse onto the kitchen counter. "I did promise you could get a dog. I was hoping we could go on Saturday."

"But this one *needs* us," Lily persisted. "We wanted a dog, and this one just appeared. It's like it was meant to be."

Erin reached out to stroke the dog's damp, silky

head. He smelled suspiciously like her twelve-dollars-a-bottle shampoo, and a glance toward the kitchen revealed a very wet floor littered with her best company towels.

"He's darling. But what if there are kids just like you who are crying over their lost friend?"

Tyler bit his lower lip. "We figured we could post some notices."

"Yeah. I could do that," Drew said quickly. "All over."

"If someone loved him, how come he's so skinny?" Lily reached out and ran her hand along his ribs. "Just look. And he was covered with burrs, and one of his paws had dry blood on it. Anyway, there aren't even any houses close to here, 'cept the man up on the hill."

"And he already saw Scout, and he didn't say anything about *not* letting us keep him here," Drew added triumphantly.

"Connor—Dr. Reynolds—was *here?*"

"Just on the road." Drew felt his smile droop into a scowl. "I don't like him much."

Erin's senses sharpened. "Why do you say that?" she asked, carefully keeping her tone neutral.

"He kept saying stuff like we shouldn't be disappointed, because Scout probably has a home. I bet he hopes it's true!"

Erin's heart tightened. "Maybe he was just trying to help."

"So can we keep Scout? *Please?*"

She gave a distracted wave. "We'll see. I'll, um, call the animal shelter, and put an ad in the local paper."

Tyler blanched. "An *ad?* For everyone to see?"

"Honey, wouldn't that be fair? What if you lost a dog you loved very much? You'd always wonder and worry about what happened to him."

The children's expressions fell into deep despair.

"There's always the possibility that someone just dumped him on the side of the road, though," she added. "People can be very cruel, or ignorant—they think it's better than taking a pet to the shelter, and never consider that the animal may starve or be injured. If no one claims this guy, we'll keep him. If someone does, we'll go to the shelter and find another dog. I promise."

While she put away groceries and started supper, she watched them through the kitchen window.

Lily, the limp from her poorly repaired clubfoot so much more noticeable when she tried to run with the pup, beamed with a joy that lit up her sweet face.

Drew so rarely smiled, but now his shouts of laughter echoed through the meadow. And Tyler had for these past few moments seemed like any other carefree child you'd see playing in a backyard, instead of one who'd lived through hell. *Please, Lord, let this dog stay with us,* she whispered.

Bracing her hands on the sink, Erin closed her eyes and rolled her head from side to side, working out the tension in her neck.

No easy day, this. Poor Frank Willoughby—who'd been on the verge of discharge—should have been back at the nursing home with his wife by now, eating supper. And Connor...

Ignoring the uneasy feeling in her stomach, Erin washed her hands, unwrapped a pound of ground beef and began forming patties.

She'd never expected to run into Connor, much less end up as his neighbor, but she'd made a promise to Stephanie and she planned to keep it.

Even if her premonition of trouble was growing with each passing day.

CONNOR GRIMACED as he hesitated at the door of Ollie's Diner on Thursday morning, even as the aromas of bacon and coffee and hot, caramel-drenched cinnamon rolls beckoned.

When deciding to come up to Blackberry Hill, he'd planned to cover Ed's clinic, take good care of the patients and spend the rest of his time in blessed solitude up on Hadley's Mountain. He'd sworn not to become involved in local hospital politics.

God knew he just wanted to be left alone, especially after the incident at the hospital in Green Bay.

But Grace Fisher—an unopposable force if there ever was one—and his own deceptively sweet office nurse, Linda, had conspired against him, and here he was, walking into a meeting he'd planned to avoid.

Sighing heavily, he stepped inside the small entryway and right into the 1940s. On one side, red vinyl stools faced the long lunch counter with its old-fashioned soda fountain, while high-backed booths lined the other, and Formica-topped tables filled the space between. War posters, antique kitchen utensils and curling vintage calendars covered the walls.

Every available seat was taken, and the din from clinking china, bustling waitresses and the lively conversation of patrons was nearly deafening. He scanned the room for a familiar face.

Guess not. Smiling to himself, he turned to go.

"Wait," a deep voice boomed from the rear of the room. "Come on back—we're right here!"

All conversation ceased. All eyes turned to the entryway. Feeling like a burglar caught in the act, Connor stopped and looked over his shoulder. Arnold Olson, a local family-practice GP, waved vigorously from an arched doorway at the far end of the diner. Behind him, Connor glimpsed the edge of a booth set apart from the others.

Wishing he'd moved to the door a little faster, Connor made his way through the crowded room, nodding to the tables full of people welcoming him every step of the way.

"Hey, Doc—I seen your picture in the paper," called one beaming, white-haired old gent in overalls and a red flannel shirt. "Mighty glad to have you here while Hadley's gone!"

Clapping him on the shoulder, Connor side-stepped between the last set of tables and a waitress laden with an armload of overflowing plates.

"Good to see you again," murmured Leland Anderson, a thin, fastidious GP from nearby Portville. He sat in the booth next to Arnold, whose belly barely fit behind the table.

Dr. Jill Edwards, a brunette with her hair caught in a classy twist, glanced up at Connor as she started to slide out of the booth. "Hi, Connor. If you're joining everyone here, you can have my place. I need to meet my husband."

"Hold on, you can't go yet. We won't have a quorum," Arnold snorted. He waved impatiently at Connor. "Come on, pull up a chair. Your opinion is important, too."

Connor grabbed an empty chair from a table in the main dining area and brought it to the back booth. Only then did he notice Erin in the corner, her short, dark hair gleaming in the dim light and her delicate features nearly hidden in the shadows as she studied the documents on the table in front of her.

He caught unexpected surprise—and wariness—in her eyes when she finally looked up at him.

"Connor. How…nice of you to join us."

Wariness? Where the hell did that come from? Then again, she'd been distantly related to Stephanie and would have known her parents. He could well imagine what Regina and Victor would have said about him to anyone who would listen.

Erin glanced at her watch, then picked up the stack of papers in front of her and tapped them into a neat pile. "We were just talking about the needs of the staff and patients at the hospital."

"And possible ways to improve its financial outlook," Jill added. "With exponentially rising costs and decreasing revenue, the board has some grim projections for the future."

"You mentioned an MRI unit," Erin said, lifting a cool gaze to meet Connor's. "And a dialysis program."

"That's impossible," Arnold blustered. "We don't have the facility, we don't have the patient base. And we sure as hell don't have the money."

"Most things are possible," Erin countered. "It just depends on the level of community support, and how hard people are willing to work for it to happen."

"Equipment costs are astronomical," Leland pointed out, wiping his fingertips on a napkin. "You'd need additional trained staff, yet I hear you're already looking at *cutting* hours."

"I am," she said slowly, "looking at every conceivable way to operate the hospital with greater efficiency, in ways that will ensure the viability of this facility—and this community—in years to come. When I'm fully prepared, I'll present my findings and my recommendations to the board. That's why I want to involve all of you. As physicians with hospital privileges, you've seen what works and what doesn't, and know what you need to practice medicine most efficiently."

Mollified, Leland leaned back. "Then you must know that in the past grand ideas have proven to be great mistakes. *Very* great."

Connor fought a smile as he listened to Erin calmly meet one question after another. He was strangely proud of her fast, intelligent responses and her patience with even the most pointed of Leland's queries.

The Erin he remembered from college had been a shy little thing—lost in Stephanie's overpowering shadow. That certainly wasn't the case anymore.

"So," she continued, "I'd like you all to develop a list of improvements the hospital needs. Equipment, remodeling, new programs you feel would be of benefit to your patients. We're already into September, and I'd like to campaign for a tax levy. We need to bring this hospital into the twenty-first century."

Arnold gave a dismissive wave of his hand. "The elections are in *November.*"

"And likely too soon for us to campaign heavily enough to convince the voters. If it doesn't appear possible, we could have the proposal withdrawn and request a special election. I'm also looking into some grants, and guaranteed low interest loans being offered to health care institutions by the government."

"We've gotten along before now," he retorted. "What's the rush?"

"The hospital, along with the schools here, are a key element of this town's future. Arnold and Leland, you're both on the board. You know that there have been concerns about the budget."

"This is a very small community, Mrs. Lang." Leland gave her a bored look. "There isn't a lot of extra money. We've even had trouble making payroll from time to time."

She dropped her attention to the papers in front of her and ran a slender forefinger down a column of numbers on the top sheet. "And if the hospital goes under, there are going to be nearly a hundred full-time, part-time and pool employees without jobs. People who may need to move elsewhere, taking their schoolchildren, their purchasing power and their tax dollars with them."

"It's worth looking into, don't you think?" Jill argued. "We've lost a lot of business to Henderson Regional. They offer more services, even if they are farther away." She glanced at the two older doctors across the table. "People moving into a community want to be assured of good schools and good medical care. If we can't offer them, the town loses. And we can't afford that."

Leland polished his coffee spoon with a napkin, his brow furrowed. "You weren't here back in '95. Big plans—everything fell through. People lost money and they lost faith."

"I'm not looking at finding a few big private investors," Erin said quietly. "Fund-raising options will be important—but this won't be the type of situation you experienced before."

Arnold studied her for a moment, his eyes narrowed. Then he threw up his hands. "Hell, I'm not going to be around here much longer. Should have retired five years ago and moved to Florida after my wife died. If you want to give this a try, more power to you—and I'll do what I can."

"I agree." Jill stood and gave Erin a wink. "Go for it, and we'll start working on a proposal for you to look over. Connor?"

"If you want the hospital to be competitive, you'll need to update the equipment and the physical plant. It should have been done years ago." He shrugged. "I won't be around long enough to see it happen, but you certainly have my support."

"Leland?"

Placing his spoon neatly across the saucer in front of him, he raised a brow. "It wouldn't hurt to look into this further, I suppose. The doctor's lounge has certainly been a disgrace for the past twenty years or more."

Erin's hands tensed on her coffee cup, but she merely gave the older man a nod.

Leland's mouth softened into a faint smile. "Good, then. We'll get back to you, say…by the 25th of the month?"

"How about the 18th, right here. We'll have more time to take action—especially if we need to petition for a special election."

"We'll try." Jill waved and headed for the door. Arnold and Leland followed, leaving Erin sitting in the booth, an elbow propped on the table and her forehead resting in her palm.

Connor hesitated. "Headache?"

She started, then gave him an embarrassed look. "I, um, thought you'd all left."

"On my way." He grabbed the back of his chair and shoved it toward the neighboring table. "Ambitious plans you have here. For a newcomer and all."

"It's my job, and I need to do it well."

The determination in her voice was unmistakable, and he thought back to the evening he'd stopped by the cabin. He'd seen the kids and her, but no evidence of another adult. Certainly not a second car. "Your husband…"

"My ex is back in Wausau." Her mouth quirked at one corner. "Enjoying midlife freedom with a girl half his age, who probably ought to take a closer look at the kind of guy she 'won,' bless her."

Connor cleared his throat. "It can't be easy for you, so far from town—with a full-time job and three kids. If you need to break the lease on your house…or if you want to be closer to town…"

"Actually, I couldn't be happier." She briskly tucked her documents and calculator into a portfolio, dropped a five-dollar bill on the table and slid out of the booth. Standing in high heels, she barely came up to Connor's shoulder. "Thank you for joining us this morning, Doctor."

She gave him a brief, businesslike smile and strode for the door without a backward glance. If he'd had a communicable illness, she couldn't have seemed more eager to escape.

Shaking his head, he made his way through the crowded room. She didn't need to worry.

Stephanie's family had shunned him ever since her death, and he had no wish to reestablish a connection with any of them now. He had no intentions of starting any *personal* relationships, either. He'd been down that road already, and it sure hadn't been a success.

Erin was simply a link to his past, nothing more.

GRACE RUBBED THE BACK of her neck as she stepped out of the pharmacy department, pulled the door shut and started down the administrative hallway toward the front desk. Another long day…and she felt it in every joint. At the door of George's old office she slowed to glance inside, then stopped and rapped on the frame when she saw Erin at her computer.

"It's four-thirty—don't you usually head home now?" The girl looked drawn, and Grace's bone-deep instincts for mothering kicked into high gear. "This will all wait."

Erin looked up at the clock on the wall. "Guess I'd better. The kids have been home for a half hour already." She closed out of the Excel program on her screen, shut down the computer and retrieved her purse from a file drawer. "They called me the minute they got home, but I still don't feel comfortable having them there alone for very long."

"They're what—fourth and fifth graders?"

"Tyler's in first, Lily's in fourth and Drew is a fifth grader."

"So they should do okay then—lots of kids manage alone for a while if their parents work."

"It still makes me nervous. Until yesterday I was taking them to and from school, but Drew *totally* rebelled over that. He said he'd taken care of his brother for years just fine, thank you very much, and that they all thought the bus would be fun. So yesterday, we tried using the bus after school—and the driver left them out way down on the highway." Erin shuddered. "Heaven knows who could see them out there, alone—and the walk home is a good mile. That's too far for Lily."

Remembering that fragile child, with her awkward limp, Grace nodded, feeling instant sympathy for the young woman shuffling the papers on her desk into some semblance of order.

"So the bus driver agreed to take them right up to our door from now on." Erin stuffed some files and her planner into a battered leather briefcase, then gave an agitated wave of her hand. "We're giving this idea a trial run—but the first sign of trouble, and they'll be going to a sitter after school."

"There could be another option." Grace studied her thoughtfully. "Do you know Jane Adams, one of the nursing assistants on third shift? She has five kids including a daughter who's a senior in high school, and her husband is disabled. I'll bet Haley could use some extra spending money. They're good people. Trustworthy."

Erin's face lit up. "Really? I've been asking around, trying to find a dependable high school student, but haven't had any luck. They're all either busy with after-school activities or have jobs already."

"I remember those days well. It's hard to find good sitters—and then they finish school, leave town, and you have to start all over."

Erin cocked her head slightly, then faint color washed into her pale cheeks, and Grace chuckled. "No, you're right. I'm still 'Miss Fisher,' but I had dozens of foster kids over the years."

"That's amazing." Erin's voice was filled with admiration. "You've been a busy woman."

"And enjoyed every minute. I'm past those days, though. Raised my last set of kids a few years back, and now I'm looking forward to retiring from here soon." Ignoring the wave of loneliness that always rushed through her at the thought, she gave an offhand shrug. "I might do some traveling—and go see some of my 'chicks.' They've moved from coast to coast now."

"That sounds wonderful."

Ah, yes…wonderful. But what about the days and weeks and months after that? The years? "Jane is on the schedule tonight—I'll put a note on the time clock for her," Grace said briskly. "They haven't had a phone for a while, but it should be back in service soon. Jane could check with her daughter and then call you from here."

Giving her a grateful smile, Erin fished her car keys from the depths of her purse. "You're a life-saver."

"No problem. You'd be doing Haley a favor, I think. That family doesn't have it easy." With a nod of farewell, Grace started down the hall toward her office, thankful that she still had her beloved job. The hustle and bustle of busy days.

What on earth would she do with her life when she had to retire? She'd never been one to sit idle, and she had no one left to share those interminable years ahead.

A brief, poignant image flashed through her head, of the one man she'd always loved.

Maybe…

But who would ever imagine that Grace Fisher, Director of Nursing, could even entertain such fool-ish thoughts? The years had left her hefty, gray-haired and entirely too practical for such nonsense.

She'd made her choices, and she'd lived with them well. Regrets were a waste of time.

CHAPTER SIX

"I *DIDN'T* LET SCOUT LOOSE," Drew hissed.

"Did, too. I bet you left the door open." Lily, who almost never stood up to him, jammed her hands on her skinny hips. "Now he's gone. Maybe that wolf will get him."

"And if Erin knows we lost him again, she's gonna be mad," Tyler whispered. "She already said we weren't being careful enough."

Tyler, Lily and Drew exchanged worried glances, then turned as one toward the half-closed door of Erin's home office. On Saturday mornings she usually worked between breakfast and lunchtime, and she'd just gotten started.

Which could, Drew figured, give them a half hour before she might get suspicious about the silence and come out looking for them. "Lily, you stay here. Turn on the stereo. Make noise."

"We all gotta go find him." Gnawing on his lower lip, Tyler shifted his weight back and forth. "If we all hunt, we have a better chance. Won't take so long, either."

"Right." Lily grabbed her jacket from its hook and held the door open. "We can be back before she knows we left, and then Scout won't be in trouble."

Already, he'd taken off three times, and Erin had talked about building a pen for him. *Dog jail.* What fun was that? Brushing past Lily, Drew hurried across the porch and down the steps. "Tyler, you and Lily stick together. You go that way—" He motioned toward the lane that led down to the road. "And I'll go—" At a distant sound of barking, he grinned. "Nope—let's all go up the hill. That sure sounds like Scout."

He took off at a run. At the edge of the clearing he looked over his shoulder, belatedly remembering that Lily and Tyler couldn't keep up. "I'll run ahead," he shouted. "Just in case he keeps going."

"Wait!"

Tyler's voice followed him as he charged through the underbrush, but Drew didn't stop. If Scout got as far as the house on the hill, Dr. Reynolds might be home. He'd told Erin about the last time they'd trespassed on his land, and just yesterday, she'd warned them all about staying well clear of the guy's house. *He was nice about letting you kids have a dog—but he doesn't want company, so respect his wishes and don't bother him.*

At the top of a steep climb, Drew stopped and leaned over to catch his breath, his hands propped on his knees and his lungs burning.

The only sound he heard was some stupid squirrel chattering from the top of a tree. "Scout! Here, boy!"

He whistled, then called again. *Nothing.*

Frustrated, he plowed past prickly raspberry vines and some sort of spiky bush, sweeping away low-hanging pine bows and stumbling over jagged rocks that poked up through the pine-needle carpet under-foot. And still there was no sound of a puppy bark-ing.

His muscles ached. All around, the heavy timber seemed to press in on him, dark and threatening, with deep shadows that seemed to form and then re-form into looming creatures waiting to attack.

Off to the left a long dark shape slid through the underbrush, silent as a ghost. *A wolf?*

Then a much larger form silently materialized—towering high above him at the top of the next rise, blocking the scant rays of light filtering through the dense canopy of branches.

Sucking in a sharp breath, Drew cried out as he stumbled backward, half fell, then caught himself with an outstretched hand against sharp-edged rock.

"It's only me. Your neighbor, Connor. Remem-ber?"

Blinking, Drew scrambled to his feet. Blood pounded in his ears as images crashed through his thoughts of another time. Walking into another place he wasn't meant to be, where a man had loomed over him like the very devil, a gun gleaming in his hand and evil glittering in his small, dark eyes.

The sickly smell of blood, and death.

The taste of his own fear.

"Whoa, kid. I'm not a boogeyman." Giving him an odd look, Connor took a careful step back, and then Scout bounded out from behind him, his tail wagging. "I was just bringing your puppy back."

"Uh—thanks." Embarrassment flooded Drew's cheeks with heat as he accepted the end of the leash, so he ducked his head as he knelt down to let Scout leap into his lap. The pup wiggled wildly in his arms, smothering him with excited kisses. "I'll bring your leash back."

"Just leave it on your mailbox. I'll get it next time I drive by. By the way, I saw your notice about the dog on the billboard at the grocery store, and an ad in the paper," he added. "Had any calls?"

"Nope." A flicker of joy danced through Drew's middle. "Not even one—and this is the third day."

"Congratulations, then. Looks like you've got a dog." Connor turned to leave, but at a rustle of branches behind Drew, he looked back over his shoulder.

Lily and Tyler, both breathless, shouted with excitement as they rushed forward and dropped to their knees. Scout scrambled over them, too. Lily laughed and kissed him, then Tyler wrestled him away and they rolled on the ground.

"Thanks, mister," Tyler squealed as Scout licked his ear.

"Yeah, thanks." Unable to hold back a grin any longer, Drew looked up—and felt his joy fade away.

Connor frowned down at him. "Just keep him safe at home, and you three all need to stay there, as well. Tell Erin I have to talk to her."

"B-but we didn't do anything wrong," Lily whispered, her eyes welling with sudden tears.

"We just came looking for Scout," Tyler added. "We had to. Are you g-gonna tell?"

Drew handed the end of the leash to Tyler, then helped Lily get to her feet. "C'mon, let's go," he snapped.

But then his anger grew, fueled by Tyler and Lily's pale faces and by the memory of all the times he'd helplessly taken crap from the druggies who'd hung around his real mom, until he'd felt as if he might explode into a million pieces.

He whirled around and glared at Connor's back as the man disappeared through the trees. "Bet it makes you feel real important to make a little girl cry."

He didn't bother to wait for an answer…didn't even know if Connor had heard him. But by the time they reached the stream bordering the clearing, Lily had tears running down her cheeks and she was limping more than she usually did.

Tyler looked up at her uncertainly. "Are you hurting?"

Scrubbing furiously at her damp cheeks, she shook her head.

But Erin would take one good look at Lily's face and want to know what was up, and then they'd all be in trouble for leaving the yard again. Drew reached down for a rock and pitched it across the stream. "Uh…we're close enough now. Maybe we just better stay out here awhile. Let's look for min-nows."

Scout tugged at his leash, then bounded back and jumped up against Tyler, wanting to play. "Were you *scared* of that guy?" he whispered to Lily.

"N-no…" She shook her head again—more slowly this time—and plopped down on a boulder. Her lower lip trembled. "It's all my fault if Erin finds out we left, and gets mad."

Tyler frowned. "What is?"

"*Everything*. You didn't let Scout out. I—I did." The dog licked her hand, and she leaned over to bury her face in his soft, warm fur. "I—I want ev-erything to be perfect, like in the stories. A family. A dog. A house where I can stay and never have to move, ever again. But I keep messing everything up."

Drew gave an exasperated snort. "We got Scout back. No big deal."

"But now that guy is probably mad at Erin and us. What if he makes us move, or says we can't have a dog, after all?"

"That's crazy."

"Oh, yeah?" Lily lifted her tear-streaked face and met his eyes. "Sam moved out and divorced her, 'cause of us kids. How much is she gonna put up with before she just decides to send me back?"

"She can't." But as much as he wanted to believe it, there'd been a big, empty place in Drew's heart ever since the night the social workers had come to take him and Tyler away from Mom, and now that painful place grew until it filled his whole chest. Nothing was certain. Not ever. He forced a smile. "Sam didn't leave because of us. He left because he was a big fat jerk."

"Oh, yeah? I heard them argue. Lots." Lily's lower lip trembled. "About how we took up all of her time, and how she loved us better than him. And how she wasn't fun anymore. He…mostly complained about me. Then he left."

Tyler's eyes widened. "She *can't* send any of us back. She *adopted* us."

"If Sam could leave us, why couldn't she?" Lily drew her knees up to her chin and wrapped her arms tightly around her legs. "'Specially me. You've been with her longer than I have."

"She won't do that," Drew insisted.

But Lily dropped her forehead to her knees, and Drew could tell she was silently crying. He awkwardly patted her on the back, wishing he knew what to say to make her feel better.

But no one could help with the *really* bad things. He knew all about pain and anger and fear, and the kind of nightmares that never went away.

He knew it well, because he'd done the worst thing a kid could do, and nothing could change that fact. If Erin ever found out about it, he'd be back in a foster home in a split second—and maybe he'd never see his brother or Lily again.

Because who'd ever want a kid like him?

A FUNERAL SURE WASN'T a good way to start out a new week.

Erin swiveled her desk chair to face the window overlooking the hospital grounds. Outside, enjoying the crisp mid-September sunshine, a nurse's aide pushed an elderly man in a wheelchair along a cement walkway. A couple of other aides on break were perched on a picnic table, hunched over their cigarettes and matches, fighting a stiff breeze.

Normal, ordinary activities, because life went on.

Yet she only had to close her eyes to be back at St. John's Catholic Church, with its intense scent of lilies and roses, and the somber faces of Frank Willoughby's family.

His frail little wife had appeared overwhelmed, even a little shell-shocked, as well-wishers approached to press her hand and murmur condolences. After sixty-two years of marriage she was alone, poor thing, though in her mild dementia she had continued to refer to her husband in the present tense.

Perhaps, Erin mused, confusion could be a kind friend.

Two of Willoughby's children—grown men now, with well-cut suits and an air of quiet success—had conferred at length at the back of the chapel. And as their voices rose, Erin had heard one of them say, "Dad was sharp as a tack, and he was doing much better. He should have pulled through this."

Losing a loved one was tough, and unexpected death even harder. There were always the what-ifs, and the self-recriminations over what should have been done faster. Different. *Better.*

And there were the regrets over words left unsaid, because it had seemed as if there'd always be another day to share them. The family clearly was still struggling with Frank's death. Seeing their grief had made her reconsider every aspect of the case as she sat through the service.

But every policy and procedure had been followed.

The documentation was complete.

He'd been one of just a few in-patients at the hospital that day, and had received close nursing supervision.

And, after all, the man was ninety-three, with congestive heart failure and a pacemaker. He might well have passed away at the nursing home…right?

At a light tap on her open office door, she shook off her melancholy thoughts and swiveled away from the window. "Hi. What can I do for—"

It was Connor Reynolds.

Dressed in Levi's and loafers, with a stethoscope hanging over his open collared black polo shirt, he looked the perfect urban yuppie doctor. One who worked out a lot, given that broad chest and those muscular forearms. "I just want to talk to you for a few minutes."

"Sure." She waved toward the two leather-upholstered chairs facing her desk. "Anytime."

He sauntered in and glanced at the bare walls of her office, the haphazard stack of cardboard boxes in one corner. "Still moving in?"

"Trying." She laced her fingers on the desk and dredged up a smile. "Is something wrong?"

He settled into one of the chairs and gave her a weary grin. "This is…a personal situation."

It took every ounce of concentration to keep her smile in place. "Yes?"

He crossed one long leg over the opposite knee. "We've got some history between us."

Erin's heart stumbled. *Oh, God.* Her mouth went dry.

"And apparently, it's not good." He studied her for a long moment. "I ran into your kids again on Saturday, Erin. I'd like to know what's going on."

Lily. Had he noticed anything? Had he caught that dimple in her chin—or the pale gray shade of her eyes? Taking a deep, steadying breath, Erin recalled the promises she'd once made to Stephanie, and gave a vague wave of her hand. "I—I'm not sure what you mean."

"They were way up in the woods."

"Oh." Closing her eyes, she leaned back in her chair and pinched the bridge of her nose. "I was working in my home office that morning. I'll bet there wasn't a half hour between the times I checked on them, and they never said a *word* about being gone. But things will be better now—I have a new babysitter who will work every day after school, and on Saturday mornings when I need her."

"The kids don't bother me," he said shortly. "It's what could be out in the woods that might hurt them. I've seen more than just tracks now—I saw a large black wolf at dawn on Saturday morning, loping along just north of my house."

"I'll talk to them right away," she said fervently, rubbing her arms against a sudden chill.

"While you're at it, I get the feeling that they've got the wrong impression of me. As much as they must believe it, I'm not the monster who lives up on the hill." There was no recrimination in his eyes, only a hint of sadness. "I may prefer my solitude, but the last thing I want is for them to think I'm a dangerous guy."

"N-no. Of course not."

"Yet when I brought their puppy back on Saturday, Lily started *crying* after I said they should try to keep him at home. And Drew…" Connor shook his head, a glimmer of a smile lifting a corner of his mouth. "That's one spunky little kid. He yelled at me for upsetting her."

A few years ago, when Stephanie revealed her darkest secret, Erin's opinion of Connor had plummeted. But the gentleness in his eyes was not what she'd have expected from someone who apparently had been so cruel. Had he mellowed—or could Stephanie have been wrong?

"It's true that I've told them to leave you alone," she said slowly, measuring her words. "They need to stay home for safety's sake, and they shouldn't bother you. I've never portrayed you as an evil guy. But these kids…" She pushed away from her desk and stood at the window, looking out at the early morning sunshine. "They've had a tough time. All of them. Drew and Tyler came from a very troubled situation, in a bad part of Milwaukee. Drew tends to be defensive, even belligerent. Tyler is just…scared. When they first came to me they hoarded food in their rooms, and Tyler had constant nightmares. They've been with me for over a year now. And Lily—" Erin swallowed hard, then turned to face Connor. "I've had her for just about six months. With her various problems, she has bounced around in the foster care system all her life."

"They've all had it rough, then." He shook his head slowly. "At least they're in good hands now."

She gave a humorless laugh. "Oh, yes—good hands. A chance to grow up in a real family, with two loving parents. Sam wasn't able to father a child, so he agreed to adopt—then he left because parenthood was 'too demanding.' A great example for them all, right?"

"But they've got you, and that's something they didn't have before. How many single moms are out there working hard and raising fantastic kids on their own? Millions."

Touched, she leaned against the windowsill and rested her palms against the cool marble surface, and for the first time felt herself truly relax in his presence. "I keep hoping that being with me is the best thing for them. The two happiest days of my life were when I signed the adoption papers."

"They're very lucky kids." Connor glanced at the clock, then rose. "Guess I'd better be on my way."

He was almost out the door when she found herself calling out to him. "Maybe it would be good if you came over sometime. I—I don't suppose you'd be free this week. For supper. With, um, the kids and me. Maybe Wednesday?"

He intended to decline. She could see it in the set of his mouth when he hesitated. Then he smiled, and the flash of those deep dimples made her pulse skip a beat. "Seven?"

"Sounds good to me."

After his footsteps faded down the hall, she sat down behind her desk and dropped her forehead into the palm of her hand. *What was I thinking?* This was definitely not a good idea. Careful distance, not proximity, was going to get her through the next three months. Lily had become a beautiful little girl. If he recognized certain traits in her, would he try to fight for Lily?

Maybe he'd changed. Maybe he was a nice guy.

But he was also the man who'd angrily told his future wife to abort the baby he'd fathered. Who'd refused to acknowledge that child. And then Lily had languished for nearly eight years in foster care, because no one else had ever come forward to accept a child who wasn't perfect.

And that was a decision Erin could never forgive.

CHAPTER SEVEN

ERIN WAS JUST A NEIGHBOR. Nothing more than that. She'd offered a neighborly invitation for supper, and he'd accepted on those terms. It was certainly not any sort of a date.

Connor told himself that on the way home from the clinic on Wednesday afternoon. As he took Maisie for a quick run up the trail. While he showered, and changed into khaki Dockers and a nubby black L. L. Bean sweater.

He couldn't even remember the last time he'd had a date, but this wasn't a date…even though he would be having dinner with a woman he'd found utterly appealing, in a winsome sort of way, back in college.

The intervening years had done amazing things to the sweet young thing she'd been back then. Stephanie had once blithely discounted her as a little bookworm, but now Erin's shyness had evolved into confidence, and her wholesome, girlish features had matured into something far more striking and evocative.

He no longer had to remind himself that this was a nondate when Lily opened the door and he found himself nearly flattened by a wet, soapy dog and an overweight teenager who barely managed to tackle the animal as it raced across the porch.

Clutching the struggling dog to her chest, the girl gave him a megawatt smile. "I'm the babysitter, Haley. You must be Dr. Reynolds. Come on in—but watch out for the floor. It's kinda wet."

"I take it Scout doesn't like bath time."

She rolled her eyes. "He escaped when Drew opened the door to go after more towels. I'll be right back." She headed across the living room toward the back of the house. "Drew, get back here!"

Heavy footsteps thundered down the stairs from the second level. The older boy gave Connor a brief glance and mumbled something that might have been a greeting, then he disappeared around the corner.

Lily stepped aside as Connor walked in. "Scout made a big mess, so we gotta give him a bath," she said somberly. "Before Erin comes home."

And it looked as if the bath had made an even bigger one. Connor hid a smile as he glanced at his watch. "I'm early?"

"Nope." A delicate blush rose in Lily's pale cheeks. "She had to run to town, because of Scout. I think she's bringing home a bucket of chicken and dessert. And," the girl added glumly, "she's buying a tie-out stake and chain until we can figure out a dog pen. We're supposed to tell you to come in."

"Thanks." Connor glanced to the left, where the kitchen table was set with a cheery red tablecloth, ivory stoneware and a pot of bright yellow chrysan-themums—so apparently Scout hadn't wreaked havoc there.

Lily led Connor into the living room area to the right, then wavered uncertainly, clearly shy and un-comfortable in her role as hostess. "Um…do you want the newspaper? Or a glass of water?"

"I'm fine." He sauntered over to the fireplace mantel, where a number of framed photographs were displayed. School photographs of all three kids; one of them posed stiffly in front of a ranch-style house with a profusion of flowers blooming along the foun-dation. Another photograph was of Erin and the chil-dren standing before a rocky cliff. "Where was this?"

"Lake Superior. We went there in the summer, after…" Her voice hitched, then trailed off as she studied the tips of her shoes. "After school was out," she finished lamely.

After Erin's jerk of a husband took off with his bimbo, probably. "I'll bet you had fun. It's beautiful up there. Did you see the Split Rock Lighthouse? And Gooseberry Falls?"

She nodded, but even from across the room, he could see her lower lip trembling. "Let's see…did you go to the big aerial bridge in Duluth?"

At that, her chin lifted and she gave him a trem-ulous smile. "We heard a ship's horn, and then the bridge guy answered with his own horn. Then the whole bridge went straight up in the air so the ship could go into the harbor."

Tyler, who looked as if he'd gotten at least as wet as the dog, appeared in the hallway door. And a second later, Drew and the babysitter followed.

Haley gave a gusty sigh. "We've done what we can, but Scout sure didn't like that hair dryer very much. I don't know where to put him to finish drying, unless you boys have a long rope."

Drew and Tyler looked at each and shrugged. From the bathroom came the sound of the dog clawing frantically at the door.

"I might have some rope in my trunk. I'll go check," Connor offered.

Drew went back for the dog, and they all stepped out onto the porch as Erin came up the steps with two grocery bags in her arms and a harried expression on her face.

"I'm sorry—I never meant to be so late." She blew at her wispy bangs, murmuring her thanks as Connor reached for the bags. "We had just a *little* problem in the kitchen."

Shifting the damp dog in his arms, Drew gave Erin a contrite look. "I'm really sorry. We didn't know he could jump that high. Honest."

"And we'll pay for the slow cooker with our allowances," Tyler added earnestly.

Erin reached into a grocery bag and withdrew a large plastic package filled with chain. "If Scout is in the house, you kids need to watch him all the time. If he has to go outside, you must tie him so he doesn't run off. He can be loose if you're playing with him, but otherwise—not. Promise?"

Drew nodded solemnly as he took the package from her, then he bounded down the porch steps. Tyler and Lily followed him out into the yard.

"Come on in," Erin said as she opened the door for Connor. "I'm afraid this isn't the menu I planned, but the kids probably like Kentucky Fried better than beef burgundy over rice, anyway. How about you?"

"I'm not hard to please." Connor thought about his solitary meals up at the house on the hill. The individual frozen entrées that he bought by the dozen when he bothered to stop at the local grocery store, his stockpile of tuna or canned soup when he hadn't. "I can't even remember when I last sat down to a home-cooked meal."

"Have a word with Scout before you leave—he can tell you what it tasted like." Erin tipped a tall carton of hot fried chicken onto a platter and dumped mashed potatoes and coleslaw into bowls. "Though I'm guessing that a whole potful of meat and a cherry cobbler has given give him a whale of a stomachache."

Connor tried to imagine what Stephanie would have done about a ruined dinner and a dog like Scout. God rest her soul, she probably would have called a caterer and the humane society, and then she would have had a nervous breakdown. "I appreciate the invitation."

"It's the least I can do, as a neighbor. After all—" Erin gave him a brief, wicked smile "—you did give us permission to keep that dog."

"A privilege you must be very thankful for." Until now she'd seemed businesslike, perhaps even a little wary. Her smile surprised and delighted him. "Maybe you'd like two."

"Mention that within hearing range of these kids, and you're dead."

The front screen door squealed open, then slammed. "I'm leaving, Mrs. Lang. You still want me to pick up the kids after school tomorrow on my way out here?"

Erin rounded the kitchen table and met the teenager in the living room. "I'd appreciate that, Haley. I'll start paying your mileage."

"Thanks!" She grabbed her purse and backpack from the sofa, waved and left with another squeal and slam of the door.

"I think you need some oil for those hinges," Connor said mildly.

"Or possibly a geriatric babysitter who doesn't move quite so fast." Erin moved to the refrigerator and pulled out a gallon of milk, poured it into the glasses on the table, then went to the door to call the kids for supper. "Though I am thrilled to have Haley. She comes every day after school now, and she's great with the kids. I'm not sure an older adult could be paid enough to keep up with them."

Throughout supper, Connor sat back and absorbed

the ebb and flow of conversation—slow at first, perhaps hindered by his presence, but then Lily hesitantly talked about a rabbit a classmate brought to school, and Tyler asked about joining Cub Scouts again.

Only Drew stubbornly refused to respond to Erin's tactful prompting. He didn't so much as meet Connor's eyes, though they sat across the table from one another.

Whatever had happened to the kid in his former life must have been damn tough, Connor mused after he tried and failed to get the boy to talk about school, in-line skating or the last *Matrix* rerun on TV.

After the meal was cleared away and the kids headed off to their rooms to do homework, Erin went out to get Scout and let him thunder up to the loft to be with the boys.

"Sorry," she said lightly as she took a last glance at the kitchen, poured two cups of coffee and handed Connor one. "You're used to peace and quiet. Your ears are probably still ringing."

"I've enjoyed every minute." How long had it been since he'd spent time like this—with an intelligent, amusing woman who both challenged and delighted him? With anyone, beyond those he worked with at the clinic or hospital?

"It's chilly out on the porch," she murmured. "Let's just have our coffee in here."

The embers in the fireplace cast a flickering glimmer across the honey-colored, half-log walls. She reached over and flipped on a small stained-glass lamp at one end of the sofa, then curled up in an overstuffed upholstered chair. The amber light cast a soft glow, warming her skin to soft peach and adding a sparkle to her eyes.

Clearing his throat, Connor settled down on the end of the sofa near her and cradled his coffee cup in both hands. "I never would have guessed that I'd run into you again, much less end up having dinner here."

She laughed. "And I wouldn't believe that you'd ever given me a thought. The surprise is that you remembered my name."

"I remember. You were so serious about school—I'd see you lugging armloads of books across the campus, or I'd go to the dorm to pick up Stephanie, and see you studying at one of the desks off the common room." She'd been such a pretty girl, he'd often wondered why she didn't have three or four guys trailing after her like hopeful puppies.

"I had to work hard to keep my scholarships, or I wouldn't have been able to continue." She grinned. "And the rooms had barely enough space for two beds and two tiny desks, so I didn't even try to study there. Stephanie was luckier. She had a private room—though she had so much stuff in there I'm not sure if she could even turn around."

Charmed by the light sound of Erin's laughter, Connor wondered about how difficult life had been for her. She'd come from less money, yet as far as he knew, she'd never shown resentment toward her wealthier cousin. "I'm sorry that Stephanie and I lost track of you over the years."

"Me, too." Erin took a slow sip of her coffee. "Our families were barely on speaking terms, so it was nice getting to know her better while we were at college. I'm just thankful that I heard about her accident in time to make it back to Wisconsin for her funeral."

Images of that day flashed through his mind like a disjointed slide show. "I don't even remember half of the people who were there…but I know you came up to me and offered your condolences."

"What a terrible day that must have been for you. How can anyone ever prepare for something like that? Right out of the blue…and then having to make it through the funeral…"

The sympathy in her eyes touched him, but Stephanie had been wild. Out of control. And that night…

The pager on his belt vibrated, startling him back into the present. He grabbed it and read the text message on the small screen, then stood with a sigh. "Hospital. I have to be on my way."

Erin unfolded her legs and rose. "You can use our phone if you just need to call in."

"I admitted a young woman with asthma this afternoon. I want to get back down there to take another look at her, because her oxygen sats are a little low."

At the door, Erin flipped on the porch light and smiled up at him. "I'm glad you could join us, Connor."

"Wouldn't have missed it." He hesitated, caught in that awkward moment when a handshake is too formal, a quick embrace too personal. And he suddenly found himself wanting to kiss her. Where had *that* come from?

"I'll try harder at keeping my kids and dog home," she continued, her eyes shining. "Thanks for being patient with us."

Patient wasn't exactly how he felt right now. Her dark hair gleamed under the porch light. Her fair skin appeared almost luminous, and her mouth—

He tried to clear his head as he turned away.

He wasn't looking for any involvement. In three months he would be gone—and the last thing he needed was anything to complicate his life further. A woman like Erin, with her career and her devotion to those three kids, meant commitment. Permanence. Putting down roots.

And he'd already found out just how heartbreaking those ties could be.

"I FIGURED YOU COULD USE some moral support." Grace winked at Erin outside Ollie's Diner the next morning. "And if you didn't, I'd still go inside for the best caramel rolls ever created."

"I couldn't ask for a better ally." Erin felt some of her tension ease as she opened the door and ushered the director of nursing through the door. "I feel like I'm getting ready to face the lions."

Grace snorted. "At my age, I've ceased to be intimidated by anyone…except maybe my ninety-eight-year-old mother."

Erin started to lead the way to the back of the busy café, then pulled up short. The back booth was empty. "I thought the doctors met here every Thursday."

"That's right." Grace sidestepped between several sets of tables filled with retirees, murmuring greetings as she passed. "Because there are just a few things in life you can count on—death, taxes, and the absolute bliss of breakfast at Ollie's."

"I hope so. They agreed to talk over my suggestions and come up with a list of useful equipment, supplies and remodeling projects. We need concrete goals for fund-raising."

Grace grabbed a couple of menus from an empty table without breaking her stride. "Good plan."

"So where are they?"

"Sometimes they run a little late. Let's sit a spell."

Grace slid into the side of the booth facing into the restaurant, and signaled to one of the waitresses bustling back and forth between the kitchen and the crowded tables. "The usual—times two," she called out.

Moments later, the waitress delivered two cups of steaming coffee and a couple of warm, dinner-plate-size caramel-cinnamon rolls.

"Whoa," Erin murmured. "I'm not even sure where to start."

"Local opinion is divided. Some argue for extra butter, to turn the top all melty." Grace reached for three pats, peeled away the papers and dumped the butter dead-center on her warm roll. "Others say nothing else is needed. Personally, I think that sounds boring. Don't you?"

Caught up in her first taste of Ollie's specialty, Erin could only nod as an intense explosion of feather-soft yeasty bread and cinnamon hit her palate. "This is heaven," she murmured a minute later. "Absolute bliss."

"And with luck, we'll be finished before the doctors show up, so these beauties don't get cold." Grace sectioned off another bite with her knife and fork. Then her hands stilled.

"What? Who is it?" Erin looked around the edge of the booth, but didn't see any familiar faces. A tall, distinguished man in a charcoal suit was headed their way, though. She ducked back inside the booth. "This someone you know?"

Grace gave an offhand wave that belied the faint pink blooming in her weathered cheeks. "Dan Travers. The high school principal."

"Ahh." Erin bit back a smile.

"With so many foster kids through the years, it seemed like I always had someone in high school, so I ran into him now and then." She set aside her fork, fluffed her short gray hair and smiled as the silver-haired man stopped at their table.

The eye contact between them appeared to hold more than casual interest. Had this been going on for *years*?

"It doesn't seem like our school is complete this term, Grace. We don't have any of your kids enrolled."

"I'm done with foster care," she murmured after making the introductions. "My final two boys graduated last spring, and I'll be retiring from the hospital soon."

"That's hard to believe." He grinned at Erin, though his gaze veered back to Grace. "She and I were classmates, and I refuse to believe we've reached retirement age already."

"But you have, what—three kids of your own spread across the country, and six or eight grandchildren?" Grace's voice turned a shade wistful. "You'll be busier traveling to see them than you ever were at the school."

"Which reminds me—I'd better run. School assembly this morning, first period." He nodded to Grace, then Erin, and he made his way back through the tables toward the front door.

"Nice guy," Erin said blandly. "A good friend?"

"Not what you think. Dan and I were neighbors as kids, but he was in a whole different sphere. He was the football star and he married the prom queen. Perfect wife, lovely home, pretty children. Linda was just the nicest gal—she passed away a year or so ago."

And if Grace hadn't held him in special regard all these years, Erin would eat her place mat. "So, I'll bet he's lonely now. Just think—his kids are grown, his wife is gone. You and he ever think about getting together?"

Grace glanced down at her own sturdy build. *"Please.* I'm not in the market for anyone to sweep me off my feet. And at my age, I don't think anyone could do it."

"But—"

"Here's one of the doctors now." She raised her arm and motioned, then slid farther into the booth. "I'd appreciate no more mention of Dan Travers, okay?"

Dr. Jill Edwards appeared at their table a moment later, too thin in her loden-green wool dress, and more than a little distracted. She gave them a strained smile. "I've been sent as a messenger. Leland was late starting his rounds at the hospital, and Arnold left early this morning for a seminar in Chicago. I don't know about Dr. Reynolds. He—"

Connor appeared at her elbow. "He's here. A little late, but present."

And he must have had to rush, too. His overlong dark hair was windblown, and he brought with him the fresh, cold scent of a blustery fall day.

He pulled off his leather jacket and hung it on a hook at the end of the booth, then slid in next to Erin, while Jill sat down across from him with a legal tablet in her hand. They both ordered coffee from the waitress who had hurried over.

Erin scooted a little farther into the booth, but still his broad shoulders brushed against hers. "Glad you could join us," she murmured, ignoring the physical jolt she'd felt at his touch. Praying that no one noticed her reaction, she edged away.

Across the table, Grace gave her an all-too-knowing look.

Jill pulled a pen from her trendy little Dooney & Bourke handbag and made a checkmark next to number one on her list. "All four of us sat down and discussed what we see as the major deficiencies of the hospital, and the stumbling blocks for change. Leland and Arnold agree that we should try to lure more specialists up here to run clinics, maybe once or twice a month. It won't be easy to attract them, given the history of the hospital. Redecorating the doctor's lounge, which is still a horrid 1950s mint-green, would help. Remodeling the clinic's exam rooms would be even better."

"I'd been thinking of concentrating on equipment and expansion, but that's a valid point about the lounge," Erin said, jotting notes as she spoke. "Maybe a local furniture store would be interested in taking on the project…for free publicity, and exposure to professionals who might well become customers."

"Good idea. We've also discussed the need for digitalized PACS X-rays, and a new MRI. A new CT scanner. A few circular beds for treating decubitus ulcers. An updated cardiac monitoring system. More equipment for rehab. We've got a long list of equipment and supplies for the O.R. and the lab." Jill paused, her pen just halfway down the list in front of her. "Most of it is impossible, yet this hospital hasn't had any improvements for years. Leland," she added with a slight shake of her head, "insists that we need to landscape and update the facade, so patients will at least *feel* we're in the twenty-first century. I'd rather spend the money where it counts. That's assuming there's any money to be found."

"My opinion shouldn't count for anything," Connor said. "But I agree, though I won't be here long enough to see it through." He shifted in the booth to look at Erin. "Have you found out anything more on funding?"

The reminder of his plans to leave jarred her, and it took a moment for the rest of his words to register.

"Yes. Yes, I have."

He was so close that she could feel his warmth and could detect the faint, masculine scent of his aftershave. Maturity had carved such striking cheekbones and deep, sexy dimples in his tanned face. Coupled with those silvery eyes and long, dark lashes—*Lord, have mercy.*

Suddenly aware that she'd been staring, she riffled through her papers to cover the awkward moment. "I, um, spoke to another hospital here in Wisconsin. They were able to pass a county levy of half a percent sales tax for five years, and have been using it strictly for capital equipment and major building repairs. Another hospital administrator said that they received a half-million-dollar USDA grant for their state-of-the-art X-ray system."

Her eyes widening, Grace craned her neck to see the numbers on the page. "Is that kind of money still available?"

Erin nodded. "We have some additional options. Our local auxiliary is willing to work on a variety of fund-raisers, and I'm wondering if the local garden club might be willing to take on a beautification project for the grounds."

Grace gave a low whistle. "We're talking major money here."

Connor nodded. "In this business, you have to keep up with the technology and stay competitive, or you fail. Frankly, it's a wonder that Blackberry Hill Memorial is still in business." He gave Erin a wry smile. "Some of the other docs are having a... *minor* disagreement regarding where funding should go, but at least most of them concur that improvements are needed. Politics and pet projects don't mean anything to me. I'll help for as long as I'm here."

Relieved, Erin gave Grace, Jill and Connor a smile of gratitude as they all stood and tossed a pile of dollar bills on the table to cover the check.

But all the way back to the hospital, the words that replayed through her mind were not about changes at the hospital. *"I agree,"* Connor had said, *"though I won't be here to see it through."*

They were merely neighbors. Barely friends. It didn't matter if he stayed or moved away. Did it?

CHAPTER EIGHT

"GOOD HEAVENS!" Erin faltered to a stop just outside the movie theater on Saturday night and stared at the sheets of rain pouring off the overhanging marquee. The kids huddled next to her. "I didn't hear about *this* on any forecast."

But even if she had, she probably would have braved the elements. Ever since that last breakfast meeting with the doctors, she'd been putting in ten-to twelve-hour days at the hospital, working on grant writing and fund-raising projects, and overseeing the auxiliary's efforts to add a tax-levy issue to the November elections.

Haley's babysitting had been a lifesaver, but after two weeks of late hours, it definitely had been time to take the kids out for some fun.

"Cool," Drew announced. He stuck his hand into the rain. "Maybe we'll have floods."

They'd all worn light jackets, and now Lily wrapped her arms around herself. "It's *cold*."

"Might even snow tonight," said an elderly man behind them. "The fourth of October is a mite early, but you never know this far north."

Snow. Even in good weather their snug cabin was a long drive from civilization. In bad weather... Erin shuddered, considering the steep, winding lane leading up from the highway. "We'd better hurry, before our road turns to mud. Are you kids ready?"

They made a fast dash to her van a half block away. Her hands wet and numb with cold, Erin fumbled with her car keys and dropped them twice before managing to open the driver's-side door and hit the unlock button so everyone could pile in.

"Good thing we left Scout inside the garage," she murmured as she turned on the ignition and slipped the heater up to high.

The wipers beat back and forth, sweeping away sheets of moisture. Glistening black asphalt blended with the rain and the night into impenetrable darkness that the headlights barely pierced. She hunched over the steering wheel, trying to make out the edges of the road ahead.

It was so dark that even the random houses and businesses along the lakeshore and the solitary streetlamps marking the intersections were invisible.

No—not just because of the heavy rain, she suddenly realized as she glanced in the rearview mirror. The entire town behind them was dark, as well.

"I think there's a power outage in town," she announced. "If ours is off, too, we'll start a nice blaze in the fireplace and roast marshmallows. We can pretend we're camping. Does that sound like fun?"

"If we can *get* home," Drew grumbled.

In the front seat, Lily looked over at Erin. Reflecting the dim glow of the dashboard lights, her face was even paler than usual. "What if our road is too muddy and we can't make it?"

"Well, everything seems to be dark back in town, so we'll just keep going. If we get stuck up on our little road, we should be close enough to make a quick run for it." Erin forced a note of cheer into her voice. "This can be an adventure—just like the movie we saw tonight. Right?"

"But *those* people were actors. It was fake," Drew said.

"Then think of the pioneers, with their covered wagons. They were outside all the time, without much shelter."

"And most of *them* died on the way."

"Drew!" When she glanced in the rearview mirror, she saw him sink lower in his seat. "Aspen Road's only a mile away. We'll be okay."

But five minutes later, when the headlights finally picked out the small sign for their turnoff, she wasn't quite so sure.

The minivan fishtailed and skidded as they left the paved road. Its tires spun in the mud not twenty feet from the highway, in a low-lying spot. And a half mile farther, at the bottom of the first steep rise, the tires bogged down and turned uselessly when she tried rocking the van between Reverse and Drive to gain momentum.

Erin draped her wrists on the steering wheel and

stared out into the rainy darkness. "If we could've made it past this one place, we would've been okay," she sighed. "But there's just a half mile to go. That's around six city blocks, and the rain is bound to let up in a little while so we can walk."

She turned up the heater, then searched for a radio station, finally finding one with static-filled reception that inexplicably promised "clear and cold" for the entire weekend.

"We'll be in front of our nice, warm fire soon, guys," she promised after a few minutes.

From the back came the sound of whispers, then Drew cleared his throat. "It doesn't, like, matter if the wood is sorta wet. Right?"

She turned in her seat to look back at him. "You didn't bring in any logs today?"

"Uh…no."

Images of a cold, damp and dark cabin made her shiver. At least there were flashlights, but how long would the batteries last? "That's one of your chores, Drew. Making sure that the log bin by the fireplace is *full*."

"Yeah, well…I forgot."

"So we have no logs to burn. And the furnace igniter and thermostat won't work without electricity."

From the silence in the backseat, she figured Drew and Tyler were contemplating that last bit of news.

Bright headlights flashed behind them, disappeared behind a wall of trees, then filled the interior of the minivan with blinding light. Startled, Erin swiveled in her seat and saw those headlights pull to a stop so close to her bumper that they disappeared beneath her tailgate.

The boys looked back, then met her gaze with wide eyes, their mouths open.

"That guy almost hit us!" Tyler whispered.

Lily whimpered. "What if it's somebody with a gun, and he—"

"Hush, Lily." Her own fear rising, Erin hit the door locks, then reached over and laid a protective hand on the child's arm. "No one else lives on this road. It has to be Connor."

At a sharp rap on her window, she jumped.

"What in heaven's name are you doing out in this weather?"

It was Connor's voice, thank goodness. Relief washed through her as she pressed a button and rolled down her window a few inches. "We're stuck. We were going to walk the rest of the way when this lets up."

"You haven't been listening to the weather reports in the last few hours? This is just the start."

She bristled. "We were in a movie, and the weather was fine before we left."

He leaned down and peered over her shoulder at the kids in the back. "Come on—you can all fit in my Tahoe, if you don't mind being cozy."

Over the past two weeks he had stopped by, now and then, to fix odds and ends around the house, such as leaky faucets and troublesome drains, and occasionally dropped off a treat for Scout or something for the kids. One day, he'd even put up a basketball hoop on the big telephone pole near the house, so the kids would have something to do. Thoughtful things, little things.

Now, the boys didn't hesitate to race for the backseat of his Tahoe as Connor swept Lily up in his arms and carried her, with Erin close behind. In a few moments they were buckled in. Throwing his vehicle into low gear, he inched around their van and then carefully navigated the treacherous road.

He slowed at the drive leading to their house. "None of us have electricity because there's a transformer out in town. How's your wood supply?"

"Wet."

"Thanks to Drew," Lily muttered.

"What about your dog?"

"He's closed in the garage," Tyler piped up from the backseat. "He has water and food in there, and a nice box with blankets."

"You're all welcome to come up to my place," Connor said. He glanced at Erin, then concentrated on the curvy road ahead. "The forecast changed out of the blue. The temp is dropping to the low twenties tonight, and now there's a prediction of up to four inches of snow. My place isn't fancy, but at least it's warm. I've got dry logs and a backup generator."

Of all nights, she'd chosen this one for a trip to

town. If Connor hadn't come along… Erin closed her eyes briefly. She and Drew would've been okay in a chilly cabin, but Lily and Tyler's health were far more fragile. "Thanks so much," she said quietly. "I really appreciate this."

He shot another quick glance at her, and the corner of his mouth lifted into a brief smile. "No problem—I'm just glad I didn't rear-end your minivan and send you all to the hospital."

"I THOUGHT YOU SAID THIS place wasn't fancy," Erin breathed as she turned around slowly to study the great room.

Banks of windows filled three walls. The soaring, steeply pitched ceiling rose a good three stories above them, its massive log framework glowing like amber in the light of the fireplace below.

Above the main-floor kitchen and bedrooms, a spacious loft held several more bedrooms, a den and a whimsical cupola with windows on all sides, similar to their cabin. In the spacious kitchen, another fireplace opened into a family room, where the kids were bent over a Monopoly game.

"This is truly beautiful."

"It is, in a rustic way. But no one has ever taken the time to bring in a decorator." Connor leaned over to arrange another log on the fire. "Ed didn't care, and I'm not staying."

"I'll bet the view is incredible in daylight."

He straightened, and braced one arm on the mantel as he watched the flames flicker. "This hill is high enough that on a good day you can see Canada on the horizon."

Through the skylights overhead, she could see lightning snake across the sky. The wind had picked up, battering the house with sheets of rain.

Here inside, the warmth of the fire felt so good against her chilled skin. "Your uncle must have a big family."

"Intended to, but it didn't happen. This was his dream home. His wife hated it. She said the town itself was too isolated and the house too far away from town. She finally just packed up and moved back to Minneapolis."

"He never remarried?"

"His divorce was very bitter. I think he decided marriage wasn't worth the risk."

"Too bad. This would've been a fabulous place to raise a family."

"For someone, maybe. When I move on, Ed will probably sell up and head south. He's been complaining about his arthritis and these cold northern winters."

Erin reached for a colorful patchwork afghan draped across the back of a rocking chair, wrapped it around her shoulders and snuggled down on the sofa facing the fireplace. "It's a shame, seeing this place leave your family. Don't you want to settle down again someday?"

"After Stephanie…" His voice trailed off, and he

abruptly pushed away from the mantel to pace along the wall of windows to the north.

Now and then he turned to look toward the sounds of the kids laughing in the other room, and she wondered what he was thinking. Did he still mourn for his late wife?

"I can only imagine how hard it's been for you," she said softly.

He moved like a caged animal, silent and restless and angry, and even in the flickering light she could see his muscles bunch and release beneath the snug fabric of his navy knit pullover.

"She was a distant cousin of mine, Connor. I missed a lot of years in her life, but I cared about her." Erin patted the sofa cushion next to her. "Please. Just sit down by the fire and warm up for a minute."

After a long silence, he moved to the couch and sat next to her with his head bowed, his forearms braced on his thighs and his hands clasped.

"I should've been able to save her," he said, his voice so low and raw that he seemed to be talking to himself.

Erin hesitated, then tentatively reached over and rested a comforting hand on his shoulder. "It was a car accident. She was alone, going too fast on a dangerous road. You couldn't have done a thing."

He was silent for so long that she figured he wouldn't say anything more.

"She was *drunk*."

Erin stilled, disbelief pouring through her as she remembered the elegant, sophisticated girl Stephanie had been in college. But then again, there'd been that fateful day at their uncle Theodore's funeral, when she'd obviously had a few too many. She'd started talking…

And then she'd made Erin promise to never, ever tell her secret.

"Didn't you know about her little problem?" He gave a humorless laugh. "I suppose not. No one did. She'd been a social drinker in college and had always liked her cocktails in the evening. It just got worse and worse. And then when she got pregnant…"

Shock hit Erin like a pitcher of ice water. "P-pregnant?"

"Yeah. Two years ago."

Confusion swirled through Erin as she sorted through his words. "She was pregnant…when she *died?*"

"Pregnant. An emotional mess. Drank when she thought I wouldn't catch her, but I found bottles stashed everywhere." His voice lowered, filled with bitterness. "What kind of woman would do that to an unborn child?"

Perhaps a woman reliving her old guilt…with regrets about a previous pregnancy she'd never dared talk about. "I know she had some problems with depression."

"That one word sounds so simple, doesn't it? But it was hell for her. She couldn't stay away from the bottle. We fought more often than not. I stayed home from work. Begged her to take better care of herself. I hid the car keys, poured liquor down the drain. I even got her admitted to a rehab unit, but she refused to stay. And then…after an argument one night, she grabbed the keys to my car and took off before I knew she had them."

"My God."

"I'll never know if that last drive was a suicide, or if she really hated me so much that she had to drive eighty on a mountain road to get away."

"I'm so, so sorry." Erin moved closer, hugged him tighter.

"You asked why I don't want to settle down and fill this place with a family. Well, now you know. The thought of going through hell again just isn't very appealing."

"But you did everything you could." Erin bit her lip, her oath to Stephanie warring with the side of her that felt his pain. "Maybe…there were other things that had happened in her life. Very difficult things…"

"What, in her charmed life, could have been so bad? She grew up wealthy. She was popular. Beautiful." He straightened, then leaned back against the sofa with a disgusted shake of his head. "Hey, once when she was drunk and angry, she told me that she'd planned all along to marry a doctor, and that's why she married me. Great romance, there. Right? What Stephanie wanted, she got."

But not everything.

Yet what was the point of adding to his guilt? Decisions had been made. Stephanie was gone. And nothing could change the past. "Then maybe it's just time to move on," Erin said softly.

He rolled his head against the cushions to look at her. "I'm not sure why I told you all of this."

The firelight cast shadows beneath his cheekbones, changed his eyes to a turbulent deep gray. With the sensual cut of his mouth and dark sweep of his brows, studying the lines and planes of his face nearly took her breath away.

Ignoring the rising awareness, she shrugged. "Maybe it was time to talk about it, so you could finally let it go."

The creases in his cheeks deepened, with just a glimmer of a smile. "You're a very special person, you know that?" He brushed his fingertips across her jaw, then gently rubbed his thumb across her lower lip. "Those kids of yours are very lucky to have a mom like you. And your husband was a fool to walk away."

The reality of Connor's touch was far more potent than Erin had ever imagined.

In college, she'd fantasized about him. Imagined Connor leaving everything behind and coming for her—just for her. But of course, Stephanie had been the beauty, the gifted one…. There'd been no contest.

But whatever Erin wanted right now, no matter how foolish or reckless, Drew, Tyler and Lily were in the family room and could walk in at any moment.

And any touch, however innocent, could easily be misconstrued.

What she wanted was Connor. What she needed was distance.

"I—I'd better go check on the kids," she whispered, forcing herself to pull away.

"No. I'll go." He got to his feet. "It's pretty quiet in there."

She followed Connor to the family room. Here, too, a fire sent shadows dancing across the walls.

Two lumpy shapes on the sofa were bundled up in the sleeping bags. A smaller one—Tyler, though Erin could barely see the top of his head—was on the floor next to his brother.

"He's afraid to sleep alone," she whispered as she stopped at Connor's side. "He had night terrors for six months after he came to live with me, and if he wakes up and Drew is gone, he becomes nearly hysterical. I don't know about everything he went through before, but I can guess."

Connor watched them for several moments, his eyes somber. "Life isn't fair. Luck of the draw—a devoted suburban family, or living through hell from the time you're born."

Erin nodded. "These kids are tough in ways they never should've had to be. And when they defend each other? You wouldn't believe it."

Connor gave a low laugh. "I've had a small taste."

"I'm just so proud of all three of them for what they've overcome, and for how normal they seem."

"And you've made it happen." Raising a brow, he slid an arm around her waist, then pulled her closer. "You are one amazing woman…and I've wanted to do this for a very, very long time."

He glanced once more at the sleeping children, then searched her face before lowering his mouth to hers for an exquisitely gentle kiss.

And with just that light touch, every rational thought fled.

CHAPTER NINE

SHE HAD NO BUSINESS kissing Connor Reynolds. Given what she knew about him, a wiser woman would have stepped back and fled.

But she'd dreamed about him, years ago, when he'd belonged to someone else, and nothing during her ill-fated marriage had ever come close to what she felt right now.

Her imagination hadn't come that close, either.

She could no more have broken Connor's kiss than she could have flown to the moon in her '98 minivan. She leaned closer to the hard wall of his chest. Reveled in the strength of his arms, the possessiveness of his mouth.

At Drew's sleepy yawn from the couch, Connor stepped back and stared at her, his breathing unsteady, his eyes dark and intent. "I shouldn't have done that." His voice dropped so low that it felt like a deep rumble against her skin. "Not here. Not now. Not…ever."

"You stole my lines." She conjured up a faint smile. "Maybe we should just blame this on the late hour and let it go at that."

He searched her face. "You understand…I'm not looking for anything here."

He'd already made that more than clear, and though her nerves still tingled and her pulse still tripped over itself, she smiled for real. "I'm not a little college girl anymore. Don't worry—I won't throw myself at your feet over one kiss. Tenant. Landlord. Nothing more." With an offhand wave of her fingers, she moved past him and into the kitchen, where a three-wick candle bathed the room with soft light. "Guess we can't make any coffee, unless you have a camp stove handy."

"Somewhere out in the garage, probably. Or the storage shed, with Ed's camping gear." Connor followed her and headed for the oversize refrigerator at the end of a long, emerald-veined marble counter. "There's soda in the refrigerator…bottled water… maybe a beer."

"Water would be great."

Accepting the bottle he handed her, she leaned a hip against the edge of the center island that provided more counter space than she'd had in her entire kitchen back in Wausau.

High above them, huge skylights were set in the slanted ceiling, and at the far end of the room, behind a rustic oak table and ten matching chairs, rain streamed down a wall of windows that stared out into the night. "This kitchen is even nicer than the rest of the house. Are you a gourmet cook?"

"Right." He twisted the tab off a can of Coke, then

tipped it back and took a long, slow swallow. "Gourmet all the way."

He leaned over and caught the door of the massive side-by-side refrigerator with one hand, revealing a freezer compartment filled to the top with neatly stacked red boxes of frozen entrées. "This is dinner, until the middle of next month."

"I suppose you—"

A bloodcurdling scream from the family room sent a shock wave through the stillness of the house.

Erin froze for a split second, then slammed her bottle on the counter and ran for the other room. Connor beat her there.

The two lumpy forms on the sofas stirred, mumbled groggily. Lily peered out from the edge of her sleeping bag, groaned and flopped back down. Drew started to reach for Tyler, then stopped and looked gratefully at Erin and Connor before lying down and pulling his own bag tighter over his head.

Connor slipped down on the floor next to the younger boy, who was sitting next to the couch, his face a mask of sheer terror as he screamed. His bloodless hands clenched the edge of the coffee table next to him, then flew into the air as if he were fighting away an unseen assailant.

Whispering soothing words to him, Connor gently curved an arm around the child's back to protect him from banging against the furniture—though Erin knew Tyler wasn't really awake, and didn't even realize Connor was there.

She dropped to her knees next to them. "He has these night terrors often," she murmured after Tyler finally calmed. "I do the same thing you did, trying to keep him safe, but I always feel so helpless."

Connor settled him back down in his sleeping bag. "It's unusual to see this so early in the night. He hasn't been asleep very long."

"Maybe because he's here instead of his own bed. Sometimes these episodes will last for a half hour or more, though the next morning he has no memory of them happening. It scares the other kids, though, and it drove my husband crazy. He kept saying to just 'wake the darn kid up,' but that doesn't really work."

Connor stood up and looked down at the sleeping child. "Tyler's panic probably just escalated."

"Exactly." Erin followed him back into the kitchen. "Sam is a good man, but fatherhood was a hard adjustment for him—and adopting older children was an even bigger challenge. He expected too much of them, and he wasn't very patient."

Though Connor was. She'd seen him gently restrain and protect Tyler from harm despite the child's frantic screaming, and there'd been no sign of impatience in his calm voice.

"You would have been a wonderful father," she murmured.

He shrugged. "Just pediatrics 101."

Not true. She knew how lacking in parenting skills a man could be.

Later, she curled up under some blankets in a guest room just off the family room, so she could be close to the children. Unable to fall asleep, she stared up at the ceiling as old memories mingled with what she'd seen of Connor tonight.

He wasn't just skilled. He was a caring and thoughtful man, a man who'd been deeply wounded by his failure to save his wife.

And now, Stephanie's tearful claims on the day of Uncle Theodore's funeral began to ring false. "He wanted me to have an abortion—we broke up over it. When we got back together a few years later, I told him I'd had his baby. He swore he never wanted to see her or hear about her—even when I told him she was physically challenged and in foster care."

Would Connor really have rejected his own child? It no longer seemed possible. And if Stephanie had lied, did that change the oath of secrecy she'd demanded before releasing Lily for adoption?

Connor had relinquished his rights to his daughter long ago…but he didn't know she was now in Erin's care.

Torn and uncertain, Erin puzzled over the situation. It was nearly daybreak before she realized what she had to do. Whatever he'd decided in the past— whatever trouble it might now cause—surely Connor had a right to know.

MORNING BROUGHT A THICK blanket of snow, bright sunshine and unexpected sounds and aromas emanating from his kitchen. The clatter of pans. The scents of brown-sugar-cured bacon—which must have been in the freezer behind the ice cream and TV dinners.

Connor blearily stared out the large windows next to his bed, then rolled over and reached for the digital clock on the nightstand. He studied the blinking numerals. *Electricity.*

Which meant that he could plow the lane, bundle up the Langs and take them back where they belonged.

A good thing, because hearing the laughter of children echo through this empty mausoleum of a house, and having Erin's company last night, had been…nice. Too nice. The sooner they were gone, the less they would disrupt his peaceful, solitary world. Already, he knew just how painfully quiet it would be when they were gone.

Having company was definitely unsettling. Having Erin here was even worse. What on earth had possessed him to *kiss* her? Big mistake. Big, *big* mistake, and one he hadn't stopped thinking about since. He'd given up on sleep when his wristwatch said 2:00 a.m., and had started reading the latest McMurtry novel by flashlight. At five he'd finally dozed off for a couple of hours.

Ridiculous, dwelling on a simple kiss like some randy teenage boy. But it had been so long since he'd been with a woman, so long since he'd even thought about it, that the sweet scent of her and the lush feeling of her mouth beneath his had apparently slammed his body into overdrive. *Damn.*

Throwing back the covers, he pulled on his jeans, a heavy cabled sweater and thick socks, then fumbled for the shoes he'd dropped at the side of the bed.

Tossing the down comforter across the mattress, he turned to go downstairs, make it through breakfast and see about rounding up Erin and the kids.

One of them appeared at his door just as he did. Lily looked up at him with eerily familiar pale gray eyes.

Shaking off *that* thought, he gave her a brief smile. "Did you sleep okay?"

"'Cept for Tyler. He wakes us up a lot." She ducked shyly. "Erin says breakfast is ready, so you should come downstairs."

"Then I guess I'd better do that." He couldn't help but grin back at her. An angel couldn't have appeared more fragile or innocent. He reached out to tousle her silky, superfine hair. "Don't want your mom getting mad at us, right?"

And then his gaze dropped to her little bare feet. One was misshaped, but the other had a graceful high arch and long, slender toes, the second toe longer than the first, all with perfect little nails. So much like...

A weight settled on his chest, making it hard to breathe as he studied her oval face. The dark rim around her silvery irises. The swirl of cowlick at her right temple, one that everyone in his family had fought for generations. *How could he have missed so many clues?* They were all there, in Lily's delicate features. Yet how…

Anger surged through him, followed by a deep sense of betrayal—one that burned through his gut with the force of a wildfire. "Maybe," he said evenly, "you could ask Erin to come up here for a minute first."

Searching his face with a worried frown, Lily nibbled at her lower lip as she took a cautious, halting step back, clearly aware of his abrupt change of mood. "But your pancakes are done. We made 'em just for you, and I even made the batter. You don't wanna come?"

At the hurt in her eyes and the touch of fear in her voice, he softened. "Of course. Lead the way."

He'd watched her awkward ambulation before and had mentally assessed the problem as equinovarus—clubfoot. One that had been inadequately treated with manipulation, bar shoes and a series of casts to bring her ligaments and bones into correct alignment.

But then he'd seen her as simply someone else's child—a potential pediatric patient. A medical case, not something more personal.

Now, his heart ached as he watched his daughter's uneven stride. He'd seen the Ponseti method of treatment work in dozens of cases, but time was of the essence when a baby was born with this abnormality. Being in foster care, there might not have been much continuity if she'd been moved from one family to the next, but why hadn't some caseworker followed up to ensure that she was properly treated?

Erin had said that she'd adopted Lily less than a year ago…but there were other surgical procedures that could be done for an older child….

In the kitchen, Lily moved across the room to stand next to Erin at the stove. "He's here," she announced. "Tyler and Drew already went outside to play in the snow. Can I go, too?"

Erin reached for a paper towel and dried her hands, then turned to bring a heaping plate of pancakes and bacon to the kitchen table, setting it down in front of Connor. "You don't have your warm snow pants," she chided. "Go outside and get chilled, and you could be sick tomorrow."

"But Drew—"

"Drew and Tyler wore their snow boots when we went to town. You said you could only find your sneakers."

"I could *borrow* boots."

Lily turned and gave Connor a beseeching look, and he realized that he would have done almost anything to fill her small request. The thought that she'd been without a family to call her own, without a mother who loved her and all the security of a permanent home for so much of her young life, made him feel as if a fist had clamped down on his gut. "No one here is your size, honey. My boots are way too big."

She flopped into a chair at the end of the table and slumped down, as forlorn as a child who'd lost her best friend.

Erin poured two cups of coffee and put one in front of Connor, then sat next to Lily. "I'll clean up the kitchen, and then we can go home if Connor doesn't mind giving us a ride back. Then you can put on all your warm clothes and we'll make some snowmen before this snow melts. Okay?" She glanced up at the skylights, where already the snow was starting to drip in the bright morning sunshine, then reached over to give the child a quick hug. "This is an unusually early snow, but believe me—this far north, we'll have *lots* of it this winter."

From outside came the whoops and hollers of the other two children, and Lily slid even lower in her seat. "Not fair."

No, life wasn't fair, and Connor knew that more than most. Especially now. "You know what? You don't have cable down at your house, but there's a big dish on this one, and there must be a hundred channels that come in up here. Would you like to go into the family room and have the big-screen TV all to yourself?"

She peeked at him from under her bangs. "Really?"

"Come on—I'll show you how to use it." Connor pushed away from the table and led her into the family room, where he handed her the remote and gave her a quick lesson, then watched as she turned on the

TV, found a zoo veterinarian show on *Animal Planet*, and curled up under an afghan on the love seat. "Like animals, do you?"

"Oh, yes." Her eyes sparkled. "I'm going to be a veterinarian when I grow up. I want to work in a zoo, just like those guys. I *love* cheetahs."

"Sounds like a cool job."

"The best part would be those little orphans, the ones you get to take home, and love, and be just like their mom. That's so awesome."

He wanted to ask what it had been like for her, without a mom and dad. Had she been moved often from one foster family to the next? Most of those homes were wonderful, loving, yet sometimes a county had too few options, and had to overcrowd the limited number of families available. And what if the other kids had been cruel about her disability?

But the opportunity to talk would come later. He'd make sure of that.

"Don't you want your pancakes?" Lily said, tearing her attention away from a pair of lambs frolicking across the screen.

He wanted to just stay and watch her.

Yet, with the boys outside and Lily entranced by an animal show, it would be a perfect time to find out a few things, too. "I'll be back in a little while," he said. "Just holler if you need anything, okay?"

Back in the kitchen, he found Erin standing at the windows watching the boys throwing snowballs at the trunk of a tree.

She looked over her shoulder and smiled. "Reminds me of when I was a kid. Snow forts, snowmen—and with every big snowfall, we'd make snow ice cream. Small-town stuff, but every minute was such fun. You grew up in…Green Bay, wasn't it?"

"Close by."

She studied his face, her smile fading. "I think we must be intruding on you too long. I'll do the dishes quickly while you eat, and then we can be on our way. I'm sure you must have a lot to do."

Moving closer to her, he leaned a shoulder against the refrigerator and folded his arms across his chest. "I don't think I could eat anything, but thanks anyway."

"Oh. Well, then, I'll just clean up the kitchen and—"

"I'll get to that later."

Now she appeared flustered, uncertain. "It…was so nice of you to rescue us last night. I can just round up Lily and get her coat on—and the boys are already outside. Do you think your SUV can make it down the road?"

"I don't want you to leave right now, Erin."

She froze, her hand halfway to his breakfast plate. "Why?"

"I think you know why." He bit out the words, one by one, but took no satisfaction at the shocked realization dawning in her eyes. "I'd stake my medical license on the fact that Lily is Stephanie's daughter—and I'd like to know why the hell no one ever bothered to tell me."

CHAPTER TEN

ERIN FELT THE BLOOD DRAIN from her face as she reached blindly for the back of a chair to support herself. "I—I planned to tell you."

Anger flashed in his eyes, coupled with disbelief. "Oh, yes. I'm sure you did." He glanced at a calendar on the wall. "You've been here, what—a month? We've run into each other almost every day at the hospital. At Ollie's twice. At your place, here and on the road. You never said a word."

"I thought about it." She gripped the chair until her knuckles turned white. "Last night."

He gave a low, derisive laugh. "Convenient. And you'd planned to discuss it this very morning, no doubt."

"I did." She took a deep breath. "Though I'm sure you don't believe me."

A muscle ticked along the side of his jaw. His eyes narrowed. "Lily is *eight years old*. Isn't that just a little late?"

"Look, until moving here, I've seen you exactly once since college—and that was at Stephanie's funeral. I barely know you, really, and she didn't tell me about Lily until we ran into each other just a few months before she died. With Stephanie's blessing, I started looking into the adoption."

"You didn't think to say anything about this to me at her funeral?" His voice was raw, hoarse. "You didn't think I'd want to know that she had a child?"

"I think you should look a little closer to home before passing judgment."

He blinked at that. "I don't know what you mean."

"Think about it, Mr. Perfect. You made your choice a *long* time ago. Maybe you've had a change of heart, but it's a little late." Erin glared at him as she strode to the kitchen counter, grabbed her purse and stalked to the door of the family room. "Lily— it's time to leave, honey. Let's get your coat."

"But this is a *good* show!" Lily burrowed deeper under her afghan. "Can't we stay just another ten minutes? It's almost over."

"Yes, Mom—stay a little longer." Connor had followed her. "We need to talk."

Erin wavered. Lily rarely asked for much of anything. Yet with every passing minute Erin spent talking to Connor, it would be harder to rein in her rising temper. On the other hand, running would only delay the inevitable. "Ten minutes, Lily. No more—and no more arguments. Deal?"

At Lily's vigorous nod, Erin pivoted and paced to the farthest point in the kitchen, by the dining room table. "I repeat," she said firmly, "that it's rather late to change your mind, don't you think?"

"Change my mind about something—or someone—I never knew existed?" He shook his head in obvious disgust. "If I hadn't noticed a family resemblance, I might never have suspected."

"Then maybe you should've been a more loving and responsible guy." She could see that he was thinking, sorting through past history—as if anyone could forget. "Stephanie told me she was six weeks pregnant when you broke up with her in college. Some boyfriend you were, dumping her and telling her to get an abortion."

"I…" His voice trailed off in stunned disbelief.

"Oh, come on, Reynolds." Erin threw up her hands in disgust. "No one could've forgotten that."

"Forgotten something that *never happened?*"

"Right." Erin gave him a narrow look. "But then she couldn't go through with the abortion…and she didn't tell anyone in her family about the baby. She made sure they never knew."

"But when she and I got together again a few years later…"

Unless the man was a consummate actor, he couldn't possibly be showing such a range of emotions—anger, bitterness, a soul-deep sense of loss. Had Stephanie *lied?*

Frowning, Erin studied his expression. "She said she told you about Lily being in foster care, and having lots of medical problems. She said you were furious, and refused to have anything to do with the child—it was either you or Lily. And Stephanie loved you too much to let you go a second time."

"Either that," he said bitterly, "or she was just afraid she might lose her chance at being a *doctor's wife,* so she let my daughter languish in foster care. Status and money were all that mattered to her, in the long run."

"She couldn't have done that—she *wouldn't.*" But even as Erin defended her cousin, she had only to remember the shallow person Stephanie had been in college, or to recall her wealthy and influential parents, who'd snubbed Erin's own family for years.

"Ironic—something she said once made me think that maybe she'd had a child with some other guy after we broke up, but she flatly denied it." He gave a short, humorless laugh. "She struggled with major depression, true…but she was also diagnosed with a personality disorder, and I was still fool enough to *believe* her. I just never guessed that she'd go so far as to deny her own daughter a home."

"Lily was in foster care from the day she was born. Stephanie never went to see her, but never signed the papers to release her for adoption, either. Then Lily needed surgeries and had long convalescence periods, she grew older, and no one wanted to adopt her."

He swore under his breath. "And you knew this all along?"

"I found out about Lily two years ago—just

months before Stephanie died, Connor. When I mentioned Sam and I were considering adoption, she *begged* me to take Lily, too. Believe me, I was more than willing."

His gaze narrowed and his jaw hardened, and Erin felt an uneasy chill.

"Then why didn't she finally tell me? Why didn't you?"

"She said she was afraid you'd leave her. And she made me promise that I'd never tell anyone—especially you—because you'd supposedly demanded that abortion in the first place. But now…well, she's gone, and her parents are gone…."

"So Lily spent years in foster care, because no one in your family seems to have more than a passing acquaintance with the truth." His mouth flattened to a grim line. "You can bet this won't be the end of our discussion. I'm contacting my lawyer."

BEFORE, ERIN HAD SAVORED each step of their bedtime ritual as she tucked Lily in at night. Breathing in the wonderful little-girl scents of the child's shampoo and bath powder, she'd assumed that the routine would go on through countless weeks and months and years ahead, until Lily was grown. The thought had filled her with peace and contentment.

Even now, sitting at her desk at the hospital, Erin felt her eyes burn when she thought about Lily's sweet prayers and their traditional big hug and kiss at bedtime.

Life had been easier when Erin still thought of Connor as the cold, selfish, insensitive jerk who'd denied the existence of his beautiful daughter. But there was no denying his stunned response at finding that he was Lily's father—he'd clearly never known about her, and Erin could hardly fault him for being shocked and angry.

Now, she couldn't help but think of him as an innocent victim in all of this, and her sense of impending loss grew with every passing day. Could he still stake a claim? Take Lily away?

The threat was there—looming like an ominous mass of storm clouds on the horizon—and she found herself jumping with every ring of the phone, whether she was at home or at work.

The fact that she hadn't seen Connor since Sunday made it worse. For the past three days he'd either been taking care of his hospital rounds earlier or dropping in much later, so she hadn't encountered him at work, and she hadn't met his car on the road.

If they could just talk it over, so she knew where he stood on the issue, maybe she wouldn't need to worry so much. But he hadn't returned her phone calls, either. Just to be safe, she'd checked around for a good lawyer.

"Hi. Are you ready for him?" Dr. Jill Edwards stood in the doorway, a tall handsome man dressed in a navy blazer and khaki slacks at her side. "This is my husband, Grant."

With his thick, dark blond hair and lean good looks, it was no surprise that Erin had heard the second shift nurses sighing over him one evening. He'd handled one of their divorces, and was known around town as a straight shooter who worked hard and treated his clients well.

"I'm so glad you could stop by." Erin stood and motioned toward the round table and chairs at one side of her office. "I certainly wasn't expecting you to come here, though."

Charming laugh lines deepened at the corners of his eyes when he smiled. "No problem. I needed to have some blood work done at the lab for my annual physical, so this works well for both of us."

Jill lingered at the door. "I have to do rounds and get back to my office, so I'll let you two talk. Honey, do you want to pick up something for supper on your way home tonight?"

With a wave of his hand, Grant stopped at the table and started riffling through his briefcase. "Maybe you'd better do it, because I'm not sure when I'll get home. Just leave some leftovers in the fridge if I'm late."

"Okay." Jill's smile wavered. "Well…drive safe, then."

After she disappeared down the hall, he moved over to shut the door, then returned to the table and dropped into one of the chairs. He settled a pair of reading glasses on his nose and briefly glanced at a page of notes. "From our phone call, I understand that you're concerned about the possibility of a contested adoption, is that correct?"

Erin sat down across from him and folded her arms on the table. "My late cousin encouraged me to adopt her daughter, Lily. Stephanie was young when she got pregnant—just a college student—and couldn't bear to release the baby for adoption for the first couple years. After that, with Lily's medical problems, she was just too hard to place, I guess. Wisconsin law allows a child to be adopted by relatives without a court order, so that's what we did."

"The father wasn't named on the birth certificate?"

"No."

"Was he notified of the impending adoption?"

"Stephanie said that when the baby was born, she found an elderly lawyer in a distant town so there'd be less chance of any rumors starting." Erin managed a weak smile. "She figured that a lawyer might respect her privacy, but she wasn't so sure about a secretarial pool."

"And this lawyer said…"

"That as long as the father wasn't named on the birth certificate and was unknown, she didn't have to worry."

"*Really.*" Grant looked at her over the rim of his glasses and lifted a brow.

"A public notice had to be put in the newspaper, so the lawyer ran it in his own town, and after that, the state of Wisconsin terminated the paternal rights."

"But that wasn't the father's hometown, where the conception took place or where he'd been known to live?"

"No…but Stephanie told this lawyer that she didn't have any information on him. She said it was a one-night stand."

Grant sighed heavily.

"She told a lot of stories, I'm afraid. She told me that the father knew about the pregnancy and told her to have an abortion, and that later on, he refused to have anything to do with the child." A cold knot formed in Erin's stomach. "I discovered last weekend that this wasn't true. He was her boyfriend at the time, but they'd just broken up. He didn't know she'd gotten pregnant until he saw Lily recently, and recognized some strong family characteristics."

"You've been in touch with him since then?"

"I'm afraid so. He definitely wasn't happy—he's upset over not being told in the first place, and he threatened to seek legal advice." Erin tightened her grip on her arms and leaned forward. "But the adoption is legal, isn't it? We followed every step, as blood relatives."

"But you said that there's been no actual DNA testing, correct?"

"Correct, though Stephanie once told me that he was indeed Lily's father."

Grant gave her a wry smile. "With all due respect

to the deceased, I wouldn't worry too much until there's conclusive DNA proof. This man cannot pursue any sort of custody action without a report from a licensed lab."

"I...we are scheduled at the lab tomorrow. Lily thinks it's just part of her annual physical. We didn't want to upset or confuse her, just in case the results weren't a match." She took a steadying breath. "I don't even know what to hope for. He would be a good father, yet I'm half afraid to answer the phone, for fear it's his lawyer wanting to start a custody battle. How irrational is that?"

"If this man is her father, I can offer good news and bad." Grant settled back in his chair and slipped his glasses into his coat pocket. "The good news is that you are educated and well-employed. The court would likely see you as a fit mother who can provide well for her children. You are also the child's biological relative, as well as her adoptive mother, and blood ties certainly carry weight in a court of law. Also, it was the custodial parent's wish that this child be placed with you."

"But..."

"But the child's biological father—if that is what he is—wasn't legally notified. Thus, he never intentionally relinquished his rights as her parent."

"But I *adopted* her. She's my daughter now. No one could love her any more than I do."

Grant shook his head. "You've probably read about many such cases in the newspapers over the years. A birth mother gives up her baby for adoption, a fine family takes the child and ties every possible legal knot to keep it. Then one day, the biological father turns up demanding his parental rights. After a long, expensive and very messy court battle, the father often ends up winning and the adoption is overturned. The child is taken away from the only family he or she has ever known. You think that could happen here?"

"He could file for custody, or shared custody," Erin answered. "He could request visitation rights… or he could decide that it's in the child's best interest to just relinquish his rights. I don't know him well enough to say."

"I see." Grant rocked back in his chair and stared at the ceiling for a while. "Well, just so you know, my wife told me that you were looking for legal counsel, but she doesn't know the reason why, and I will not share any of our conversations with her. Your confidentiality will be preserved unless this ends up in open court."

"So what do you think? Is it hopeless? Am I going to lose her?"

"I'll do my best to see that doesn't happen."

"There's one other thing." Erin tried for a smile. "My ex-husband and I lost a lot of money a few years ago, when the stock market took a downturn. After paying for our divorce and our outstanding bills, neither of us got much." Weariness washed through her. "I'm not sure I can afford another lawyer."

He rocked forward and planted all four chair legs on the floor, and the disarming laugh lines appeared again at the corners of his eyes. "This is a small town. I stayed here because of family and friends and the quality of life, not because I planned to retire a millionaire. You can afford me—we'll work it out."

He quoted her a reasonable retainer fee, and an hourly rate beyond that, if the need arose. Relieved, she followed him to the door of her office.

"You might not need me at all," he added. "But if you do, just give me a call and I'll be sure to work you in as soon as possible."

She offered him her hand. "I appreciate this, Grant."

His handshake was warm, reassuring, though his eyes were grave. "My wife tells me you're a great asset to the hospital, so I'm more than happy to help in any way I can. I just hope it will be enough."

AFTER A QUICK CALL HOME to check in on Haley and the kids, Erin downed a stale sandwich and luke-warm coffee from the machines in the lounge. *Show-time,* she muttered to herself as she walked to the hospital's meeting room at the end of the administra-tive wing.

Tonight's meeting promised to be bigger than most because of the efforts of the auxiliary and com-munity leaders who had been working with Erin on raising funds, and who were likely to attend.

Hopefully, everyone there would be enthusiastic

about seeing the hospital move into the twenty-first century, with a revitalized business plan and enough money to make it happen.

But there were always those for whom change was threatening, or totally unnecessary—Leo Crupper, the middle-aged owner of the local grocery store, came to mind. He often walked the streets of town with his massive dog, Burt, during his lunch break and after work, and he'd stopped her several times already to rail against the new proposals. With a little luck, he might be working late tonight and wouldn't arrive in time to share his critical views.

He met her at the doorway of the meeting room, though, with a smug smile. "Are we ready for a good presentation tonight, Mrs. Lang?"

We? "Oh, so you're speaking, too? How nice." She gave him a nod and moved past him into the room. Nearly every chair was filled—a good fifty people were present, with some standing along the walls, though she searched for Connor and couldn't see him in the crowd.

She eased past them, and found a chair at the front of the room. Paul Benson, the board president, nodded to her and called the meeting to order.

Swallowing hard, she took her notes to the podium. "As you know, we've seen declining revenues and skyrocketing costs. I've been working on these issues, looking for ways to revitalize Blackberry Hill Memorial Hospital, preserve jobs and provide bet-

ter patient services. Through the purchase of updated equipment and the scheduling of more specialty clinics, I believe we can utilize our space more
efficiently and ultimately generate greater income.
Correcting our current overstaffing, with its unnec-
essarily high staff-per-patient ratio, will generate
significant savings—especially when you factor in
the benefit package costs. If you could look at your
handouts, please…"

One by one, she addressed the items on her list.
Capital equipment. Building repairs, including a new
roof and high-efficiency, triple-paned windows. A
newer, larger MRI unit. A PACS X-ray diagnostic
system. An updated CT scanner.

When she got to the end of her proposal and asked
for questions, Leo launched himself to his feet.

"This is ridiculous. Anyone here can tell you that
this is totally impossible. Our revenues are declining and we can't come up with this kind of money.
I suggest, young lady, that you take a hard look at
where you are. This isn't New York City."

A few snickers traveled through the crowd.

Welcoming the chance for rebuttal, she gave him
a patient smile. "If the hospital goes under, most of
the employees—including nurses, aides, housekeep-
ers, maintenance people, pharmacy, lab and secretarial staff—would need to move elsewhere to find jobs.
If that happens, this town will lose families, and declining enrollment could lead to a consolidated school
district. Businesses—like yours, Leo—will struggle."

Leo snorted. "And the option is for the hospital to go too far in the red, and then go bankrupt?"

"No." She glanced at the board members seated at the front table, then addressed the crowd. "We have volunteers who have already gathered eight thousand signatures supporting the addition of a tax-levy proposal to the ballot in November. We've gotten a late start on this, because I just arrived here at the beginning of September. If we don't make the required number of signatures in time, we'll work at having a special ballot this spring."

A burly man in overalls stood up, his face reddened and his jaw working in agitation. "So we're all going to get hit with higher taxes. Like any of us can afford that!"

"Just a one-and-a-half percent sales tax, for five years. A very small amount, spread county wide, but it will allow us to make all of the major repairs and improvements this building needs. I've already applied for a USDA grant for the X-ray system we need, and there are other grants available."

A buzz of conversation arose at the back. "I assure you, none of these proposals has been made lightly," Erin continued. "I've met with staff from every department and talked to consultants from both the State of Wisconsin Health Department and from the private sector. I look forward to—"

From near the doorway, she saw Grace beckoning to her.

"I...look forward to continuing to work on this

project and will have a final report available by the end of this month." She nodded to the board. "Thanks for your time."

She made her way back through the crowd, catching both positive and negative comments along the way. When she reached the door, Grace signaled her to step out into the hallway.

"What did you think?" Erin whispered, as she fell into step with the older woman. "I knew there would be some dissenters, but Leo was in unusually good form tonight. I think he was leading the pack."

"He's not our only problem tonight," Grace said in a low voice once they were well out of hearing. "We've had another unexpected death. This time, a sixty-eight-year-old man admitted for chest pain last night who was doing well, and was likely going to be discharged in the morning. He ate supper, joked with the staff. Twenty minutes later, one of the aides found him dead."

CHAPTER ELEVEN

IGNORING HER ARTHRITIC left hip, Grace hurried
down the hall with Erin at her side. "Two of the doctors were here this evening. We've tried calling both
of them back. I did a quick review of the charting—
everything seemed to be appropriate and up-to-date
as far as Milton's meds and cares were concerned.
His blood pressure and vital signs were normal, he
was eating seventy-five to a hundred percent. Fluid
I and 0's have been fine. Afebrile since he was
brought in."

"And his chest pain?"

"Resolved…possibly a severe bout of indiges-
tion. Epigastric pain can mimic certain heart symp-
toms and send people running to the hospital, but
we're always glad when patients play it safe. We always do an EKG and run some cardiac enzymes
stat, to rule out heart damage."

They stopped as they neared the deserted lobby.

"We lost Frank Willoughby a month ago—almost
to the day," Erin said quietly. "He was ready to go
home the next morning, too."

"That's true, poor man."

"Have you seen any other unexplained deaths over the past few years?" Erin asked.

"Unexplained?" Grace felt herself bristle at the implication. "We give the very best of care—just look at our records. We had two tube-feeders who were both here for over three years, each in a persistent vegetative state. Neither one of them ever developed a single pressure ulcer."

"A sign of excellent nursing care," Erin agreed.

"Most people here have known each other since childhood, and I can't think of a single nurse or nurse's aide who would hurt a fly, much less harm a patient."

"I just want to be sure."

"Many of our elderly admissions have multiple chronic illnesses. Add acute congestive heart failure, pneumonia and strokes, and there's no getting around the fact that all people die, eventually." Grace sighed. "Yes, we've lost patients—sometimes they take a turn for the worse when you think they're doing well. But no one has ever accused us of inadequate care."

Frowning, Erin started for the east-wing nurses' station. "There will be an autopsy, right?"

"In this county, deaths in a hospital, nursing home or hospice setting aren't reported to the sheriff's office, barring unusual circumstances."

"I'd say this qualifies, unless the doctor has an explanation. Whose patient was he?"

"Dr. Reynolds, I believe."

Erin's gait faltered when they reached the station at the end of the hallway and found Reynolds writing in a chart at the desk. When he spun his chair around to greet them, Erin paled...and his mouth hardened into a grim line.

"Mrs. Lang is wondering about an autopsy for Mr. Striker," Grace said, watching the doctor and the new administrator with interest. "Do you have a cause of death?"

"Even with his previous diagnoses and current reason for hospitalization, we couldn't be sure without an autopsy." Reynolds raked a hand through his thick, dark hair. "I was just looking for next of kin. There's no one close, according to the admission sheet."

"Then you agree that an autopsy is in order?"

"A man of his age and overall condition should've walked out of here on his own power." Reynolds swiveled back to the chart, flipped it open and scrawled a new order inside. "Have the unit nurse call the sheriff's office, so the county coroner can be notified. I'm just as upset about this as you are, believe me."

ANOTHER BORING MONDAY. Drew hiked his backpack higher and stomped down the front steps of the school, wishing he could snap his fingers and be back home in Milwaukee...where he could skip school easily as not, and just hang out with his friends on the street.

Here, it was like he was five years old. Haley picked them up at three-thirty sharp. They all went straight home, where they were practically confined to the house and yard. On weekends, Erin was at home all the time—working on office stuff, or cooking or cleaning.

She was cool. The food was good and the beds were soft, and the place was cleaner than any place he'd ever been. But it still wasn't the same. Then again, if he hadn't opened his big fat mouth, he'd still be back on the streets, and Tyler…

He scowled, remembering the bruises, and the way his brother had taken to hiding in the back of a closet, behind a pile of dirty clothes. Maybe it was boring here. Maybe he and Tyler didn't fit in, but at least they were safe.

He took aim and kicked a rock off the sidewalk, his anger building. Maybe Tyler was safe, but now—

At a girlie, high-pitched scream, he looked up and saw a kid from his class crouched low, clutching her knee. Blood seeped between her fingers and tears were already trailing down her pale white skin. Cara—no, Sara was her name, and she glanced up at him with such hurt in her eyes that he felt lower than dirt.

"I—" His apology died on his lips when the bus monitor, a fifth-grade teacher who watched the kids leave at the end of the day, wheeled around from her position out by the street, took one look and came striding up the sidewalk.

Everyone said Miss Pratchett was someone to watch out for. Nearly six feet tall, with long bony fingers and a permanent scowl, she could lift a guy right off the ground with one hand at the back of his neck, and shake him like a puppy, some kids said.

Drew scanned the street for Haley's car, then edged back into the crowd of kids still coming out of the building. Dread tied his stomach into a cold knot.

Miss Pratchett wasn't fooled. "Young man—you, with the black backpack. Come here. *Now.*"

The other kids, sensing a good confrontation, parted to let him pass, then stayed to watch as he grudgingly moved forward.

The teacher dug in her jacket pocket, pulled on a pair of plastic gloves and inspected the wound before looking over her shoulder at him. "What do you have to say for yourself?"

What could he say? She'd already made up her mind about him, just like everyone else always did. From the corner of his eye he saw Lily and Tyler edge forward through the circle of kids surrounding them. "I didn't mean it. It was an accident, honest."

"He hauled off and kicked something *real* hard," some kid piped up. "It coulda hit her in the face!"

Miss Pratchett's eyes narrowed. "Name?"

"Drew. Lang," he added lamely, when she continued to glare at him.

"Have you *anything* to say to this young lady?"

"Sorry," he mumbled, looking down at the sidewalk.

The teacher ripped open an adhesive bandage and positioned it over the wound, then gave Sara a pat on the shoulder. "Make sure you take this Band-Aid off when you get home, wash your knee well and have your mother take a look, okay? I'd have you go to the school nurse, but you'd miss your bus." She turned to look at Drew as she stood up. "Do you think that's enough, Drew? Just saying 'sorry'?"

Sara straightened and pulled her backpack over a shoulder, then gave Drew a shy smile. "It was just an accident. He didn't mean to do it."

"I think it was more than that." Pratchett folded her long arms over her chest and looked at them both. "Perhaps he needs to have a little talk with the principal tomorrow, after school."

"He just…tripped," Sara insisted. "Honest."

Two yellow buses pulled up along the sidewalk, and the kids surged forward. Sara joined them, limping just a little.

The teacher didn't move. "She says it was an accident, but I've seen you out here, Drew. Every day after school. You look like a kid who's just spoiling for a fight. Do you want to tell me what's going on?"

He stared down at his shoes.

"You're in Miss Vinton's class. Right?"

Of course she would know. School was like a big spiderweb, where everything connected. Trouble in one grade just got passed up to the next, until everyone knew every last thing you'd ever done wrong—and only expected the worst.

"I think I'll need to have a little talk with Mrs. Lang."

Which meant they'd probably tell her to come in for a meeting, and Erin would have a disappointed look on her face that said she'd expected better of him. *Again.*

Life sucked.

Giving Pratchett the barest nod so she wouldn't press him any further, he trudged to the sidewalk, and wished he could turn back the clock.

On Thursday afternoon, Connor paced the length of the house once. Twice. Three times, his frustration building with each stride.

There was no point in coming back here to relax after a long day. Every waking minute he heard the echoes of Drew and Tyler's voices when they'd played outside in the snow. Of Lily's voice, nearly breathless with anticipation, when she'd invited him downstairs for the pancakes she'd helped prepare.

They were all good kids. Friendlier, after he'd started taking the time to stop in at their place now and then. He missed the laughter and the boisterous horseplay…and he missed Lily's fragile, childish beauty, and her soft, sweet voice.

He'd missed too much, dammit—eight years of his daughter's life, thanks to Stephanie's secrecy. Eight years that he could never take back.

And now…what should he do now?

The letter from his lawyer lay open on the

counter. He'd been denied his rights—no kidding—
and had valid grounds for contesting the adoption.
Numerous cases before this had set a strong prece-
dent for winning full custody, if he chose.

But what was best? His selfish need to never miss
another day of Lily's life? The prospect of a home
with no siblings, without a mother who would know
how to tie ribbons in her hair and give her home-
cooked meals?

Or was there some value in growing up with her
father—her own flesh and blood—who would simply love her more than anyone else possibly could?

In the past twelve days, he'd agonized over what
was best for her. Longed to stop at Erin's place
where he could just sweep Lily up into his arms and
tell her who he was—and how he'd instantly, irrev-
ocably fallen in love with her.

But always, his more practical side warned him
what that could do to her. She'd had uncounted
changes in her young life. Long hospitalizations,
foster homes. There'd been no one person in her life
who'd loved and cared for her every day—until Erin
adopted her.

Surely the child had bonded so thoroughly with
Erin that to wrench her away would be an unpardon-
able sin. Yet there could be shared custody…visita-
tion rights….

The unfairness of it all burned at his soul. Stephanie surely should have known that he would have
welcomed their baby in an instant. Yet she'd stolen

that opportunity from him, and had left their child in the uncertain and changeable world of foster care, where the home Lily had one day might not be available six months later. What kind of mother would do that?

And Erin Lang had kept her secret.

As Connor paced the room several more times, Maisie lifted her head from her paws and watched with mild interest, flapping her silky tail against the floor whenever he drew near.

Uttering a soft curse, he wheeled around, grabbed his keys and whistled to her. "Come on, girl...want to go visit that pup? It's time we went for a little ride—and it may be the last time we're welcome."

CHAPTER TWELVE

CONNOR DROVE SLOWLY DOWN the lane from his house and stopped briefly at the turnoff to Erin's. Her babysitter's rust bucket of a Mustang was still there, so he took Maisie back home, gave her some dog treats as consolation, and then continued into town.

He'd skipped the weekly breakfast at Ollie's this morning, not wanting to risk an awkward encounter with Erin in front of so many prying eyes. Still, he'd driven past the diner on his way to the clinic, and her minivan hadn't been parked in its usual place. Had she decided to avoid *him?*

Surely she had to be nervous, wondering when he would make a move regarding Lily. He'd practically threatened her with that prospect, though he hadn't meant to come on quite so strong. But now…

The hospital staff parking lot was half-full, since most of the office workers left at five. He parked next to her Windstar and strode in the front door—and nearly collided with the elderly housekeeper who usually worked nights.

She jerked her scrub bucket out of the way. "Sorry, sir," she mumbled, taking a step back in obvious deference.

"My fault. I wasn't paying attention." He nodded to her and headed for the open door of Erin's office, his shoes squeaking on the damp floor.

The noise didn't jar Erin out of her concentration.

There had to be twenty old charts piled high on her desk, thick ones and thin, each enclosed in a manila folder and held with a rubber band. She chewed on the end of her pen, then jotted a few notes on the yellow legal pad by her phone.

"Got a minute?" he asked.

She jerked her head up in surprise, then her eyes widened. Her hand flew to the neckline of her pale blue sweater. "Connor."

"I drove past your house, but your car wasn't there. I should have guessed that you'd be here."

She glanced at the clock on the wall. "Not for much longer. Barring an occasional late meeting, I'm always home in time to make supper."

There was a defensive note in her voice that he hadn't heard before—a reminder that everything had changed between them, and not for the better. "Maybe I should stop at your house later this evening?"

"No...this is okay." Only the flutter of her fingertips at her throat gave away her tension as she met his eyes. "Is there something you need?"

"I need to talk to you about Lily." He dropped a

document from the Wisconsin Regional Genetics Lab on her desk. "I...got this back today."

"Already?" She blinked and shook her head as she looked at the report. "We just sent it off last Friday."

"I paid nearly double to have it done stat, and express mailed. I figured it was best to know for sure where we stood." He'd thought he might feel a sense of victory, but looking at her pale face and trembling fingers, he felt only a wave of regret over how this would change her life. "DNA tests are better than 99.9% accurate, and they say she is mine."

"But h-her adoption was legal. She finally has a stable, loving home, with brothers and a mom who loves her. Would you try to take away the only real family she's ever known?"

He walked into the room and dropped into one of the chairs in front of her desk. "The adoption actually wasn't legal. Stephanie made false statements regarding Lily's parentage, and continued to keep the child a secret from me despite countless opportunities to reveal the truth. My lawyer also discovered that my rights were improperly terminated. But," he added gently, "I'm not here to argue or lay blame."

"Your...lawyer?" Erin lifted a shaking hand to her mouth and stared at him.

"I want what's best for Lily. And for all of us." He lifted a shoulder. "I just don't know what that is."

She rallied at that. "A stable *home,* with her brothers and me."

He ignored the sharpness of Erin's tone, knowing that she was scared and worried about the daughter she'd come to love as her own. "What about her closest blood relative? A father who's missed every big landmark in her life—first words, first steps—and wants a chance to see her grow up?"

Erin closed her eyes tightly for a moment. "What do you want, really? You must have some idea."

"I want to be a part of my daughter's life."

Her eyes widened with fear. "In—in what way?"

"I'm not sure. Lily has faced a lot of big changes in a short time. Coming to live with you and your husband. Your divorce. The move up here, and change of schools."

"I've given her a loving home and family," Erin snapped. "Things are settling down for her…and you want to disrupt her life again?"

"No, I want to talk about all of this. Tell me what you think would be best for her, and I'll listen."

Erin pushed away from her desk and strode to the window, then turned and propped a hip against the sill, her arms folded across her chest. The anger in her eyes faded to weary acceptance. "I think it would be in her best interest to get to know you gradually, so she'll be comfortable with you. If you want it done through legal channels, our lawyers can arrange visitation rights."

"Does it have to be so formal right now? Maybe we can just see how things go."

"That would be fine, but understand that this isn't

like a no-strings test drive. If you don't find parenthood that much fun, are you going to just disappear from her life altogether?"

"Whoa—I didn't say that at all." Connor reined in his impatience. "Maybe I could come by as a family friend now and then. We could do things together, with the boys, too. Eventually, we could work out shared custody—especially if and when one of us moves away from here."

Erin paled.

"Look, I could take this to court and I would probably win, but I don't want to fight you, Erin. For Lily's sake, I want us to get along. Anything else would be unfair and frightening to her, don't you think?"

"Will you tell her that you're her father?"

"In time, when it's right—but you'd be part of that decision, as well."

"Then perhaps we can give this a shot." Erin moved away from the window and paced the room, then turned back to face him. "I was so angry when Stephanie said you'd refused to acknowledge your own baby. I guess I finally, truly believe that she lied to me…and to her family. And to you."

"I never would have denied my child, Erin."

"Just promise me that you won't overwhelm Lily with attention, or spoil her with too many gifts. I want her to value love and affection, not what people give her. And you have to be fair to the boys. It would be hard for them to see that she was the only child who mattered to you…especially if they came to like you a lot. Fair?"

"Fair enough." He stood and offered his hand. "Deal?"

She shook his hand briefly. "Deal. But I warn you, Lily's welfare is my only concern. If this doesn't go well, you'll need to face me in court before you have any further access to her."

"Agreed, because she's my daughter, too—my blood. I'll fight for her if I have to." He gave her a grim smile. "Believe me, I'll plan on it."

Veiled threats, promises of battle. Not the best beginning. But it would have to do.

FUMING, ERIN LUGGED the stacks of old files to the cabinet in the corner of her office and locked it securely, then jerked open the lower drawer of her desk and hauled out her purse and keys. *I'll plan on it,* he'd said.

A threat that if Erin didn't cooperate, he'd gladly take her to court, fight her for custody and quite probably win.

If Stephanie were still alive, Erin would have had a few choice words to say to *her.*

Except that given her late cousin's mental illness, much of what she'd done had probably been out of her control—the addiction to alcohol, the lies, the furtive manipulations of other people's lives. It was left to everyone else to pick up the pieces.

Erin grabbed a set of files from her desk and

jammed them into her briefcase. Looked around for anything she'd forgotten, then pitched her PDA and cell phone into her purse. She gripped it tightly and bowed her head as she took a few deep breaths.

In all fairness, Connor was being incredibly civil about this. Many men might have been furious. Demanding. Some might have walked away from all responsibility. But the future now stretched out before Erin like a bottomless chasm. So many things could go wrong. He could change his mind. Lily could be confused, and upset.

She could even decide she only wanted to be with her father. The anxiety over *that* possibility had been gnawing at Erin's stomach for days.

"Taking down the place, are we?" Jill sauntered in, her voice filled with laughter. "I could hear you clear down the hall. I thought there might be some carpenters in here ripping out the walls."

"Just…in a hurry." Erin met Jill's amused gaze and collapsed in helpless giggles. "Or maybe venting, just a little."

"I saw Connor Reynolds leave the building a few minutes ago, but I won't ask. Never pry. Um…not my business." She gave Erin a broad wink as she fluffed her long dark hair. "But that is one *handsome* guy."

"Which goes to show that looks aren't everything, right?" Erin snapped off her desk lamp and took one last look around her office. "I should add that that was a personal comment, and in no way related to his professional presence at this hospital."

Jill laughed. "I gathered that. So, are you off to feed the kiddies?"

"Not nearly soon enough. My sitter must be chewing her nails by now. I try to get home at six, but that doesn't always happen. How about you?"

"Definitely no kiddies. No husband tonight, either." There was still humor in her eyes, but there was a note of loneliness in her voice. "He's gone a lot at night. Clients...neighboring towns. Between his hours and mine, we have to check our planners to meet for dinner."

"Want to join us for supper? Give me a half hour head start, and I can get something exciting started... if you like macaroni and cheese, omelets, or the all-time favorite, hamburgers."

Jill pursed her lips as she looked up at the clock. "That's the nicest invitation I've had all week. Let me follow you there so I don't get lost, and you can put me to work."

"IF THIS IS MORE COMPLEX than boiling water, I'm going to need some help here." Jill ran a finger down a stained recipe card she'd laid on the counter in Erin's kitchen. "Who makes biscuits from scratch these days, anyway? I thought they just came in a refrigerator tube."

Laughing, Erin finished adding raw onions and a can of mushrooms to the butter in a cast-iron skillet on the stove, and nodded to Lily. "Dr. Jill is going to be your doctor here. Can you help her? You're our best biscuit maker, bar none."

Lily tucked her pale blond hair behind her ears and nodded. "What kind?"

"Garlic and cheese—with the butter melted on top," Drew said as he headed out the back door with Scout on a leash. "Not something girlie."

Jill met Erin's eyes across the room. "Girlie?"

"We did lemon-cream muffins last time, with a sugary crust and a little twist of lemon rind on top." Erin turned up the heat under the skillet, remembering Lily's determination to make each one perfect. "They were a little dry, though, and his crumbled into his lap."

"He said they were dumb and belonged at a stupid tea party." Lily rolled her eyes. "But I think he was embarrassed 'cause he made a mess."

Reaching for the flour canister, Jill gave her a playful nudge. "Men can be pretty darn particular, can't they?"

"Yeah." Lily's smile faded as she shot a quick, furtive glance at Erin. "I suppose."

It wasn't hard to guess that she was referring to Sam, who had certainly been distant and withdrawn during those last few months of marriage. Erin whisked a dozen eggs, then added cheddar cheese, milk and the sautéed vegetables, and poured the mixture over croutons spread out in a cake pan.

In minutes the casserole was baking in the oven, along with Lily and Jill's biscuits. "Not a very fancy meal, I'm afraid. When I work late, I need to figure out something easy."

"At my house, 'easy' is take-out pizza or left-overs." Jill rinsed her hands in the sink. "This is a five-star restaurant by comparison." After Lily dis-appeared into the back of the house, she lowered her voice. "And just having people around to talk to is such a treat. Have you ever noticed how the silence seems to echo in an empty house? You can sense that no one else is there. And in mine…"

"You live in that lovely Victorian up on Chapel Hill, right?"

Jill shivered. "Along with a few of the long-de-ceased inhabitants, I think. The floors creak. Little drafts swirl through and make the curtains rustle. Sometimes the place seems to settle in at night—probably just the cooler temperatures—and there'll be a loud crack that wakes me right up."

Erin paused on her way to the table with a stack of plates. "You think it's haunted?"

"No…but when I'm alone there, it sometimes makes my mind wander. I think I just need to get a dog. Or maybe turn into a crazy lady with thirty cats."

"Somehow," Erin retorted, taking in Jill's sleek air of sophistication, "I can't quite picture you with a bunch of cats. An elegant Persian, maybe, and a graceful Afghan hound draped artistically across the sofa."

"I'll keep that in mind—though a nice old dog and cat from the animal shelter would probably be more my thing." She reached for a carrot from a plate of relishes on the counter. "You're lucky, you know? You've got all the divorce stuff behind you. You're here, you're settled, you've got the kids and one particularly amusing puppy. You're all set to move ahead in your new life."

Erin hesitated as she reached into the refrigerator for a gallon of milk. Grant had seemed like such a pleasant, levelheaded man, and the two of them seemed so well matched. "Are you…"

"Headed for divorce? It would certainly startle my mother, who always thought Grant was the perfect guy. I swear, if we separate, she'll keep in touch with him and forget all about me."

"I'm sorry. I didn't know."

"I don't discuss my personal life around the hospital. Not with anyone, really." Jill shrugged. "Funny, isn't it? You find the right guy. Have the career you always wanted, the house of your dreams—even if it is a little spooky. And then out of the blue, you find that your world isn't quite as perfect as you thought. He comes home late. Later. The conversations start to fade away. You become business partners who own a house together…and soon it's barely that."

"Or it's a lot more sudden—and hits you like a bolt of lightning from a clear blue sky." Erin moved to the table and started pouring milk. At a flash of movement in the living room doorway, she looked up to see Lily disappearing around the corner. "And for the kids, it's even worse."

"I can believe it."

Erin put the jug back in the refrigerator. "Come out on the porch with me for a minute."

They both stepped outside and stood at the railing to watch Drew and Tyler, who were in the clearing throwing a ball for Scout. The pup was a flurry of motion as he repeatedly raced across the field, his tongue lolling and tail wagging.

Drew whirled around and tackled Tyler and they went down in a laughing heap with Scout bouncing back and forth over them in an obvious bid for more attention.

"They look so happy, don't they? Like normal kids. But Drew still hides a great deal of anger. Tyler is painfully shy, and still wets his bed. And Lily... ever since my divorce, she's been even quieter than she was before. Unsure. I hope that someday they'll call me Mom, but I wonder if that's ever going to happen."

"How long have you had them?"

"The boys about a year, and Lily half that."

"Still not a lot of time if you consider what they may have been through before."

Erin braced her hands on the railing and sighed. "I'm looking forward to the day when the kids can feel truly secure. We'd made such progress—and then my husband split and that hurt everyone."

"It will come, in time. They've got you, they've got this great place to live, and they have a very exuberant puppy. They're bound to make friends at school. What more could they ask?"

"I suppose you're right...."

At the far end of the meadow, a golden lab sauntered out of the woods followed by a tall, broad-shouldered man. Even before he stepped from the shadows, Erin knew it was Connor, and her heart sank at the reminder of just how complicated her life had become.

CHAPTER THIRTEEN

ERIN WOULD HAVE PREFERRED to ignore him, but Jill peered at the figure at the far side of the meadow and gave a low, appreciative whistle.

"Interesting neighbors you've got up here. From what I can see—" she squinted, then a slow grin tipped up the corners of her mouth "—*very* interesting."

"Believe me—it's not what you think."

Scout romped up to the white-muzzled old lab, crouched low and pounced, his tail wagging furiously. The boys stopped wrestling, looked over at the visitor, then scrambled to their feet and headed toward him.

Jill lifted a brow. "Looks pretty friendly to me. Does Reynolds stop in often?"

All too often, and I think it's going to get worse. Erin managed a casual shrug as she watched Connor bend down to rub Scout behind the ears. "He's our only neighbor, and he's also our landlord."

Jill pursed her lips. "Maybe I should just skedaddle. You and Doc could have a nice romantic evening—"

"*No.* I mean, he must be stopping by for…well, maybe to borrow something." Erin felt her cheeks warm at the knowing expression in Jill's eyes. "The last thing I'm looking for is any sort of relationship right now. It would be a big mistake. Very big."

One of the boys must have said something to him, because Connor tipped back his head and laughed.

"How big could it be? The guy seems to like kids. He's got a nice sense of humor. He has a job. Sounds like a winner to me."

"Only if a person is looking."

They stood on the porch and watched him step back and send the ball into a high, clean arc.

Scout and Maisie flew after it. Scout stumbled over a rough patch of ground and tumbled head over heels. By the time he scrambled to his feet, Maisie had nosed the ball out of a tall patch of goldenrod and started trotting back to Connor, clearly pleased with herself.

The kitchen stove timer buzzed. Jill glanced at Erin, her eyes full of the devil as she held open the cabin door for them both to go back inside. "That big casserole isn't going to heat up well for leftovers."

"Then we can all eat doubles. Triples."

"And," Jill continued blithely, "you know he'd probably welcome the invitation."

On the verge of explaining the entire situation, Erin hesitated, then changed her mind.

If Connor didn't follow through well on his daddy role and later chose to leave the area, would people question her about him in the future, and make her feel even more abandoned? The uncertain, complex situation made Erin's temples start to throb.

"You're right," she said finally, after she checked the casserole and biscuits in the oven and reset the timer for another five minutes. "I'll go ask him to stay. But please—don't read anything more into this than there is. He's not here to flirt, believe me."

"Not a word. I swear." Jill tapped her lips with a forefinger. "The last thing you want is a buzz of gossip floating around the hospital. And in a town this size, that can happen mighty fast."

Giving her a nod of thanks, Erin went out on the porch to call the boys for supper—and found Connor and them just beyond the porch, where Drew was hooking Scout up to his chain.

"Supper's ready." She managed a smile for Connor. "You're welcome to join us if you'd like to. Jill Edwards is here, too."

"I'm sorry. Maisie and I were out walking, so we stopped by." He gave her a wry smile. "I don't want to interrupt your plans."

"No…it's fine. Really." She swallowed hard. "What better time to start than now?"

Drew's suspicious gaze ricocheted between them both. "Start what?"

"Being *friends*."

Though being friends was not going to be an easy thing—not when the mere sound of Connor's voice had the power to make her insides warm, and when just meeting his gaze made her feel giddy.

Jill and Connor chatted easily about hospital policy as Erin set the casserole on a trivet in the center of the table and put the hot, buttery biscuits in a basket lined with a red linen napkin.

"All set, everyone?" she called out.

Drew and Tyler thundered to the table and took their places with a screech of chairs against the oak flooring. Lily joined them, her eyes downcast—feeling shy, probably, given the additional two adults at the table.

Erin stood behind Lily to rest her hands on the child's shoulders as they said grace, then gave her an extra little squeeze before taking her own place.

The phone rang the moment she sat down. "I'll just let the answering machine get it," she said with a wave of her hand.

But from across the table, she saw Drew glance anxiously toward the phone before dropping his gaze to his lap, and warning bells started tolling in her mind to the exact rhythm of the telephone's rings. *Not again.*

"On second thought, maybe I'd better check this call, in case it's someone from the hospital." She made it to the phone at the far end of the kitchen just after the answering machine kicked in. Instead of picking up the receiver, she turned the volume down low and listened to the caller's message.

"This is Miss Pratchett from the elementary school. We've had some problems with Drew...."

Erin rested her forehead against the cupboard door. *Belligerence. Careless disregard for fellow students.*

It was an all-too-familiar litany, one that had been addressed by the teachers and counselors back in Wausau. And now, despite this new start in a new school, the problems were back. After supper, she and Drew would have a talk…and tomorrow she would call the school.

With a deep sigh, she pasted a casual smile on her face as she headed back to the table.

But when she walked around the corner, Drew was gone.

HUMILIATION BURNED through Drew as he ran for the door, jerked it open and raced across the meadow to the stream. Erin had turned the answering machine volume down low as she listened, but he'd still heard every word. And from the sympathetic glances of everyone at the dinner table, they'd all heard, too.

He slid down the bank of the stream, battled through a tangle of wild raspberry vines and jumped from one slippery, moss-covered rock to another until he reached his favorite—a broad, flat boulder in the middle of the creek, just big enough for him to sprawl across and dangle his hands in the icy rushing water on either side.

On it, he could close his eyes and be on a boat cutting through the waves of the Pacific toward some secret island…or in a canoe, paddling through a dark and dangerous part of the Amazon.

Or, on bad days, he could just come here to get away from everyone and everything, and let the sound of the water drown out his anger and the fear that sometimes grew in him until he thought it might explode, like the creature that burst out of some dude's chest in *Alien*.

At the rustling of branches behind him, he looked over his shoulder and saw Dr. Reynolds standing at the top of the bank.

"Cool place," he said mildly. "I bet you come out here a lot."

Great. Another adult, thinking that suddenly being a "best friend" would solve everything. It was so totally fake that Drew wanted to barf. He didn't bother to hide his scowl.

"Erin has dinner on the table. Are you coming back?"

Drew shook his head.

"Mind if I join you?"

Like I have any choice. Drew jerked a shoulder impatiently, hoping the guy would take a hint, but he came down the bank and settled on a boulder at the water's edge. "Think there's any trout in there?"

"Dunno."

"Ever gone fishing?"

"No."

The doctor fell silent, and after a few minutes

Drew ventured a glance at him. He was studying the creek, his mouth curved in a faint smile.

"Seems to me," he said, "that a boy who lives here ought to be fishing a lot. Look up there." He pointed to the opposite bank, a dozen or so yards upstream. "See that old tree that fell in the water? The current is quiet there, and the branches under the water provide nice structure for the fish. I'll bet you could land a fly just a little north of there and catch some fat rainbows."

Drew had expected a stupid man-to-man talk. One of those behavior lectures thinly disguised as friendly conversation. That, he was prepared to ignore. But fishing...

Some places in the stream were shallow. Some were so deep that you couldn't see the bottom. He stared at the dark water swirling past him, imagining for the first time all of the creatures that might live in its depths. Huge, slithery fish. Slimy things with long tentacles and big squishy suckers. Ancient fish with armored plates and dagger-sharp teeth.

And maybe they were watching him, from just below the surface.

Suppressing a shiver, he pulled up into a sitting position. "What else could be in there?"

"Brook trout, probably. Browns. Large- and smallmouth bass. When I went to buy my trout stamp and license last month, a guy at the store said someone caught a big muskie out of a stream not far from here. That's pretty rare, though."

The types of fish meant nothing to Drew…except that the rainbows sounded pretty, and the browns sounded sorta dull. But at the thought of catching them, he couldn't hold on to his scowl any longer. "Here? *Really?*"

"Maybe." Reynolds gave him a measuring look. "But a guy has to develop his technique, then learn to read the streams—so he can outguess the fish. And he's got to have a lot of patience."

"You could show me how?" Drew's excitement faded as he saw through the doctor's intent. Another little life lesson, hidden in a bunch of stupid talk about fishing—something Drew wouldn't ever get to do, because most guys had dads that did those things with their sons. And he had…no one.

He turned away and flopped back down on the rock, tuning out the conversation…until he caught what the guy was saying.

"—I'll check on the license regulations for youths and get back to you. Oh, and Erin says she wants you home in thirty minutes. She'll keep your supper warm."

When the words sank in, Drew twisted around to look at him, but Doc was already halfway up the bank. Regulations? A *license?* Did that mean…

Nah. Big words, careless promises. Drew had been down that road before. And believing any of that crap was just a waste of time.

THE EMPTY DEPTHS of Drew's eyes haunted Connor all night.

The kid held absolutely no hope that anyone

would ever follow through with a promise. Sure, he'd probably come from rough circumstances, and he'd been adopted at the late age of nine or ten. His adoptive father had split. But had Drew faced even more disappointments with Erin? Was she truly a fit mother for the two boys? For *Lily?*

The thought made it nearly impossible to fall asleep. And then he'd awakened at dawn, to impatiently watch the clock until the time when he could reasonably track her down at the hospital. Eight o'clock had never taken so long to arrive.

Now, at the door of her office, he felt ready to take her on, to challenge her with a long list of questions. If he didn't like what he heard, he wasn't waiting around to "get to know Lily better"—he would contact his lawyer about custody.

"Erin, we need to talk."

She peered over the stack of charts on her desk, her sunny yellow sweater in direct contrast to her tired smile. "It was nice of you to come over last night."

"I didn't mean to drop in during supper. Thanks, though…it sure beat one of my frozen entrées."

"No problem." She hesitated. "Thanks for talking to Drew."

The boy had shuffled into the house just as they were finishing dessert, his eyes downcast, and had gone straight up to his room. "I'm not sure it did any good," Connor stated.

"With Drew, that's often the case." She sighed and

leaned back in her chair. "After you left, he said something about fishing."

"*Fly*-fishing."

"Ah, yes." She laughed. "Definitely a different plane altogether, from what I hear."

"I offered to teach Drew. He seemed attentive for a while, then shut me out."

"That's not a surprise, believe me." She waved toward a chair in front of her desk. "Have a seat, if you can take a few minutes."

She waited until he'd settled into it, then shoved a stack of charts to one side and met his eyes squarely. "I have to ask you one thing—and it means a great deal. It isn't important that you give these kids anything tangible. But if you tell them something—if you say you'll do something with them, or promise to come back on a certain day—you've *got* to do it."

"I'm not so sure he was interested."

"Believe me, he was. I could hear it in his voice when he mentioned fishing to his brother after you left. He hides behind a tough attitude because he's afraid to show much emotion about things. I think," she added slowly, "that he must have faced endless disappointments before he came to live with me."

"How much were you told?"

"Enough to know that he and Tyler are two of the strongest, bravest little boys I've ever met…and to know that I never want another adult to betray their trust." The thread of steel in her voice was unmistakable. "If you talked to Drew about fishing with him, you absolutely have to follow through. Not next year, not next month. *Soon.*"

With her delicate features and gleaming cap of dark hair, she hardly appeared threatening, but the glint in her eyes promised a serious battle if he didn't measure up.

She reminded him of a petite Viking warrior, defending her family, and his worries about her eased. Satisfied, Connor leaned back into his chair. "I'll look into the license requirements for kids this afternoon. In some states, they don't even need one."

"There's a bait-and-tackle shop on the edge of town, and I'm sure they must sell licenses there. I can get it, though. The responsibility is mine."

"No, I'll do it. I'll probably be going past before you, anyway." His gaze fell to the stack of charts on her desk. Old ones and new, there were several dozen, and they all bore one unifying feature: the lime-green sticker on the spine of the folder indicated that they were all Hadley patients. And by default—at least for the next few months—his own.

Connor frowned. "Something wrong?"

"Research." She gave an offhand wave. "Just research."

"On Ed's patients?"

"On the past in general." She looked up at the clock. "And I've got quite a few old charts to cover before I meet with the office staff at nine. I'm glad you could stop by, Connor."

He rose, stepped closer to the desk and lifted several of the folders on top. From the dates on the outside covers, they all went back three to five years. More curious now, he opened several and discovered that the top sheet in each was a copy of a death certificate.

"You're checking up on my *uncle?*"

"I've been reviewing everything. Everyone."

Incredulous, Connor stared at her. "But you had stacks of charts in here before, and the spine stickers were a variety of colors. I can't help but think you're narrowing your search. Hell, he hasn't even been in town for the past month."

"As I said, I'm simply doing a review. Now, if you'll excuse me…" She stood and propped her hands on her desk. "I really do need to get back to work."

A dozen images flashed through Connor's mind. Ed's jovial laugh. The way his face glowed as he talked passionately about his career. His sorrow when he'd mentioned a patient who'd died the previous year.

"You are *definitely* following the wrong scent here. I can't think of a doctor more dedicated to his patients, or his profession. Hell, he's the one who *inspired* me to think about medicine."

"I met him. He's a very personable man." She drummed her fingers on her desk. "I'm reviewing those two unexplained, unexpected deaths in this hospital since I arrived, and I've found several others during the last few years. They all happened to be his patients."

"And that's never happened with another physician?"

"Of course it has. People do die. I'm simply looking for patterns, that's all. I had to start somewhere."

"You're an administrator, not a doctor." He tried to control the edge in his voice. "What do you think you can find?"

"Possible med errors. Breakdowns in charting protocol. Failures in care procedures, or follow-up. *Anything* that could place patients at risk. I was," she added evenly, "a surgical nurse for three years before I went back to school. I do know my way around a medical chart."

"Then let me help. I can go through these charts, too…and the other ones you're checking. Surely two pairs of eyes are better than one."

"Thanks. But, given the circumstances, I really need to do this review on my own. When I feel comfortable with the information I find, I'll take it to the board."

"The *circumstances*." Anger simmered through him at the implication. "You don't want my help because you've already decided that Ed is guilty of some sort of malpractice."

"I didn't say that."

"And you think I will *cover* for him?"

"I didn't say that, either."

"Then I guess we now know exactly where we stand. But I promise you, I won't let you use false accusations to railroad Ed into a lawsuit. This is going to be fair and impartial. And you'd better have ironclad facts before you take another step."

CHAPTER FOURTEEN

GRACE SHUFFLED THROUGH the stack of mail on her desk at noon on Saturday, tossing the envelopes into the appropriate piles. She hesitated over the last one, addressed to the Blackberry Hill Director of Nursing from the Lakeview County Medical Examiner's Office, then slit it open and spread the contents out on her desk.

Milton Striker. Height 177.8 cm. Weight 82 kg. Mild congestive heart failure. Marginally elevated BUN, indicative of mild renal failure. The other lab results were within normal range, including those values that would have indicated a myocardial infarction. No evidence of a CVA—stroke—or heart attack or internal bleeding.

She gathered up the papers and headed for the nurses' station in the hospital unit, where she found Dr. Edwards standing at the desk writing a progress note, and the unit secretary working at her computer.

Grace handed the papers to the secretary. "Put a copy of this in Milton's chart, and send copies to Dr.

Reynolds and Mrs. Lang. Then you can take his chart up to the front office."

Jill closed the folder in front of her. "Are those Milton Striker's autopsy results?"

"There wasn't much to report. The cause of death was listed as 'chronic illnesses of old age.'"

"Nothing unusual?"

"Not at all. I'm sure Mrs. Lang and Dr. Reynolds will be happy to see the results." She lowered her voice. "They were concerned, you know."

Jill nodded. "Understandably so, after that other death a few weeks ago."

Their gazes met, and Grace knew Jill was thinking the same thing. These days, litigation was all too common—even when there seemed to be no good cause.

"Which reminds me that I need to make an appointment with your husband one of these days. I've been meaning to have my will revised for ages." Grace stretched a little, to relieve some of the arthritic pain in her back. "Facing retirement has reminded me of a lot of things I need to do…and of things I wish I'd done."

Jill chuckled. "Like what?"

I wish I'd had a wild fling…with the only man I ever wanted to be with…. Grace gestured vaguely. "I'm going to pitch all of my sturdy nursing shoes and uniforms. Lose fifty pounds. Buy new clothes and go to Europe. Not one of those regimented, hand-holding tours for old folks, either. I want to stay in hostels and go at my own pace."

"Somehow," Jill said dryly, "it's a little hard to

imagine you leaving this hospital. Here you are, working through another weekend. I must see you here seven days a week. The only person who works longer hours is Mrs. Banks, and she's practically lived here since her husband died."

"I never had one to go home to, or to mourn. And seeing how her husband's death affected her, maybe I was lucky. When I retire, I'll be free as a bird. No ties, no one holding me back. No sad memories to drag me down."

"You vagabond, you—I'm jealous."

"You've got that handsome husband of yours, though. I don't imagine he'd be thrilled to see you take off on an adventure for months."

"I'm not sure he would even notice, frankly."

"I suppose he's as busy as ever?"

"I imagine so. Not that I have much firsthand knowledge."

"Long hours?"

"Long and late. The last two mornings I just found a note on the counter, since he got in after I went to bed. You can call his secretary and set up an appointment to see him, but I honestly couldn't tell you how long it will take for you to get in. I'm half tempted to make an appointment myself. For all I know, he might have dyed his hair orange or gone bald."

OUT OF THE BLUE, Connor stopped by Erin's on Sunday afternoon towing a utility trailer filled with chain-link fencing materials.

She put the last of the lunch dishes in the dishwasher, rinsed her hands and dried them on a towel as she watched him from the kitchen window. The kids had run outside the moment they heard his SUV pull to a stop by the garage, and now they stood at a respectful distance, watching him lay materials out on the ground.

Lily apparently asked him something, and he turned to look down at her with a grin that bracketed his mouth with deep dimples. Whatever he said to her made her smile.

Erin wavered, then tossed her dish towel on the counter and went out onto the porch to watch them for a few minutes.

Maybe she and Connor hadn't parted on the best of terms at the hospital a few days earlier, but that didn't mean she was going to hide in the house when he showed up. She'd seen the disbelief in his eyes at her suspicions about his uncle. She'd seen that disbelief turn to indignation, then cold resolve. He'd been offended by her refusal to accept his help…but that was hospital business, and nothing to do with the process of being good neighbors.

Tyler glanced over at her and waved vigorously. "He's making a pen for Scout! A cool one—with lots of room, and a house! *And,*" he added with obvious relish, "he says he's gonna come over to teach us how to fish with *flies.*"

"Really." Erin grinned down at him. "That sounds truly fascinating."

"He says we'd do better with bobbers, but we want to learn how *he* does it."

Connor glanced up at the house and acknowledged her with a nod before turning back to pull a toolbox and a battered wheelbarrow from the trailer. He slammed the tailgate, then motioned Drew over. Together, they began digging a rectangular space, evening out the dirt.

When Erin came back out onto the porch twenty minutes later, they were pounding stakes into the ground to create a wooden form. Both Tyler and Lily were watching with rapt attention.

It would have been all too easy for Erin to watch, as well, for however long Connor stayed out there in the meadow.

The bright October sun gilded his skin, highlighting the strong angles of his face. With each powerful, downward stroke of the mallet, his black polo shirt stretched over the muscles playing across his upper back. His faded jeans molded his trim hips and strong thighs.

And his hands were definitely not those of a pampered city boy. They were lean and strong and tanned, and he handled the mallet as if he'd spent a career framing houses and building barns.

That masculine capability spoke to her on a level she knew she'd better ignore, right along with his easy rapport with Lily and the boys, and the sound of his warm laughter floating to her on the late afternoon breeze.

Foolish thoughts, she chided herself, as she went back inside and gathered a tray of chocolate chip cookies, lemonade and cups. Out in the yard she sidestepped Scout, who bounced against her legs as she walked over to the kids. "Anyone thirsty?"

Tyler and Lily jumped to their feet and each grabbed a handful of cookies, then waited impatiently as she poured them some lemonade.

Drew, who was kneeling in the dirt next to Connor and pounding in a stake, shook his head. "We gotta get this done before the truck comes."

"Truck?"

"Cement truck—he's gonna pour a kennel floor this evening."

"On a Sunday night?"

Connor rocked back on his heels and surveyed the angles of the two-by-four framework, then pointed toward the opposite side. Drew moved over there and began pounding in another stake.

"The cement truck driver is one of my patients. We're doing a little bartering, because his son has medical problems and they don't have insurance."

Erin raised a brow. "This looks like quite a project."

He didn't look up. "The pup can't roam. It isn't safe up in the hills, and he doesn't stay home very well."

"But this is such a *permanent* structure." She surveyed the rolls of fencing materials. "Are you sure you want to do this?"

"Absolutely. Drew, you've been working really hard. Take a break while Erin and I chat a minute, okay?" Connor rose to his feet, met Erin's eyes and tipped his head toward the garage. "I need to talk to you."

Great. She put the refreshment tray down on a tree stump and followed him to the back of the garage. "Look, if this is about those Hadley charts—"

"It's about another wolf sighting."

Surprised, she lowered her voice. "Close by? Just one?"

"East of my house—not a hundred yards away—and some people living on the edge of town reported that their small dogs have disappeared. One of them spotted a gray wolf in the area that evening. I'm guessing that it's the one I've seen up here."

Her defensiveness faded. "I thought wolves avoided populated areas."

"Livestock is easy prey for them, and there are large deer herds around here. I don't want the kids to be frightened, but if wolves are going after small pets, you'd better keep a close watch on Scout."

"And the kids?"

"Usually wolves avoid people, but I wouldn't want them to take any chances."

Erin shivered as images of huge, silent creatures flashed in her mind. "Thanks for the warning."

She turned to go, but he caught her elbow gently. "Don't take any chances yourself, either. Promise?"

"Yes. Of course."

"I wish…" His eyes were intent, searching, and for just a moment, she imagined that he was going to move closer and kiss her. Erin felt a thrill race through her that made her knees go weak.

But then he released her arm and stepped back with a grave smile. "I understand your concern about the hospital…and its patients. But I want you to know that Striker's autopsy results came back yesterday and were ruled as natural causes. I hadn't seen the man until he was admitted through the E.R., but he had an appointment with Ed two months ago. All of his prescribed medications were appropriate, and the dosages were correct. None of them could have potentiated or otherwise interfered with the others."

"Was he being seen regularly at Hadley's clinic?"

"Striker had mild hypertension. A hiatal hernia. Arthritis. Diet-controlled diabetes. Ed carefully followed up on everything."

"You think very highly of your uncle," Erin said.

"He's had a long, successful career. He established a free clinic for low-income mothers and babies—one that I'm covering while he's away. He's been well thought of by his peers, and he's not a careless man."

Yet she'd found records of several unexpected deaths at the hospital over the past five years. They'd occurred at seemingly random times, without a discernible pattern that might alert hospital officials, except that so far, every patient had been Hadley's.

"I understand that you want to defend your uncle,

and I can appreciate your loyalty. But I'm just trying to cover all the bases."

"And I want to make sure that your…investigation doesn't harm a good man." Connor's voice took on a definite edge. "He doesn't deserve it, and it's a damn easy way to ruin a reputation."

"I'm not making any wild claims, Connor, and I certainly don't have a vendetta against anyone."

"Before you assume too much, promise that you'll be careful. And if you need any help, call me."

"Fair enough."

But if malpractice had occurred, Hadley's fine reputation wouldn't matter. Erin owed it to the people of Blackberry Hill to see justice done.

ON TUESDAY MORNING, Connor pulled into a parking spot in front of the hospital, turned off the motor and rubbed his stubbled face with both hands.

He'd been called to the hospital the last two nights, and the late hours had taken their toll—hell, last night he'd never even made it back home. Right now, the thought of a good hot shower and then hitting the sack sounded so inviting that it would have been all too easy to throw the Tahoe back into gear and head for home.

But the box in the back of the vehicle was too important. He'd worked too hard, lost too much sleep, to risk delaying its delivery now.

He unfolded himself from behind the wheel and

stretched, then rounded the back of the Tahoe and opened the tailgate, grabbed the box and strode into the hospital, ignoring the startled receptionist at the front desk and brushing past a nurse's aide who scuttled out of his way.

A vaguely familiar form appeared in front of him as he turned down the administrative hallway.

"Well, well, *well.*"

The nasal tone hit Connor like the sound of fingernails scraping down a blackboard, and he nearly lost his grip on the slippery plastic box in his arms as he pulled to a halt. Revulsion snaked through him. "Wayne?"

"What a surprise." The younger doctor gave Connor a sweeping glance, from his old running shoes to his faded jeans, then smirked as he met Connor's eyes. "Doing deliveries now, I take it—of another kind. How appropriate."

A dozen sharp replies shot into Connor's mind, followed by the temptation to ram a fist into Wayne Bloom's doughy midsection. But a moment of satisfaction would mean assault charges, and the spineless bastard just wasn't worth it.

Connor adjusted his grip on the box and stepped around him. "Excuse me."

Wayne moved directly into his path. *"Excuses."* He tapped his lips with a forefinger. "Interesting choice of words, Reynolds. Do they know about you here? Do they know what you did? Or is that your little secret?"

Connor glanced over his shoulder. The hallway

was deserted. "Tell me, *Wayne.* What did you get for your 'efforts' on my behalf? A nice Rolex? Money? Or did you do it out of the goodness of your heart?"

Wayne paled, but at the sound of voices coming from far down the hall, he reached up and coolly adjusted his collar. "I did the right thing."

Connor lowered his voice. "No, you didn't. And if I'd stayed around to prove it, you would have been in *jail.*"

"Really." Wayne stepped aside and smiled as two nurses walked by. "Funny, but I'd say that entire hospital in Green Bay has a different opinion."

"One not based on fact, believe me." Connor leaned closer. "If you share your stories here, you'll be hearing from a lawyer. Fast."

Wayne's mouth pursed into a smug smile. "Not my intent, buddy. Not my intent at all. In fact, I hope we will stay in touch. A good idea, don't you think?"

His blood still simmering, Connor swore under his breath as he watched the man saunter through the lobby and out the front door. *Not his intent—but something was.* Connor spun on his heel and headed down the east wing corridor to the nurses' station. Why had he shown up here?

Carl Miller looked up from his charting. "Hey, Doctor—what's up?"

"I just passed a man in the hallway. Early thirties, maybe. Sandy, thinning hair. Packing an extra twenty pounds of belly. Wire-rims. Do you know what he was doing here?"

"I asked him that myself, because visiting hours don't start until nine," Carl said with a grin. "He said he'd just stopped in town to visit with his Aunt Maude in room 12, but she wasn't in the mood for company so he didn't stay long. Knowing Maude, she probably swore at him and sent him packing after the first hello."

"Thanks." *So running into him had been a chance encounter, then. Nothing more than that.*

At least, not yet.

Connor strode to Erin's office. Rapped once on her door, then walked in and headed straight for her desk.

Her welcoming smile faded. "What—"

He dropped the box on her desk, then folded his arms across his chest. "You didn't want my help, but you've got it. Now tell me, where do we start?"

CHAPTER FIFTEEN

ERIN STARED AT THE BOX on her desk, then lifted her startled gaze to the man standing in front of her. Yesterday, she'd heard his laughter and had watched him banter with her children.

There was no sign of that humor now.

She stood and ran her fingers across the edges of the hanging files neatly suspended inside the container. "What is this?"

"You seemed so sure that Ed is guilty of malpractice—"

"No," she said quietly. "I'm not sure at all. I'm just checking old records."

"But you've singled him out, based on just a few cases out of the thousands he's admitted to this hospital during his career."

"He wasn't even in town when Frank and Milton died, but yes—I'm looking for any possible pattern."

"I've been researching his old records, and these are photocopies of hospital admissions from 2000 to the present day. The histories and physical summaries. The physician's order pages and progress notes.

In most cases, the labs. With more time, I could go back another five years."

He paced to the windows, then back again. "This is, of course, privileged information, but as hospital administrator you have access to all of the originals that have been filed. I just wanted to make it easy to review the overall statistics, so they would be very clear."

Erin felt her heart turn over at the hours of work he'd put in to defend his uncle. Connor was really a far different guy than he'd seemed back in college. Had he changed, or had she just failed to recognize him for the person he'd always been?

"Since I'm here at least once a day seeing patients anyway, let me know when you're free and maybe I can help you review the records."

"I don't think—"

"For starters, we could go through these page by page. Together. I'm new here, and I'm not staying, so God knows you won't find anyone more impartial."

At the twinkle in his eye, she couldn't help but smile back. "Except where Dr. Hadley's concerned."

Connor turned his hands palm up. "If something went wrong in the past, I'm sure he'd want to know about it. So…are you busy right now? Midafternoon? I can't later, because I promised Drew and Tyler that I'd stop over and show them some fly-fishing techniques tonight. It's not the season for it, but they wanted to try."

"Thank you, but—"

"In fact, you could have a go, too." He gave her a disarming grin. "I picked up some smaller rods for the kids, so that size would work for you."

"I'm sure the boys will love it, but I'd just be in the way."

"Not at all. You could help supervise. It would be safer that way, don't you think?"

She frowned, realizing just how neatly he'd cornered her…and just how nice his offer was.

Time and attention were invaluable, and she knew how little of either Sam had shared with the kids. There'd always been something he'd had to do, someplace he'd had to go, or he'd been glued to a sports channel on the TV.

She lifted her gaze to meet Connor's. "I suppose… Just tell me what time and I'll be ready."

At a light tap on the door, she glanced over his shoulder and saw Carl standing there, his brow furrowed. "Yes?"

"Excuse me—I don't mean to interrupt your meeting." He gave Connor a curious look as he walked in and handed him a sealed, business-size envelope. "I didn't want to miss you before you left."

Connor turned the package over. "There's no name on it. This is for me?"

"Yeah. You know that stranger you asked about—the man who was wandering the hallway earlier? He just came back and handed this to me. Said it was for you, and had a real attitude about it. He said you needed it right away."

Frowning, Connor tapped the envelope against his open palm. "Thanks, Carl. He…mentioned something about getting in touch, though I'm not sure why."

"Strange guy. He said he'd been visiting Maude…but when I took in her ten o'clock med, I asked her about him. She may be cranky and forgetful, but I think she'd remember something that happened a few hours earlier. She said she hadn't had any visitors at all."

CONNOR GRIMACED as he thought about Wayne Bloom's visit this morning.

Despite what the man had told Carl, he could have strode down the halls with his trademark doctor-as-God style that few staff members would question, caught Maude's name on the morning's menu selection form tucked in the file rack outside her door, and then used her name as an excuse to be in the hospital.

Another doctor in town had admitted her, but Connor had overheard the staff discussing her early-stage Alzheimer's. Had Wayne actually gone to see her, and had she simply forgotten his visit?

This was a less troubling scenario, though given the veiled threat in the note he'd left, it was also unlikely. The cryptic message simply read, "Your secret is safe…for now."

Connor swore under his breath. There'd certainly been no secrets kept over what happened back at

Green Bay General Hospital. It had all been intensely public, from the first move by Stephanie's father, who'd been chief of staff.

It had been *intentionally* public, designed to humiliate Connor and seed doubt about him throughout the medical community. There'd even been articles in the newspaper, albeit small ones tucked back in the community news section.

Rather than stand and fight, Connor had simply chosen to walk away. Denying Victor Ralston the satisfaction of even greater focus on the situation had seemed like the right decision at the time.

Maybe that had been a mistake.

Connor withdrew a handful of fishing rods and a tackle box from the back of his SUV and strode up to Erin's porch, where she and the children were all sitting on the front steps. "Let's go down by the stream, okay?"

"That, um, sure looks like a lot of equipment," Erin ventured. Lily hurried to catch up to her and then walked beside her, hand in hand. "What do you think, honey—are you going to try?"

"Not today."

The child slid a shy glance at Connor and he smiled back at her, his heart too full for him to speak.

Her snow-blond hair shimmered in the early evening sun and her skin was so fair, her eyes such a startling silver, that she seemed more fairy princess than child—a sugar-spun creature too lovely to be real.

What had she looked like as a baby? Were there photographs of her back then? At age one? Age two? On her third birthday or fourth? Or had she drifted through the government system without anyone ever bothering to record those precious memories on film?

The thought filled him with inestimable sadness for what he had lost…and for what she would never have. A history. Someone to lovingly recall her first steps, first words.

He glanced over her head at Erin, and caught her watching him. "I'm glad you could all come to the stream." *I'm glad Lily came along.*

Erin seemed to read his thoughts. "Lily wanted to join you," she said lightly. "None of the kids ever want to be left behind if there's an adventure in store."

A dozen yards from the tree-lined bank, Connor stopped and set the rods and tackle box on the ground. "It's easy to fish like Tom Sawyer, with a big old pole, a fat red-and-white bobber and a hook." He handed both boys a fly rod. "You plop your bait out in the water and just watch for that bobber to dip."

Drew slouched, as if with blatant disinterest, but his gaze never wavered from Connor.

Tyler nodded, his eyes wide.

"Another style is spin casting. That's what we'll do when I take you guys fishing. You use a lure, and you do a single back cast like this…." Connor picked up a rod and reel from the ground, flipped the tip of the rod behind him, then snapped it forward. "And your lure goes flying far into the lake. Have you seen people do that?"

Tyler silently shook his head. "No...except maybe on TV."

"Drew?"

Drew gave a sharp jerk of a shoulder.

"Well, that's an art in itself, and we'll fish that way if we go to a lake." Connor grinned at him. "These ole Wisconsin fish won't know what hit 'em."

"But you like fly-fishing best?" Tyler leaned over to study the box of tiny flies Connor had set on the ground.

"I do for rivers and streams, especially in shallow water. I think fly-fishing is the hardest to master and the most fun."

Drew gave him a bored glance. "So how hard can it be?"

"You think it's easy?" Connor handed him a fly rod. "A skilled fisherman can land a fly in front of a trout's nose from thirty feet or more. It's called 'presentation' of the fly, and it takes endless practice to develop it to perfection. That's what makes it so interesting—the challenge."

He walked several dozen yards away and spread a sheet of paper on the ground, weighting it down at each corner with small rocks. When he got back to the boys he lifted his own rod and demonstrated the whipping, back-and-forth blind casting motion that built up the speed of the line, then landed his weighted fly squarely in the middle of the paper.

"Who's next?"

Tyler looked up at him in awe. "I think I need a bobber pole instead."

Connor chuckled and moved behind him, with his hand on the rod just behind the boy's. "Just relax. There's no fly on the end, just a very small weight. Rod in your right hand, coil this extra line in your left…let me move the rod. Okay…there you go. Good job! Now, I'm going to let go, but you keep practicing your cast. Okay?"

Tyler's motion was awkward. The tip of the rod wobbled wildly in the air. But when his fly landed some twenty feet away and off to the left, the delighted grin on his face would have charmed the hardest heart. "Wow!" he exclaimed, pumping his fist in a victory motion. "This is cool!"

"Great job, Tyler!" Erin called out. "Now, Drew—how about you? Are you ready?"

He glowered at her as he gripped the rod with two fists and awkwardly waved it back and forth over his head. Given the set of his jaw, he was probably embarrassed and very afraid of appearing foolish, especially in front of an audience.

"Just relax, Drew. This rod has a good amount of flex to it, so it doesn't take much effort. Just let the line float—"

The tippet at the end of the line snaked past Drew's head. The tiny weight snapped against his ear. With a yowl, he dropped the rod.

"This *sucks*," he yelped. A small drop of crimson

blood welled at the crest of his ear. "Who wants to do such a stupid thing, anyway?"

"Oh, Drew!" Her voice filled with dismay, Erin started toward him, but Connor gave her a pointed look and shook his head.

"I got myself in the eye when I first started," he said mildly, leaning over to pick up the rod. "I had a shiner for a week...and I was in med school. Looked like I'd been in a gang fight, but the girls all thought it was cool."

Drew wavered, his bravado slipping. He was clearly on the verge of stomping toward home.

Connor leaned over to look at the wound. "Bet that hurts. Ears are mighty sensitive, but it's just a little nick." He clapped the boy on the shoulder, man-to-man. "Ready to try again?"

Drew's mouth worked. His gaze slid to Lily and Tyler. Then he set his shoulders and accepted the rod. "I guess."

"Good." Connor slipped behind him and placed his hand on the rod next to Drew's. "The key is to start right, so you don't have to unlearn the wrong technique. Even adults have one heck of a time when they start out."

Drew grunted in assent.

"Now, follow the motion. The rod is like an extension of your arm. Feel it?" Connor coached him through a dozen dry casts, then stepped to one side, well out of the way, and watched in satisfaction as the boy became smoother, more adept.

"Excellent! Now, you boys can just keep practicing for a while. Drew—you move way over by the tuft of tall grass. Tyler—stay right here."

Connor gave them a wide berth and headed over to Erin and Lily, who'd settled on a grassy spot along the bank.

"Very nice, Connor," Erin murmured. "Drew needs small successes like this. Learning is hard for him, and he tends to be impatient—especially in school."

Connor dropped onto the grass next to her. "The boys wanted to try this, or I wouldn't have started something quite so challenging. Still, maybe he'll have fun working at it. Do you want to have a go?"

"Another day, maybe. I need to get Lily back up to the house so she can do her homework, and I need to do mine."

Connor leaned forward to catch Lily's eye. "Do you have lots of schoolwork to do?"

She wrinkled her nose. "Math and a book report."

"What's your favorite subject?"

"Science." She beamed. "I got to go to a science fair last year, with my frogs."

"Science was always my favorite, too." He wanted to ask her more.

About what she liked to watch on TV.

What she liked to eat.

He wanted to find out everything about her, to savor each detail and then catalog it away for the future, but Erin was standing up and motioning to the boys, and the sun was already slipping behind the trees.

Frustration welled in Connor's chest as he realized that there never would be enough time—not while he was merely a guest, who might stop by for a meal or a brief visit, then go back to his own, silent house.

"Connor." Erin gave him a curious half smile. The boys were already halfway across the meadow toward home, carrying the fishing poles, and Lily was lagging along behind them. "You sure are quiet tonight. Are you coming with us?"

His thoughts jerked back into the present. "Yeah." He grabbed the handle of his tackle box and tucked the spare rods under his arm. "I guess it's been a long day."

"Thanks for coming over. I know it's Lily you want to see, but this meant a lot to the boys, too."

"They can keep those rods." He fell into step with her and they walked back to the house. "I'll come again as soon as I can and work with them some more, and then we'll try out the stream."

The kids had already disappeared into the house by the time Connor and Erin reached his Tahoe.

"By the way, I had the strangest visit from the security guard at the hospital today," she murmured.

He faltered, then caught himself as he began stowing the equipment in the back of the vehicle. "Really?"

"He was outside the hospital early this morning

and noticed a Lincoln Town Car with a Green Bay General Hospital parking sticker in the window. It was in one of our staff spaces, so he went over to tell the driver that he could park even closer—in the visitor area—if he came again."

"Oh?"

"The man didn't answer, and he took off down the road like he was possessed. The guard thought it was so odd that he wrote down the guy's license plate number. What do you know about a Dr. Wayne Bloom?"

CHAPTER SIXTEEN

CONNOR HESITATED, debating over just how much to say to Erin about Wayne Bloom.

Wayne had been resentful of Connor from their first encounter—a situation in the E.R., when Connor stepped in to help with a severe trauma patient and had been, perhaps, a little less than diplomatic about Wayne's lack of speed and decisiveness.

The patient survived. Wayne's resentment festered, and apparently deepened when he was passed over for the coveted chief of internal medicine position three years later.

That the man was too volatile for the position had been Connor's private opinion. That the man imagined that Connor would try to influence his former father-in-law, the hospital's chief of staff, had bordered on the bizarre.

"Bloom," Connor said after a long pause, "is an internist in Green Bay. I think he's been there for several years."

"So you know him, then." She visibly relaxed. "You practiced there, too, right?"

"Yes, I did." Connor slid his fly rod into its case and snapped it shut, then put it in the back of his SUV. "He's not a friend, but I do remember seeing him."

"Good, then. I had a word with Beth—she'd left the reception desk for fifteen minutes and didn't have someone cover for her, so nobody saw him walk in. We just can't be careful enough these days." Erin handed him the last fishing rod. "Are you coming to the meeting at the hospital next Monday night?"

"Wouldn't miss it," he said dryly. "From what I hear, some people have definite ideas as to what should be done with any money you raise."

She hooked her thumbs in her front pockets and leaned against the vehicle. "Such as?"

He closed the back of the Tahoe and turned toward her. "Well, Leland thinks…"

The last, rosy hues of sunset warmed her skin, wrapping her in a soft glow and adding mysterious depths to her dark eyes. The scent of her—wildflowers and fresh linen—compelled him to move closer.

His gaze locked on hers, and he simply forgot to speak.

"Leland?" she coaxed. But her eyes sparkled with feminine awareness, and her voice sounded low and sultry. "Not that I, um, care much about him right now."

Anticipation rushed through Connor, even as

warning bells sounded at the back of his mind. He ran his hands slowly up her arms, watching as her breathing grew shallow and her lips parted.

He was in deep trouble, he thought dimly, as he lowered his mouth to hers. She melted against him, curving her arms around his neck and drawing him even deeper into the kiss, until arousal burned through him. He wrapped an arm around her lower back and pulled her closer, wanting…

From someplace far away came a distant voice, but he ignored it and lost himself in the deep pleasure of her sweet mouth and soft, sensual curves.

And suddenly she was gone. Her eyes wide, she stared at him from an arm's length away. "Oh, my…"

"Erin—*phone!*" Drew stood on the porch of the cabin, silhouetted against the lights inside. "Are you out there?"

She gave Connor a regretful smile. "Sorry, do you want to come in for a while?"

He wanted to stay, but what he craved right now was something he shouldn't wish for. Not when they had no future together. Not when there were children in the house. And after that kiss, he was in no condition to be seen.

"Another time, maybe."

She reached up, framed his face with her hands and kissed him lightly. "Maybe so."

And then she turned and headed for the house, leaving him standing in the dark. Alone.

IF NOTHING ELSE, Connor learned a good lesson on Tuesday night. Play with fire, and you could get burned. Give in to temptation, and you might as well chuck the whole idea of sleeping well in the foreseeable future.

Each evening after supper, he stopped by Erin's place and took the boys down to the stream, where he helped them work on their casting skills while Scout and Maisie romped with Lily nearby. Erin joined them, sitting some distance away while she worked on a lapful of documents, but now and then he would glance her way and see her watching pensively.

She'd carefully avoided being alone with him since that last kiss, but he found himself thinking about her at night, after he turned the lights out. During the day, whenever the rush of appointments at the clinic slowed down. And when he came to spend time with the kids, he found himself seeking her out for hours of conversation long after the children went to bed.

Stephanie had dressed impeccably. She'd never stepped out of the house without flawless makeup, perfectly coiffed hair. Who knew that faded jeans and an old red Wisconsin Badgers sweatshirt could be so appealing?

On Friday evening, he arrived at six o'clock with two large pepperoni pizzas, a couple of bottles of pop and a plan.

"Supper's ready," he announced when Erin answered his knock on the door. "This is for Haley and the kids. Would you like to go to a movie with me and have dinner after?"

Startled, she backed up a step and let him walk in the door. *"Pizza."* She inhaled the aroma and smiled. "It smells heavenly."

The babysitter appeared at her shoulder with her backpack slung over one shoulder and car keys in one hand. "Wow—that's Luigi's pepperoni supreme," she breathed. "People drive clear over from Henderson to order it."

"So I've heard." Connor handed her one of the boxes. "How would you like to stay awhile longer and earn some extra money? Say…until midnight, at double your day rate?"

"You've got a deal!" She swung her backpack to the floor and headed for the kitchen. "I'll get the plates."

"Wait a minute." Erin watched Haley disappear into the kitchen, where all three kids whooped with joy. Plates clinked, silverware rattled as they set the table in record time. "This is really nice of you, but—"

"When was the last time you went out?"

"Um…"

"With *me.*"

She sputtered into helpless laughter. "I guess that would be…never."

Haley popped her head around the corner. "Go, Mrs. Lang. On Friday nights the theater in town runs 'blockbusters from the past' as double features, and they have the best popcorn in the whole world. You can even butter it yourself."

Connor watched an array of emotions play across Erin's face, but before she could say no, he stepped closer and caressed her arm. "Consider it your good deed for the day. I can't even remember when I last went out on a weekend."

"Well…"

"Good! I'll go home and change, and let Maisie out of the house for a few minutes." He bent down and brushed a kiss against her cheek. "I'll be back by six-thirty."

Grinning at her startled expression, he jogged out to his SUV and whistled as he drove on up to his place, took care of Maisie and headed for the shower.

The phone in his bedroom blinked at him as he stripped off his clothes. Impatient, he wavered for a split second before hitting the message button.

His mother, wondering when he was coming home for a visit.

Leland, wanting to discuss the upcoming meeting at the hospital.

Ed, making his weekly call to ask after his patients.

And then a voice he hadn't ever expected to hear again.

"I hear you're at the hospital in Blackberry Hill." Victor Ralston's voice dripped venom. *"Do they know what kind of man you are, Reynolds? What you're capable of? My daughter and grandchild*

*would be alive today if not for you. Sleep well, you
bastard."*

With a towel around his waist, Connor sank down
on the edge of the bed, braced his elbows on his
thighs and buried his face in his hands.

There wasn't a day when he didn't think about the
accident, or quietly mourn the loss of his unborn child.

There wasn't a day when he failed to remember
every detail of that last night, that last argument, or
the sound of tires squealing out of the driveway.

And Victor was going to make sure that never,
ever changed.

CONNOR DIDN'T SHOW UP at six-thirty, or at six forty-
five. At seven, Erin tried to call his home number and
got a busy signal. At seven-fifteen, the same.

Frowning, she grabbed her car keys and cell
phone from the kitchen counter. "I think I'll drive up
and see what's going on. Maybe Maisie went wandering when he let her out, or something."

The kids and Haley had polished off the first pizza
and were busy with the second. Scout sat next to the
table, his tail waving back and forth against the polished oak floor, his eyes eagerly following each
piece of pizza as it traveled from plate to mouth.

Haley glanced at the kitchen clock and blissfully
took another bite. "The movies start at seven-thirty,
so you guys better get going," she said around a
mouthful of pizza.

Erin nodded. "Ten o'clock bedtime, everyone.

And Haley—you can call my cell anytime. I'll keep it in my pocket and set it on Vibrate during the show."

Locking the door behind her, Erin stepped out into the crisp evening air. Already a haze of frost had silvered the long, bowed grasses in the meadow, and overhead the sky was a sea of stars.

Shivering, she zipped up her light jacket and strode to her minivan. An eerie sense of awareness prickled at the back of her neck as she opened the door.

A dark shape materialized not twenty feet away, at the edge of the clearing, visible in the dim glow of the interior lights. She fumbled for the headlight switch and flicked it on.

Black on black in the deep twilight, a wolf—a huge wolf—stood staring at her, its eyes burning like pale yellow embers. She stared back from the shelter of her open car door, entranced by the animal's sheer, primitive beauty and incredible size.

"I finally got to see you," she whispered, wishing it would linger. "And you are *amazing*."

But in that brief moment the wolf dissolved silently into the shadows. Were the stories true, about small dogs disappearing? Were there other wolves closer to town, or would this one range that far?

On her way up to Connor's place she phoned home and told Haley to let Scout out on the long chain fastened to the porch for a just a few minutes before everyone went to bed, and to bring him right back in.

At Connor's place she parked next to his Tahoe.

Several lights glowed in the windows. The front door stood open, yet the porch was unlit. Uneasy, she studied the house for several minutes, then tried dialing his phone number once more. *Busy.*

She turned off her headlights and scanned the area as she opened her car door. The absolute silence of the surrounding forest enveloped her. The thought of huge creatures lurking there, with golden, glowing eyes and empty bellies, made her pulse quicken as she judged the distance to the house.

I could call 911, in case something is wrong in there...but he probably just has his phone off the hook and is in the shower.

Wavering, she stared up at the house—and felt immeasurable relief when a familiar dark form lumbered out of the shadows on the porch. *Maisie.*

The old dog came to the top of the steps and woofed a polite sort of greeting, her tail wagging madly.

Erin strode across the yard and up onto the porch, and bent to give the dog a hug. "You sweetheart," she said fervently. "I'll bet you'd like to come in."

She opened the screen door for the dog and then followed her inside, shutting the door behind them. "Connor?"

Maisie headed for a soft rug by the fireplace and flopped down, her head on her front paws.

"Connor, are you here?" Erin checked the kitchen, then the family room, where she dropped her purse on an end table. She hesitated at the bottom of the stairs. Only the old dog's nonchalance gave her the courage to continue on up.

Connor was still a young guy of thirty-five, but visions of early heart attack or stroke raced through her mind as she reached the top landing and considered the three doorways along the open gallery that overlooked the living room below. Or diabetes—could he be diabetic, and in trouble?

The door at the end was ajar, and a dim apron of light spilled out onto the pine flooring of the hall. She headed that way and pushed the door open wider with her fingertips. "Hello?"

The room was dark, though light from the master bath picked out the highlights of the massive bed and dresser, and reflected in the windows that formed most of one wall. She didn't see him until she took a step inside.

"Connor?" She fumbled for a switch along the wall by the door and flicked it on.

Light blazed from an ornate crystal fixture hanging in the middle of the room, momentarily blinding her. Pine log walls rose a good twenty feet to the top of a steeply pitched ceiling set with a trio of skylights. Wildlife prints and an antique quilt hung on the walls.

But it was the beauty of the man sitting in a corner that nearly took her breath away.

"Not exactly dressed for town, are we," she said, masking her awkwardness with a smile. "Are you okay?"

"I will be." He tipped his head toward an unopened bottle of bourbon on the lace-draped table at his side. "In time."

She swallowed hard. *Okay* was certainly a relative term.

He appeared to be dressed only in a towel knotted at his narrow waist. His long, muscular legs were stretched out in front of him, crossed at the ankle; his hands folded loosely on his lap. Above the towel, his flat belly and broad chest flared out to even broader shoulders.

He looked powerful. Intensely masculine, with that dark swath of chest hair narrowing to a thin ribbon that disappeared beneath the towel. His lean jaw was still shadowed with stubble. He was two hundred pounds of sheer sensual promise, but it was the bleak look in his eyes that touched her.

"I see you didn't get very far," she murmured, fighting an urge to grab the bottle and dump the contents down the bathroom sink. "Can I assume that our date is off?"

He tipped his head back against the chair and closed his eyes. "I don't think I'd be very good company tonight."

"I tried calling you," she ventured, as she scanned the room for clues. The receiver was off the phone on the bedside table, but the room was immaculate. "The line was busy every time."

He rolled his head against the back of the chair to give her a heavy-lidded glance. "Guess I forgot to hang it up."

"Right. So what's up?" When he didn't answer, she sat on the edge of the bed near him and waited. "You know, sometimes it works better to talk things out."

He apparently didn't agree, because he just leaned his head back again and closed his eyes. "I think you should go. Maybe…another time."

"Drew does this, too—he tries to tune me out. I discovered something interesting, though. The longer I wait, the more likely it is that he'll finally break down and talk to me. And you know what? He always seems to feel a lot better after he does. Just a thought," she added after a long pause. "Not that you have to, or anything."

Five long minutes ticked by before he spoke.

"Imagine your life…stretching out before you. A career where you truly make a difference. A wife you love. A baby you've longed for."

"You lost a great deal, Connor."

"Imagine…" A muscle in his jaw ticked. "Losing everything."

"It's been nearly two years," she said gently, when he fell silent. "I can only guess at how hard it's been. The grieving…and the guilt. But it wasn't your fault."

"Really." He gave a dry, humorless laugh. "Not everyone would agree."

She reached over and took one of his hands in hers. "I've seen you with kids over the past few weeks. You're patient and kind—even with Drew, who isn't always the easiest child to deal with. You've given them time and attention they never experienced until they came to live with me." She gave his hand an extra squeeze. "You could've concentrated on Lily, but you've been equally attentive to the boys, and many men wouldn't have bothered. In short, you are—as Drew says—one very cool dude."

A corner of his mouth lifted. "Cool?"

"And Lily thinks you're…" Erin hesitated, then realized that she didn't owe Sam anything but the truth. "A lot nicer than Sam ever was."

Connor's gaze zeroed in on hers. "She said that?"

"Her words exactly." Erin started to take her hand back, but he held on and began caressing it with his thumb. Ignoring the warmth of his touch, she met his eyes squarely. "And I can't think of another man who would've handled the news about his unknown child as well as you have—without demands, and with only her best interests at heart. If you're ever feeling down, remember that the four of us think you are a very special guy."

Silence lengthened between them, his eyes still intent on hers, his thumb still rubbing against her hand in lazy circles that no longer seemed like just a friendly, comforting gesture, but something promising much more.

She shifted nervously, suddenly entirely too aware of the fact that he was sitting before her in nothing more than a towel. She closed her eyes, trying to block the vivid images that flew into her mind.

"So," she said brightly. "We can still make that second feature. What do you think?"

The air between them changed. Sizzled. She swallowed, her mouth suddenly dry.

"We can go to that movie if you'd like," he said quietly.

She knew he meant it. She could walk out and he would get dressed and take her into town if that's what she chose, because he was an honorable man.

But his heated gaze burned into hers, and the undercurrent of sexual tension seemed to explode between them, sending a rush of adrenaline through her veins and erasing all thoughts of leaving this room.

She hesitated for only a moment. "I imagine we've already seen whatever is playing," she murmured.

"We could always rent a DVD." He rose and pulled her to her feet. His warm arms curved around her waist and pulled her close. "Or we could catch the last show."

But when he lowered his mouth to hers, nothing else mattered.

CHAPTER SEVENTEEN

ERIN SAVORED the exquisite pleasure of Connor's mouth on hers. The sensual slide of his hands on her back. The way he cradled her head with one hand to angle in for a deeper kiss that sent shivers skipping down her spine, and made her feel empty and wanting in her most intimate place.

But he didn't rush to the next step as if he had a plane to catch. In wonderment, she felt him hold back, explore, his eyes hot and dark and possessive as he groaned with pleasure at her own rising response. And he *talked* to her…whispering hot, sexy words in her ear, making her feel as if she were the most desirable woman he'd ever known, until she was nearly engulfed in white-hot desire, wanting more, *needing* more.

When he finally drove into her, everything inside her turned to a fire that consumed her, body and soul. "Connor," she breathed.

Exquisite pleasure swept her away.

GRIEF DIDN'T DISSIPATE like morning fog in the heat of a summer sun. It wore away slowly, like granite dissolving over the eons beneath a trickling stream, so gradually, so imperceptibly that it seemed as if nothing would ever change.

The cruel finality of death offered no second chances. No opportunities to make a different choice, to try a little harder. It had offered no chance to ever escape the fact that Stephanie had driven herself over a cliff and taken their child to his death.

Connor propped his head in his palm to look at the woman nestled against his chest.

For almost two years, he'd carried that grief in silence, as atonement for what happened. He'd accepted that it was his fault, and that he would never escape the enormity of that fatal crash. Nothing could ever change, because nothing could ever bring Stephanie back.

But now…the crushing weight of that grief lifted.

Connor stroked Erin's silky hair. She'd brought happiness into his life. She'd brought Lily. And what he felt for her he'd never expected to experience again.

She opened her eyes and stretched languorously, her soft mouth curving into a sleepy smile.

And then her eyes opened wide with horror and she shot straight up in bed. "Oh, my God—what time is it?"

"A quarter of midnight." He reached up and rested a hand against her cheek, then slid it behind her neck and drew her down into a deep and soul-satisfying kiss. "Which means that we need to get you home."

A pink blush darkened her cheeks as she felt around on the bed, then stared at the trail of clothes across the room.

She pulled the top sheet tight against her chest. "I…don't believe I did this," she murmured, grabbing for more of the sheet. "I mean, I don't usually—"

"I know."

"I never…" Her eyes widened with renewed horror. "Did you—I mean—did you have—"

He nodded toward the torn packets on the bedside table. "Yes, I did."

She rolled her eyes heavenward and mumbled what sounded like a prayer of thanks as she jerked the sheet from its moorings at the foot of the bed and wrapped it around her, then retrieved her clothes from the floor en route to the bathroom.

So much for savoring the moment, he thought dryly, as he rose and found his own clothes. Erin burst out of the bathroom as he was stepping into his shoes. "I'm all set," she said, averting her eyes as she headed to the door.

He caught her elbow and brought her back to him, caressing her upper arms as he searched her face. "I'm sorry if this wasn't what you wanted to do…if I took things too far."

"I think it was *me* who did that. Believe me—" Her blush deepened. "This is the first time since my husband left. I don't even know how to act afterward anymore…."

Connor chuckled and drew her into an embrace, savoring the lemony scent of her hair and the sweet warmth of her against his chest. "I want you to know that there's been no one else for me, either. That this meant a lot to me. And…" he brushed a kiss against her temple "…I never would have made love to you if I didn't care for you very much. Okay?"

She nodded. "I feel almost like a high school senior who's been making out on the front porch, and is afraid her dad will find out. The kids are going to ask about the movie tomorrow. Maybe they're even still awake, and now I'm going to be late. What kind of example am I setting?" She glanced around the room and caught her reflection in a mirror over the dresser. "And I look like I've been in a wrestling match!"

He laughed and hugged her tighter, then released her and took her hand. "Then let's go, Cinderella— and get you home by midnight."

"Follow me in your truck, and I'll treat you to the best hot cocoa anywhere."

They raced down the stairs and outside, laughing as she lost a shoe and had to stop to retrieve it, and in ten minutes both of them pulled to a halt in front of Erin's cabin. The lights were on. Four faces peered through the windows as they stepped out of their vehicles.

"I *knew* it," she whispered. "Tell me what that movie was. Quick! No—I'll just say we decided to have a quiet evening instead."

But the moment they came up the porch steps into the light, the door flew open. Haley and the kids tumbled out, all talking at once.

"I tried to call you," Haley said. "I tried and tried."

"Scout's gone," Lily wailed. "We put him out for just a minute, and he was gone!"

"We heard barking and yowling," Drew added. He scrubbed furiously at the moisture in his eyes. "But we couldn't see any sign of him, anywhere!"

Behind them, Tyler sniffled and backhanded his own tears away.

"I'm so s-sorry." Haley's mouth trembled. "He pulled away as I was trying to snap the chain on his collar. I wouldn't let the kids run out into the dark after him, and they've been so upset with me!"

"You did the right thing." Erin opened her arms and welcomed the children into an embrace. "He might turn up tomorrow, safe as can be." But the look she gave Connor over the tops of their heads was anything but hopeful. *I saw the wolf tonight,* she mouthed. *Here.*

"There's some messages for you in the kitchen, too," Haley said. "Some guy called, and he sure wasn't very friendly. And the hospital phoned twice."

Erin's eyes widened in dismay. "Let's go on inside, everyone. Everything will work out." She shepherded them through the door, then turned back to Connor and lowered her voice. "I can't believe that I was so careless. I left my purse in your living room, and my phone's in it. Haley probably called while we were…upstairs."

"I'll get it and bring it over." He dropped a swift kiss on her mouth. "And I'll bring a flashlight so I can look for Scout, just in case. If anything happened, it'd be better if the kids didn't find him."

CONNOR RETURNED THAT NIGHT with Maisie to search the meadow and surrounding woods for over an hour, then came back at dawn on Saturday and continued looking for any sign of Scout.

He stayed close by throughout the weekend, enticing the boys into fishing. Playing catch with Lily. He took everyone to a children's matinee. He did everything he could to cheer the kids up, and for that gift Erin was more than thankful. She'd realized that, despite every intention to the contrary, she was falling in love with him.

But Scout didn't turn up, even though they searched through the underbrush surrounding the meadow, and by Monday morning all three kids were completely disheartened as they got ready for school.

"If Scout was hurt, he probably died by now," Drew said glumly as Erin pulled to a stop in front of the school. "We'll never see him again."

"Or maybe he ran away," Tyler added, his head bowed over the backpack he held in his lap.

Lily sniffled into a tissue. "I bet he's scared if he ran away. And hungry."

"The hardest part now is just not knowing for sure," Erin said. She reached across the seat and pulled Lily into a hug, then turned to give the boys an encouraging smile. "I think we should imagine that he got lost, and is safe somewhere. Maybe someone else found him, like you did. And right now, he's eating his dog food and has a warm bed by a fireplace."

"Like *that* could have happened," Drew snapped. "We heard him yelping, and something else growling. Maybe the wolves got him. Some kids at school say that their parents hate the wolves and wish they were gone. They're talking about putting out poison or shooting them."

"The wolves are protected, Drew."

"Yeah? Well, no one would know. And if I found the one that killed Scout, I'd want to shoot it myself!" He jerked the handle of the door and climbed out, then slammed it shut.

Lily looked up at Erin with sad, wide eyes. "Do you think that's what happened?"

"I don't know. But I'd like to think that Scout got away, and found someone to pick him up and take care of him. I'll call the newspaper this morning and put in an ad about him. Maybe we'll get a call."

She stepped out of the minivan to help Lily and Tyler with their backpacks, then gave them each a hug. She watched them trudge up the sidewalk and into the school, her heart heavy.

In her office twenty minutes later, she worked on

her latest revision of the budget, and then began calling the people heading up the canvassing process for signatures that could put the local tax levy on the November ballot.

They were within a few hundred signatures of succeeding, she discovered with a sigh of satisfaction. If the doctors could come to an agreement tonight regarding which projects to tackle first, the meeting could go very well indeed.

Success meant job security for the employees and far better care for the patients, and was worth every ounce of effort it took. But the success that meant most of all involved the happiness of her children, and she couldn't get their sad faces out of her mind.

"BOARD MEETINGS ARE NEVER this large," Jill whispered to Erin. "You've got the whole community interested."

"Hopefully, in a positive way." Erin glanced over her shoulder at the full chairs and crowd of people standing at the back. "This one is mostly just to share information with the public, and I think there's even a better turnout than last time."

Arnold Olson, who still had a stethoscope slung around his neck, appeared to be involved in a heated discussion with Leland Anderson at the board members' table up in front. And at the opposite side of the podium, two other officials frowned as a third spoke to them in a voice too low to hear from the audience.

President Paul Benson called the meeting to order.

Erin searched the crowd for Connor. He hadn't attended the meeting earlier in the month, citing his desire to avoid hospital politics, but since then he'd certainly seemed more interested. He'd asked questions and had offered suggestions during some of their late-night conversations…so where was he?

Leo Crupper was here, though. Sitting right behind her with his all-too-familiar supercilious smile, and his fingernails tap-tap-tapping on a manila folder in his lap.

The president of the auxiliary gave her report of the signature drive—now less than a hundred names shy of the number needed to place the tax levy on the ballot, but with just four days left before the deadline.

"You're on," Jill whispered as the woman took her seat. "You go get 'em."

Erin took her place at the podium. "I'm happy to announce that our USDA grant for a new X-ray diagnostic system has been approved as of this morning. We also have three other grants, available through the state of Wisconsin and a pharmaceutical company, that are looking very promising." A smattering of applause rippled through the audience. "At our last meeting, I promised a final report by the end of the month regarding an assessment of our needs, and the total costs involved. The report covers this, plus recommendations for specialty clinics.

We'd like to utilize physicians who'd come several times a month from the larger hospitals in nearby counties, and in particular we see a need to develop a dialysis unit as soon as possible. If you would open the packets that were on your chairs when you came in..."

The crowd rustled through the papers, and from the back of the room she heard a rumble of conversation that didn't bode well.

After she'd carefully outlined each point in her report, Paul addressed the board for their comments. Leland picked up the mike and announced that he fully supported the remodeling of the lounge, to "create a more enticing setting for the doctors coming in for rotations through the specialty clinics."

Jill groaned and leaned close to Erin's ear. "He just wants a nicer place where he can go to escape his wife," she whispered.

Arnold took the mike and announced that Leland's idea was a huge waste of money better spent on redecorating patient rooms or remodeling the 1940s E.R. entrance and waiting area.

"I thought we were on the same page," Erin whispered. "We had a consensus!"

"It's all about power. Those two have been contentious ever since I came to this town."

"They were fine at Ollie's!"

"Ah, but here we have a big audience."

The other board members spoke about fiscal responsibility and, conversely, the need to invest in the town's future, rambling on for a good half hour but getting nowhere, in Erin's opinion.

By the time Paul ended the meeting, her frustration had increased tenfold. "We've got funding for some of the changes already. We've received board approval for projects that will start if the tax levy goes through. But with all this dissension, it's going to be hard to make things happen...and I wonder just how much support we'll get afterward. You'd think that the community would be behind this a hundred percent."

Jill reached over and gave her hand a quick squeeze. "I guarantee that when this is all over, the people here will be very proud of their hospital, and will be even more proud of you for making it happen."

Erin followed her toward the back door, where a knot of people were speaking in low, vehement tones.

"I saw one of 'em near town. I'd like to know what the hell we're supposed to do to keep our kids and livestock safe."

"Yeah, and by the time the DNR arrives, it's always long gone."

"I say, someone should go out and shoot 'em on sight."

Leo Crupper nodded in agreement. He raised his voice above the others as Erin walked past. "I saw your note up in the grocery store this afternoon about your lost dog. Bet a wolf got him, too," he said with obvious relish. "But I suppose you're one of those who just think the wolves are pretty."

"Without proof, I don't think anyone can assume the wolves are at fault, Mr. Crupper." Erin nodded politely to the group as a whole and continued on out the door.

His words to his cronies followed her into the hallway as she made her way through the crowd and headed for her office. "What did I tell you, boys? She's a city gal—not someone who knows and cares about the area. The last thing we need is someone like her starting a big spending spree that will sink our town in debt."

STILL FUMING, Erin stopped by her office to drop off her files and grab her purse. She was halfway to the door when the phone rang. Glancing at the clock, she sighed and turned back to the desk. "Mrs. Lang. Can I help you?"

"You need to know who you're dealing with there," a voice growled in her ear. "Have you no idea?"

Startled, she sat forward in her chair and grabbed a notebook, wishing the hospital phone system included caller ID. The voice sounded suspiciously like one that had left a cryptic message on her machine at home, but that number had shown up as a pay phone. "I—I'm not sure you have the right number," she said evenly. "This is the hospital."

"And you're the administrator. One who sure

didn't do her homework." The caller gave a derisive snort. "You've got a doctor with hospital privileges who should have lost his license over a year ago. One who repeatedly made med errors. Failed to chart properly. Didn't follow through."

She gripped her pen tighter. "I'm sorry—I didn't catch your name."

"Do you really want a physician like that making decisions regarding patients in your hospital? He was investigated by our hospital review board three times…after patients suffered serious setbacks or died unexpectedly while under his care. Look out, Mrs. Lang. Malpractice suits can be a very ugly thing."

She scrawled notes across the paper in front of her. "You haven't identified yourself. How can I possibly take this seriously, Mr.—"

"All you need to know is the name of the man himself. And if I were you, I'd find a way to get him out of there. Fast."

"Who are you?"

He ignored her question. "I was concerned enough to look up your name on your hospital's Web site, so I could contact you directly. The longer Connor Reynolds has hospital privileges, the greater risk you take."

She took a sharp breath. *Connor?*

"Carelessness kills—and we found that out in Green Bay. Let it be on your conscience if you allow it to happen. Sleep well, Mrs. Lang."

"Wait—"

But the soft click at the other end of the line told her that she was too late.

It was impossible. The caller had to be crazy—and he'd not only tracked her down at the hospital and knew her name, but had presumably found her unlisted home number, as well. That in itself was frightening.

Surely he had to be lying. But what if…oh, God. What if it was the *truth*? She had no choice but to make sure. For the safety of the patients. For the future reputation of this hospital.

She braced both palms on her desk with her head down, trying to calm her shaking nerves and the wave of dizziness.

Then with trembling fingers she tapped in the password on her PDA, found the cell phone number of Patty Long, an old friend from nursing school who lived in Green Bay, and dialed the number.

After five rings, the voice mail feature kicked in. "Patty—this is Erin Lang. I need some information about a doctor who had privileges at Green Bay General, and wonder if you might have heard anything about him. Call or e-mail me, stat."

And then she hung up, and prayed that the anonymous caller was wrong.

CHAPTER EIGHTEEN

On Tuesday morning, Tyler awoke with a cold and a temperature of 100 degrees, so Erin stayed home with him while the other kids went to school.

Tyler spent the day curled up on the sofa watching Disney movies on TV. Erin roamed through the cabin, cleaning and catching up on laundry, plying him with ice cream and juice, and checking his temp every hour.

The day dragged. Another call to Patty just reached her voice mail again. A call to Green Bay General's human resource department yielded exactly what Erin had expected—a chilly response telling her that information about staff members could not be shared.

After a few moments of thought, she called information for the phone number of the *Green Bay Courier* and requested a search of any newspaper articles in the past five years relating to the hospital and a Dr. Reynolds. The harried receptionist promised to pass on the request.

Frustrated, Erin paced the cabin while Tyler was sleeping, then went out to stand on the porch.

It still seemed impossible that Connor might have been investigated for malpractice. She'd seen his gentle touch with the kids. She'd repeatedly heard staff comment on how thorough and caring he was with patients, and experienced nurses would be the first to know if someone wasn't receiving good care.

Erin's worries eased as the day wore on, though one concern remained—who had called, and why would he try to damage Connor's reputation? He'd claimed that there'd been newspaper coverage, so a search through the archives would either substantiate or refute his statements. Once she'd done a little more checking, she would talk to Connor and see what he had to say.

It would certainly be in his best interest to know if someone back home was carrying out a vendetta against him. If he did move on to a new community when his uncle returned, the next hospital administrator might take such statements at face value.

Erin met Haley at the door when she arrived after school with Drew and Lily. Drew dumped his backpack in the hall and trudged upstairs without a word. Lily went to the living room and dropped on the floor next to Tyler.

"Thanks so much for bringing them home for me, Haley—I'll pay for your mileage and the usual afternoon hours, but since Tyler's sick you can just go on back to town. Fair enough?"

Haley peered around her at Tyler, who was now surrounded by a sea of LEGO pieces and a rather impressive moat. "He looks okay to me. He isn't throwing up, is he?"

"Not at all. He did have a fever earlier, but that's normal now. He does have a cough."

The girl shrugged. "I can stay, if you need to go into work or something. I've got four little brothers and sisters, and I must be immune to everything on the planet by now."

Erin went to check his temperature with the ear thermometer one more time. "Still normal. You're sure you don't mind?"

"We have the rest of the week off for some sort of state teachers' conference, so I can stay as late as you want. I'd just as soon be working." The girl grinned. "At home, I watch everyone for free."

"I've got a chicken-Parmesan casserole in the oven, plus baby peas and Tyler's favorite strawberry-banana Jell-O in the refrigerator."

Haley beamed. "Good deal. *My* mom was cooking liver and broccoli."

ERIN MADE IT TO THE hospital by five o'clock, and met Grace on the sidewalk just outside the front door. The older woman looked pale and tired. "Long day?"

"Busy one. Three admits to the hospital side—one chest pain, one severe hypoglycemia, one hip fracture. One of my nurses gave her notice today, saying that she's moving to Michigan." Grace blew at her bangs. "And *three* people asked to totally change their vacation schedules during the next two pay periods."

Erin laughed. "No wonder you look so eager to leave."

"I'm getting too old for this, believe me. Sorry I had to miss the last board meeting, by the way. Two nurses called in sick, so I had to cover the floor that shift instead." She raised an eyebrow. "I hear things got a little…tense."

"A few disagreements. The good news is that we've nearly hit the required number of signatures for the tax-levy vote. The deadline is Friday, and the auxiliary ladies are working overtime to get it done."

"And if it doesn't?"

"We'll have to work on getting enough support for a special election in the spring, then. I hope that doesn't happen."

"Dr. Reynolds was looking for you earlier." The older woman gave her a knowing smile. "He asked where you were."

Erin glanced around. Though no one else was in sight, she lowered her voice. "What do you think of him—on a professional level?"

"On a personal level, I'd say he's…" She thought for a minute, her eyes twinkling. "*Hot.* Even if I *am* old enough to be his grandmother."

Hot, indeed. Just the thought brought warmth to Erin's cheeks. "Give me your honest professional opinion. Would you send your own daughter or granddaughter to him? Your mom?" At Grace's hesitation, she pressed on. "Nurses see the daily charting, the decision making. The types of tests ordered and how a doctor relates with patients and staff. An experienced hospital nurse like you should be a good judge, because you've worked with so many different physicians."

"Put that way, yes. I would send my mother to him. He's thorough. Careful. He gets along well with patients and is very pleasant to the staff. And," she added with a smile, "he listens to what we say about the condition of his patients. A good thing, because nurses are seeing those people twenty-four hours a day and a doctor sees them for maybe five minutes on his rounds."

"He's professional, then? Competent?"

Grace gave her a quizzical look. "Absolutely. Is something wrong?"

"No. No, course not. I just wanted to ask, since he's the newest doctor on the staff. I've heard nice comments from patients."

"I do think that you two would be a wonderful couple. I've seen him down in the hospital wing, watching when you walk by. I'd say there's some definite interest there."

An area Erin definitely didn't want to explore with Grace. Especially not now. "I'm sure I don't begin to match up to the sort of women he's dated before," she said lightly. "Thanks for the information, though…and have a nice evening."

As she walked up the steps to the front door, she heard Grace snicker softly behind her.

Had it been that obvious to the other staff, too? Stifling a groan, Erin nodded to the receptionist, went straight to her office and shut the door behind her.

BY SEVEN O'CLOCK, she wished she'd eaten at home before leaving for the hospital. By eight o'clock, even the stale sandwiches and soft apples in the lounge vending machines seemed like gourmet fare.

On her way downstairs to the file storeroom, Erin swung by the employee lounge, stood in front of the machines and glumly considered the day's leftovers. Soggy tuna salad sandwiches. Some sort of mystery-meat deli sandwich on an overlarge bun. Browning bananas.

"Quite a selection."

Startled, she turned around and found Connor in the doorway, leaning against the frame.

"I usually make it a policy to avoid those things," he added with a definite twinkle in his eyes as he surveyed the vending machines. "Unless I'm feeling masochistic."

"Which is…"

He laughed. "Never, actually. How come you're here so late?"

"Tyler was sick today, so I'm just here for a little while catching up. How about you? I missed you at the board meeting last night."

"Couldn't make it," he said vaguely. "I heard it was interesting."

"Yes, and I could have used a voice of reason in that room." She gave the vending machines a last look, then dropped some change into one and punched a button for a diet soda. "Leland seems set on having a home away from home in this building, and I think he turned a lot of the voters off with his ideas for the doctors' lounge. Half of the attendees were more concerned about the wolves in northern Wisconsin than they were about the hospital issues. All in all, I was ready for a good stiff Scotch afterward, and I don't even drink."

Connor laughed. "I'm covering for another practice tonight, and I have a half-dozen patients I need to go see. After that, would you like to go out for dinner somewhere?"

The complexity of the situation hit her broadside. Her deepening feelings for him were as strong as ever—yet she was busy following up on his past, needing to verify whether there was any truth to that anonymous caller's accusations.

What did that make her? Certainly not someone who was very honorable. She couldn't quite meet his eyes. "I'm sorry…another time. I…have to be home in an hour, because Haley is babysitting and it's a school night. And…Tyler doesn't feel well."

Connor gave her a searching look, the warmth in his eyes fading as he studied her. "I see. Maybe another time, then."

She could've kicked herself. She watched him turn on his heel and disappear down the hallway. *Good job, Lang.* She'd always been a terrible liar, and now she'd babbled like an idiot, which made it even worse. Even at thirty-three she couldn't pull off a credible half-truth. But when this was all over…

With a sigh, she gathered up her purse and the can of Pepsi, and headed out the door.

Surely, she would discover nothing amiss. That anonymous caller had to have had a grudge. Someone who'd made up a preposterous story as vengeance for some minor incident or an unintentional slight—perhaps something he'd just imagined.

But if he was telling the truth, and any potentially criminal negligence was evident here, she would need to call the police and the state medical board. Connor could lose his license and possibly face both legal charges and a host of lawsuits, once everyone caught up with him.

And that thought nearly broke her heart.

ERIN FINISHED GOING through the day's stack of mail and her business-related e-mail, took care of everything urgent, then wearily rested her chin on her hand.

She had over twenty Hadley charts left to review. And now a couple of dozen from Connor's hospital admissions, in fresh, new manila folders, sat on the other corner of her desk.

So far, she'd found four deaths among the old Hadley charts that could be considered suspicious. All elderly men who'd been doing well, according to progress notes, vital-sign documentation and lab reports. All had been close to discharge, but had passed away in the late evening or during the night. None of them had had local relatives. All were listed as DNR, Do Not Resuscitate.

Coincidence?

Yet two more had passed away since she'd started working here—while Hadley was out of state. Only Milton Striker had been autopsied, and that report had come back negative.

Maybe it *was* a coincidence. Why would anyone target just Hadley's patients?

A grim thought hit her. She'd pursued Hadley because of the deaths of Frank and Milton, but without reviewing every single chart, from every admission, she couldn't be positive there hadn't been unexpected deaths of other doctors' patients. And checking that could take months—unless she requested help. But who could she absolutely, unequivocally trust? And if people in the community learned of her research, what could that do to the reputations of those doctors, and the hospital itself?

The weight of all that doubt filled her chest and sent pounding waves of a new headache throbbing through her temples.

She pulled on her jacket, grabbed her purse and keys, and headed for the door. After a good night's sleep, maybe things would look better. Maybe her imagination was simply working overtime, looking for problems when there were none.

She was halfway out the front entrance of the hospital when a low, urgent voice came across the loudspeakers in the hall. "Code blue! Code blue! Room 34B, stat."

She pivoted and hurried back inside, to the sound of staff racing down the halls from every direction. The rattle of a crash cart. Tense voices. She stood aside until the stampede had passed, then went to the nurses' station in the hospital wing.

A hubbub of tense voices rose from a room two doors down. Someone shouted, "Stand clear!" There was a moment of silence, then another shouted order and renewed furor.

A young nurse's aide rushed out of the room and sped to the phone at the desk. Rapidly dialing a number, she spoke in low tones, then hurried back to the room and disappeared inside.

What seemed a lifetime later, Erin looked up to see Connor running down the hall in jeans and a sweater, his hair windblown and his face flushed from the chilly night air.

Five minutes stretched to ten, then fifteen.

And then the staff began trickling out of the room, their faces somber and their steps heavy. One of the nurses pushed the crash cart into the pharmacy store-room next to the nurses' station, where she began re-stocking its supplies.

Low, respectful voices drifted from the patient's room. *A good man...a sad loss.*

Erin sagged against the raised counter as the enormous finality of the moment hit her. *Another one gone.* Someone's husband, father, son...friend.

And when a nurse stepped out of the room with a chart in her hand, dizziness threatened to overcome Erin. In place of the bright orange DNR sticker was an unmistakable green one. *Hadley.*

The implication made her stomach pitch as she walked slowly down the hall. Something was happening here, and she could no longer hope that it was just her imagination.

At the double doors leading out into the lobby, she reached for the handle just as one swung open.

"Oh...Mrs. Banks." Erin summoned up the semblance of a smile. She held the door as the housekeeper started to push her cleaning supplies cart through, but the woman stopped halfway and peered down the hall.

"Guess I'd better wait until things quiet down."

"Maybe so."

"Another code." Mrs. Banks shook her head. "Makes you wonder." Mumbling to herself, she backed up and started off toward the long-term care unit, the wheels of her cart squeaking on the polished terrazzo.

Yes, it makes me wonder, too. And if a cleaning woman questioned it, why hadn't anyone else?

Marcia, one of the dark-haired young nurses from

the hospital wing, came up the hall, her jacket and purse slung over one arm. "Too bad, isn't it? Del was my Sunday school teacher in third grade. A really nice old guy."

Erin held the door open for her, as well, then fell in step with her. "What happened?"

Her brow furrowed. "Possibly his heart. The lab just drew a postmortem blood sample to check his cardiac enzymes."

"Did anyone mention how Del was before this happened?"

"He was doing pretty well, I guess. The nurse had taken his vitals an hour ago—just before Reynolds went to talk to him, and his cardiac enzymes were normal earlier this afternoon. Reynolds said it can happen that way—everything looks okay, then suddenly there's an acute change. He wants an autopsy, but hasn't been able to reach the family yet."

"Was anyone with Del when he passed away?"

"When the nurse went in a few minutes ago, the poor guy was already gone."

Nausea rose in Erin's throat. "Reynolds…was the last one who saw him?"

"Yeah." Marcia frowned. "Why?"

"I…" Erin faltered, then recovered. "I guess that's a good thing, right? If there'd been any sign of trouble, a doctor would have caught it. So there was probably nothing anyone could do."

CHAPTER NINETEEN

"YOU WANTED TO SEE ME?" Grace strolled into Erin's office at noon the next day, dropped into a chair and fanned herself with a sheaf of memos. "This has been one chaotic morning—what with the local newspaper reporters stopping by and that pileup out on Highway 72."

Erin paced behind her desk, then went to shut the door. "I didn't realize Del was such a figure in local politics."

"He ran for the state senate twice, though that was in his younger days. I remember seeing him kissing babies and making speeches when I was a teenager."

"His grandson called the hospital a few minutes ago with a lot of questions."

"I saw him in the hospital wing this morning, picking up Del's personal effects. He talked to the nurses for a while and complimented the staff on Del's care, then he left."

Erin crossed the room and sat down at her desk. "Well, he must have had some second thoughts, because he's requested an autopsy. Apparently he and

Del had been up north just a week or so ago, and they fished from dawn to dusk each day. Del walked two miles after that, every evening."

"He was seventy-five, and a person of forty can have a heart attack, but it's still good to know." Grace gave a weary sigh. "Gives the family a sense of closure."

Or it could reveal something that shouldn't have happened. Erin rolled a pen between her fingertips as she studied the notepad in front of her.

Sharing her concerns with the wrong person could mean an increased risk that word would spread, yet there was simply too much to handle right now, and Grace, who emanated rock-solid values and tough work ethics, was the only person she knew well enough to trust.

She just had to hope that lifelong associations, friendships, and the woman's ingrained professional courtesy wouldn't cloud Grace's judgment.

"Once before, I mentioned my concern about the elderly patients who have died here over the past few months," Erin said, watching the older woman's expression carefully. "I could be entirely wrong. Then again, as someone new to this facility, it's possible that I might have the advantage of a fresh view." She nodded toward a pile of folders on the credenza along the wall. "Now there's another one."

"Some months we don't lose anyone. On a bad month, we might have five or even six. Accidents, cancer, heart disease, stroke…I could name off another seven or eight causes we see on a regular basis. This county's average resident is well above middle age now. It's going to get worse."

"But I think I'm seeing a pattern," Erin said quietly. "I've gone back through five years of records on one particular physician's admissions. Older, male, all DNR—except the one last night—so only he was coded. Two to four days in the hospital. Normal vitals recorded for their final twenty-four hours or so, and ready for discharge in the next day or two. Then they've suddenly passed away."

Grace shifted uneasily in her chair. "What about the autopsy results?"

"Few were done. The causes were generally listed as some variation of 'old age,' or based on the admission diagnosis...mostly pneumonia or heart failure."

"Which is still possible."

"Yes, it is. It's what I'm hoping for. But it's also easier to *cause* an elderly person's death, because one tends to accept that it will happen sooner or later."

Before, she'd clearly resisted the possibility, but now Grace swallowed hard. "You said this has been related to just one practice."

"I don't know for sure—that's why I need help from someone I can trust. I've pulled old admission records from Hadley's patients, but I haven't had time to start reviewing *everything* from the past."

"Hadley? This has to be a coincidence," Grace insisted, but her eyes filled with concern. "He's a fine doctor."

"And I would love to prove you right."

Grace hesitated for just a heartbeat. "What do you want me to do?"

"I want this review to be kept absolutely quiet, for now. I don't want to risk damaging the reputations of staff members or this hospital. If I'm wrong, unfounded rumors could be catastrophic."

"Understood."

"I've used old census records to find the names of patients who passed away here, and I've started going through their charts with a fine-tooth comb." Erin picked up a folder and handed it across the desk. "This is a list for you, and I have one for myself. If we can split up the load, maybe we can have some answers within the week."

"And...then what?"

"Depending on what we find, we may need to take the information to a private meeting with the hospital board."

The woman's shoulders sagged, and she looked as if she'd aged ten years in the past five minutes. She was thinking, no doubt, about what this could mean to her lifelong friends and co-workers here at the hospital.

Images of Connor filled Erin's thoughts as she met and held the older woman's gaze. "I don't want to hurt anyone, but we have to do what's right. It's the only thing we can do."

DREW SAT ON THE TOP STEP of the porch with his chin resting on his palms, staring down the driveway. Haley and the other kids were inside, playing Monopoly until Erin came home, but he didn't dare take a chance on leaving his post.

He's gonna come today, I'm sure of it. But the minutes ticked by with no sign of the floppy-eared pup bounding up the road. No sign of him out in the meadow or in the woods beyond…and it had been five long nights since Scout had disappeared.

Drew had hated this place at first—so far away from sidewalks for skateboarding, and the crowd of kids in his old neighborhood who hung around the playground after school.

Mom had never cared much if he and Tyler didn't come straight home. In fact, it was usually better not to, because you just never knew who'd be there with her. Some of those guys had a mean streak, and the sickly sweet, smoky haze in the apartment made him dizzy. Tyler sometimes threw up or started to wheeze, and they'd both have to go out on the fire escape with blankets, where Drew would tell Tyler stories to make him stop crying.

There'd never been the time or chance to make good friends back there, but here Scout had become his instant best buddy. He'd slept at the foot of Drew's bed…though by morning, he was usually curled up on the pillow or nestled next to Drew's chest, all warm and soft.

Drew rubbed away the hot tears beneath his eyelids. *Stupid dog. Stupid, stupid dog.*

Seeing a flicker of motion through the trees, he launched himself to his feet—but then Dr. Reynolds's Tahoe appeared at the bend in the lane. Drew sank back to the step and fought the urge to cry.

By the time Reynolds pulled to a stop in front of the cabin and climbed out from behind the wheel, Drew had gritted his teeth and forced his I-don't-give-a-damn attitude back into place.

"Hey, there," Reynolds called out, an easy smile on his face. "What's up?"

Drew jerked a shoulder and ignored him.

"No sign of him?" The doctor dropped onto the top step next to Drew and rested his forearms on his knees. "There's still a chance, though. It's only been a few days."

"Yeah."

"I took Maisie and searched this area for him late Sunday night, Monday and yesterday. If he'd been killed outright, I think I would have found him by now."

Surprised, Drew turned to look at him. "You did that? For us?"

"I know Scout means a lot to all of you, Drew."

His flash of hope faded, and a hot tear escaped Drew's tightly squeezed eyes. "He could have been hurt bad by a wolf and escaped, then died someplace else."

"When a dog attacks, it tends to slash and nip.

Wolves are expert killers. They're powerful, fast, and take their prey down with a few well-placed bites. He wouldn't have gotten away. Like I said, I found no sign of him. Maybe you didn't hear wolves, after all."

"The guys at school say their dads were gonna go out and shoot the wolves on sight."

"That's against the law, because they're still on the threatened list. Once they're delisted, you could shoot them if they're attacking livestock or pets on private land, but you'd have to tell the authorities, and prove it was true."

Drew snorted in disgust. "Like that would work. No one would ever believe you, anyway. Me and Tyler—" He caught himself sharply and looked away, heat climbing up into his cheeks over what he'd nearly said.

Connor sat quietly next to him, his hands still loosely clasped. After a long silence, he leaned to the side and bumped his shoulder gently against Drew's. "Erin has never said a word, and I'm not asking. I just want to tell you, though, that I'd guess you've been through some tough times."

Drew flinched.

"And I also think you must be an incredibly strong kid to have braved whatever happened in the past. I just wish I could have made this one thing better for you, by being able to bring back your dog."

Strong and brave? Drew nearly swore in disgust over just how far wrong he was. Yet—the kindness in his voice felt good, like salve on a fresh burn. "Me, too."

"So, are you boys going to dress up for Halloween and go trick-or-treating? It's this Friday, isn't it?"

"That's *kid* stuff."

"And what are you, an old man? Why not have some fun?"

The whole idea seemed so foreign, so out of place in his world that Drew couldn't think of anything to say.

"Didn't Erin take you out on Halloween last year?"

He shook his head. "We weren't with her yet."

"And you didn't ever go trick-or-treating before that?" Connor slid an assessing glance at him. "I could sure see you as Predator. Or maybe an alien."

"I never did that crap. Go out on the street at night in my old neighborhood, and you're asking to die."

"That bad, huh? Sounds like where I lived during medical school. I saw a lot of my neighbors in the E.R. on Saturday nights."

Drew tried to never think about his own old home. About Mom, and old Miz Mendez down the hall, with her cane and wispy hair, and sugary sopapillas that were light as air. About the hot summer nights up on the roof, where the sharp smell of asphalt made his eyes burn, and music from a dozen bars down the street blared into a nightmare of sounds that could've belonged in a horror movie.

Where gunshots rang out and people screamed.

And safe places were far away from the people who should have loved you most.

He didn't even realize he was crying until Connor reached over, hung an arm around his shoulder and gave him a hug. "It's okay, kid. You're going to be all right."

Embarrassed, Drew swiped away his tears and lowered his head. And he would have pulled away, except…the weight of Connor's arm felt safe and warm, and he couldn't remember letting anyone come this close. Even Erin—because he'd been too afraid.

"I know you've had it tough, and that you've had to take care of your brother. He's one lucky little guy. If you ever want to talk, I'm here."

"Lucky?" Drew jerked away and hunched over, with his arms wrapped tightly around his middle, trying to hold back his sobs as an image of Mom's last boyfriend crawled into his mind.

"I sent our mom to prison, and she won't get out till we're both grown up. Tell me—how lucky is that?"

CONNOR STAYED ON THE porch steps until Erin arrived home from work, though Drew had long since gone inside the house and thundered up the stairs to his room.

She gave him an uncertain glance as she got out of her car, then strode up to the cabin with an over-flowing briefcase at her side. "Did you stop to see the kids? I'm sure they must be inside with Haley. They *should* be doing homework…though I wouldn't bet on it."

"I stopped to see you, actually, but ran into Drew first. I thought you should hear about it before you go inside."

Alarm flashed in her eyes as she faltered to a stop at the bottom of the steps. "Is he okay? Oh, no—did he find Scout dead somewhere?"

Connor reached out to steady her. "Not yet. God willing, that pup will still turn up."

She adjusted her grip on the briefcase and tilted her head. "Then what?"

"I was only making conversation. He was feeling down about Scout…and one thing led to another. He started crying, and said he'd sent his mother to prison. Then he raced into the house and I could hear him run upstairs from way out here."

"Oh." A hand at her throat, she leaned against the railing and let the briefcase drop.

"I didn't mean to upset him."

"He's never talked about his past with me. I've tried to give him his space, so when he feels the time is right he can tell me what he wants to share. But…I do know. The social workers told me when they were trying to dissuade Sam and me from adopting him."

"They didn't want to give him a chance at a good home?"

"They wanted us to be very sure, because they

didn't want to risk the adoption failing. They figured that at his age, with his attitude, most families wouldn't give him a shot...or they'd start trying to deal with his behavior, then want to send him back."

"He did send his mom to prison?"

"Yes. And if I had my choice, she and her boy-friend would have gotten fifty years instead of twenty-five. They were dealing. They had a meth lab in the *basement*. Do you know how volatile and dangerous those things are?"

"I have some idea. I worked in an E.R. for two years."

"His mother and the boyfriend were high most of the time, abusive when they weren't. Tyler was twenty pounds underweight for his height when I first got him. Drew tried to defend his brother no matter what—but then the boyfriend took...a special interest in Tyler."

Connor felt sick. He'd seen too much of that in E.R.s. In clinics. It never failed to make him wish he could find the perpetrator and throw him against a brick wall.

"I guess this guy wheedled. Threatened. Promised all sorts of harm if Tyler didn't cooperate. Their mother didn't do a thing, and that's when Drew loaded up a bag of drugs and paraphernalia, hauled it to school and gave it to the principal. After six months in foster care, the boys came to us."

"I'm so sorry."

She gave a small, sad smile. "The funny thing is,

I've tried so hard to let him know that I'm ready to listen anytime. That I want to help in any way I can. But instead, he told you."

She reached down and fumbled for her briefcase, and Connor reached for it, too, as it teetered on the edge of the step. Their fingers collided and sent it tumbling, its contents spilling across the grass.

She gasped and dropped to her knees to gather up the folders. "I'll get it—don't bother."

Courtesy made him lean over and capture those that had spread beyond her reach. "No problem…"

But then he blinked, focused on the name labels on the folders and the bright yellow stickers on the spines. He straightened slowly, his pulse pounding in his ears. "These are my patients—the ones I've admitted since I got here."

"Yes, well…"

He stared at her, disbelief warring with anger and a sense of loss. He'd trusted Stephanie, given her his heart. In turn she'd hidden away the only child he might ever have now—and had destroyed the other on a mountain road.

He'd fallen for Erin, more and more with each passing day, and she had so little belief in him—such a low opinion of him—that she was examining his patient records for possible *malpractice?*

"I would have thought that you might have had the courtesy to talk to me. That you would have enough faith to believe in me, just a little. Obviously, I've read far more into this relationship than

I should have." He gripped the folders, then carefully placed them on the pile in her arms. "Be my guest."

Then he headed out into the darkness for his truck.

CHAPTER TWENTY

ERIN STEPPED INTO the cabin, shut the door and leaned against it, her heart aching. *My God, what have I done?*

Her job demanded that she protect the hospital and its patients. Honor demanded that she follow through, without regard for her personal feelings. But never had she wanted to harm anyone with this quiet investigation. And never had she wanted to hurt Connor.

The look of betrayal in his eyes burned her soul. The thought of losing him was unbearable.

"Erin, is that you?" Haley wandered to the door from the living room, a European-history book in one hand and a half-eaten peanut butter sandwich in the other. "I was just thinking about starting something for supper, in case you were late."

Erin struggled to find her voice. "For once, I'm early. Thanks, though."

"No problem. Hey—you look really pale. Are you okay?"

"Just…tired. You said that your high school canceled classes for the next two days. If I needed you to stay later tomorrow night, could you?"

"Sure. Late as you want." The teenager grabbed her jacket and backpack. "Let's see...Lily is reading in her room. Drew isn't speaking to anyone—I saw him talking to Connor out on the porch for a while, then he stormed upstairs and slammed the door. Connor said he was upset about Scout, but I guess you two already talked about that before you came inside. And Tyler...I don't think he feels so good. He's just been slumped in that living room chair, staring at the TV. I took his temperature, but it was just under a hundred. I would have called you if it was any higher. Some lady called and didn't give her name, but said she would call again." Haley grinned. "Her number's on the caller ID, though, if you need it."

Erin couldn't help but smile at the girl's rapid-fire report. "You're the best, Haley. I think you need a raise."

After she left, Erin checked on Tyler, who did appear listless and pale. Then she threw together a quick supper, helped Tyler and Lily with their homework and tried to talk to Drew...to no avail.

By nine o'clock Tyler's temperature was up to 100.5. By ten, it had climbed to 101 despite a dose of children's Tylenol, and his breathing had grown labored, his eyes glassy.

Pneumonia...again? Her worry escalating, Erin dialed Jill's number and left a message with the answering service, then hovered by the phone for her return call. By the time it rang, Erin had everyone back in their jeans and sweatshirts, ready for a trip to the clinic.

"Let's just meet at the E.R.," Jill said. "Given his history, I'll need some chest X-rays and labs. It'll save time. And you might want to make overnight arrangements for the other two kids, in case we keep Tyler in and you want to stay with him."

Yesterday, Erin would have called Connor without hesitation. Now, remembering the hurt and anger on his face, she dialed Haley's number instead to ask if she could drop the kids off for a while. With two of her children on sleepovers, Mrs. Adams promptly offered a couple of spare beds if need be, and assured Erin that she and Haley would make sure the kids got to school on time in the morning.

In just over a half hour, Lily and a very disgruntled Drew were safely dropped off at the Adams house, and Tyler was on a gurney in the E.R., dressed in a hospital gown.

"That wasn't so bad, was it?" Jill nodded at the lab tech leaving the room, then rested a hand on Tyler's thin shoulder. "We should have the films and lab reports back soon, and then we'll see what's going on. I think," she added with a twinkle in her eyes, "that you just really like coming to see me."

He shook his head and gave her a weak smile. "Not here."

"Well, tiger, I'm guessing that we're maybe going

to keep you for a day or two. I'm hearing those darn old crackly pneumonia sounds in your lungs, and I know from your history that you've had this problem before. Right?"

He nodded glumly.

Jill straightened his gown. "Isn't fair, is it? I know you've had the vaccine, but you must have picked up another strain. Some kids are more susceptible than others, but you'll likely grow out of it, in time."

She clipped an oximeter over the end of his finger and read the screen, then bent over again to listen to his chest and back with her stethoscope. Smiling, she slid the side rails up on the gurney. "I think I'll order a nice room so we can keep an eye on you. Okay? Erin and I will be back in a minute." She motioned for a nurse to sit with him, then beckoned for Erin to follow her out to the nurses' station.

A few minutes later the reports arrived from the radiologist and the lab. Jill skimmed the documents, then handed them to Erin. "His oxygen sats are barely ninety, his temp has spiked to 103 and his white count tells me this is a bacterial infection. The films confirm that this is indeed pneumonia—involving both lower lobes."

Even given the years she'd spent in nursing before going back to school, Erin's throat tightened at Jill's words. "I was afraid of this."

ERIN STAYED BY TYLER'S bedside through the night, dozing fitfully, awakening every time he stirred or a nurse stepped in to check his vitals and IV line. His temperature rose during the night, then fell slightly. His breathing grew more labored by dawn. He picked at his breakfast and then rolled over, leaving everything untouched.

Erin rubbed his back and spoke softly to him as he dozed off. The overwhelming love she felt for him welled up in her chest until she could barely speak. "You made such a change in my life, sweetheart," she whispered, leaning down to brush a kiss against his cheek. "I love you so much."

At a soft knock on the door she turned and found Connor standing there, his eyes on Tyler and his brow furrowed. "Hi, buddy. Are you awake?"

Tyler mumbled something and rolled halfway over. His face brightened. "Dr. Reynolds!"

Ignoring Erin, Connor moved to the side of the bed and cast an experienced glance at the antibiotic and dextrose IV bags and rate of drip. Then he grinned down at the boy. "Looks like you're taking it easy today. I'll bet you just wanted a day out of school."

A faint smile played at the corners of Tyler's mouth. "Rather be home."

"You'll be there soon, I promise. Dr. Jill is taking really good care of you." Connor gave Erin a cursory glance. "I can keep him company for an hour if you want to go home for a shower and change of clothes. My appointments don't start until nine."

The offer was kind, the tone of his voice cold.

"You don't have to do that. I—"

"It's not for you."

"N-no. Of course not." She wavered, then grabbed her purse and gave Tyler's shoulder a quick squeeze. "I'll be back in an hour, no more. Thanks, Connor."

He didn't bother to say goodbye.

AFTER CHECKING IN WITH Jane and Haley, who said Drew and Lily were welcome to stay another night, Erin dashed home for a quick shower, clean clothes and her briefcase.

Throughout the day she alternated between her office—where she tried to catch up on her work for the day—and Tyler's bedside, though by evening he was feeling better and was less willing to have her hovering over him.

At eight o'clock, he announced that he wanted to watch a Harry Potter video, so she gave him a kiss and then settled into her office, where she began tackling a pile of mail and a deluge of e-mails.

At nine she went to spend a half hour with Tyler, then kissed him good-night and went back to her office and worked for another hour.

Each time her gaze landed on her briefcase, she sadly recalled Connor's words. *Obviously, I read far more into this relationship than I should have.*

Back in college, he'd seemed so hot, so distant and unattainable, that she'd barely dared to even dream about him. But now, she'd seen new and deeper sides to him. His gentleness with the children. His thoughtfulness.

How could she have imagined, even for a minute, that he would be capable of harming a patient? Yet after one anonymous phone call, she'd let her suspicions destroy her chances with the one man she'd ever truly wanted.

Restless, aching with regret, she fingered the stack of mail on her desk, then shoved it aside. The mail could wait. The e-mails. The copies of hospital patient records tucked in her briefcase.

"Some lady called," Haley had said. *"Her number's on caller ID."*

Patty?

Erin launched herself out of her chair and bent over her briefcase, pulling everything out and laying it on her desk. She retrieved her PDA at the bottom. She quickly called up her personal phone book and found Patty's number, then punched it into her cell phone and began to pace.

One ring…two…three…

Sighing with frustration, Erin left another message, then ended the connection and paced the room once more.

Patty could have called again and left a message on the answering machine back home. With any luck, a response from the *Green Bay Courier* could be waiting in the mailbox at the cabin, as well.

Erin called Tyler's nurse to explain that she had

to leave the hospital for an hour or so, then she hurried out of her office. The administrative hallway was dark now, with just a dim Exit sign alight at the far end. Ahead, lights glowed in the lobby, and she could see Mrs. Banks on her knees tackling some sort of persistent spot on the floor, with her mop bucket at her side.

The old woman looked up at Erin's approach. *"Gum,"* she said with utter disgust. "Oughta be outlawed."

"I'll be back, and I'll be working late, in case anyone asks," Erin said. "It could be a long night."

Shivering in the frosty air, Erin made for her car, her resolve increasing with every step.

She knew how badly Connor had been hurt by the betrayal of the wife he'd loved, and she'd seen his reluctance to even begin to become involved again. Maybe there wasn't any hope that he would forgive her own lack of faith in him.

But if she could, she was going to make things right.

TYLER FLOPPED from one side to the other, trying to get comfortable. The bed was hard. The sheets got bunched up easily, and there was some sort of crackly stiff cover on the mattress that made him feel sweaty and hot.

The big clock up on the wall said almost eleven…and for the first time in two days, he was *hungry*.

The last nurse, though, had hurried through listening to his chest and getting him to brush his teeth, saying things were really busy down in the E.R.

Tyler eyed his IV pole and the tangle of plastic tubing looped over the T-bar at the top, then scooted up higher in bed and swung his legs around the railing. He hopped to the floor, grabbing on to the bed as a wave of dizziness sent spots dancing in front of his eyes.

There was a room down the hall somewhere. One where the nurses always went to get him pop and ice cream and little pudding cups during the day. And since they were busy…

He grabbed on to the cool metal IV pole and pushed it away from the bed. It caught on a chair leg and teetered, the plastic bags swinging at the top as the chair's wooden legs screeched against the floor. He held his breath. Listened for footsteps and the irritated voice of that nurse telling him to *get to bed, now.*

But no one came. And when he stepped out into the darkened hallway, it was empty, though from somewhere outside came the sound of distant sirens.

Reassured, he slowly trundled the awkward stand down the hall and peered at each room as he passed, trying to gauge which might hold the little kitchen. The rumble of the hard rubber wheels sounded like thunder in the total silence. His steps slowed and his heart quickened as he neared the nurses' station, half expecting a nurse to pop out from behind the desk like an angry jack-in-the-box.

He held his breath and peeked around the corner. The chairs were all empty. Grinning now, he turned to look across the hall. Two doors stood ajar, each with light beaming through the crack.

Tyler's stomach rumbled in anticipation as he eased closer and nudged the first door a little wider, and then wider yet. He could see the edge of a counter, cupboards... Grinning, he gave the door another little push. Then his spirits fell as he saw the rows of medical stuff lined up behind the glass cupboard doors.

The door swung wider. Like a creature from the movie he'd watched tonight, a figure whirled around with a loud screech, with gnarled hands and a wild look in its eyes. *Reaching* for him.

Tyler's heart jumped into his throat. With a scream, he grabbed the IV pole and raced for his room, tripping over its wide-set legs, getting tangled in the tubes, the pole swinging wildly overhead. Terror clenched his chest, making it hard to breathe.

The metal pole banged against the wall as he wrestled it into the room. He slammed his door. Frantically reached for the lock...but his fingers only caught the cold, curved handle.

His heart pounded out the seconds as one minute passed on the clock on the wall. Two minutes. Three.

Something rustled out in the hall. His door swung open. He stumbled backward against the bed frame, trapped and helpless, his terror rising.

But the face that appeared around the corner of the door wasn't that of the wild-eyed woman down the hall. It was the impatient nurse who'd hurried him through brushing his teeth.

"Well, young man! What are you doing out of bed?"

"I—I…"

"You know better than to be traipsing around your room. Just look at your tangled IV lines. Do you need to use the bathroom?"

When he shook his head, she reached for the IV stand to move it out of his way, then helped him into bed and rearranged his covers. She tucked the call light within reach. "If you need something, you press the button. Remember?"

Tyler swallowed hard. "A-are you the only nurse tonight?"

"Until eleven o'clock." She grabbed his wrist and took his pulse. Pulled the stethoscope from around her neck and listened to his chest, then checked his temperature. "And it's a busy night, so stay in bed. Promise?"

He wanted to ask about what he'd seen down the hall. But if she was this mad about him being out of bed in his room, she'd probably blow up if she knew where he'd gone. "Y-you'll be here, close by?"

She gave him an odd look. "Of course. Now go to sleep."

Fear crawled like spiders through his stomach as he stared at the door after she left. Last night, Erin had stayed on the fold-out bed in the corner of his room, but tonight she'd had to leave.

He'd never wanted to see anyone so much in his whole life.

Fighting back his tears, he slid deeper into the bed and pulled the covers over his head, praying that the witch in the storeroom wouldn't know where to find him.

ERIN CHECKED the answering machine—no new messages since she'd been home this morning—and riffled through the bundle of mail she'd brought in from the mailbox. Bills. Sales flyers. Magazines. A postcard from her aunt Tilly in Florida. More junk mail.

She tossed it all on the counter and started for the door, but an uneasy feeling swept through her as she touched the knob. Something made her turn back— a niggling feeling that she'd been missing a very important clue. Something just beneath the surface.

Frowning, she went back to the counter and picked up one of the folders she'd been working on before Tyler got sick.

She'd been looking at ways to cut labor hours in the various departments. One folder held printouts on all of the current employees, including their hire dates and number of hours they worked each pay period.

Another bulged with copies of census data and the biweekly schedules for each department over the past three months—a folder she'd picked up Monday in Human Resources, on the spur of the moment.

Why didn't I think of it sooner?

So far, there'd been little evidence to indicate any element of criminal intent in the deaths of men at the hospital. As Grace had pointed out, death was expected sooner or later in the elderly, especially those ill enough to be admitted. The few autopsies done had shown no sign of anything other than natural causes.

Yet a pattern was emerging, one independent of Dr. Hadley's presence. Seemingly random, yet…not.

Erin scooped up the folders and hurried to her car. The miles flew by on her way back to town as she considered and discarded a dozen different scenarios…until one fell into place. *A few hours. Just a few more hours, and I think I'll have it.*

On the way through town she stopped briefly at the Adams house to check on Lily and Drew, who'd already gone to bed, then she drove to the hospital.

She dropped off the files and her purse in her office and locked the door, then hurried over to the east wing to ask at the nurses' station about Tyler.

The nurse at the desk flipped through papers on a clipboard. "I just came on, but at report they were saying that he's stable. He still has crackles in both lower lobes, but his white count is going down. I was just in to see him a few minutes ago. He's been restless and he keeps asking about you."

Chagrined, Erin smiled at her. "Thanks so much. I'll go down and stay with him the rest of the night. My work will hold until tomorrow."

Long after the hallway lights were dimmed and the hospital noises faded to a soft hush, she fingered her cell phone and debated making a call so late at night. She finally went to the front entrance of the building, stepped outside and speed-dialed Connor's home number. After four interminable rings the answering machine kicked in.

"Connor—I need to talk to you, soon. Can you stop by and see me sometime tomorrow? I think I've got the answer."

CHAPTER TWENTY-ONE

THE NEXT MORNING, Erin left Tyler's room early and drove to the Adams house.

"I missed you!" Lily wrapped her arms around Erin's neck in a fierce hug. "This just isn't the *same*."

"I know, sweetheart. I'm guessing that Tyler will be gone one more night, and then we can all get back to normal." Erin hugged her back and stretched a hand out to Drew, but he stood apart at the edge of the porch, too far away to reach. "I came to drive you to school today, though. And this weekend we can all go out for pizza if Tyler is feeling well enough, or I'll get take-out pizza and rent a stack of movies. Deal?"

Lily's lower lip trembled. "Why can't we go home with you now?"

"You have Drew and Haley to be with, and her mom. But Tyler's been kind of scared of some of the nurses at the hospital during his first two nights, so I've needed to be there," Erin said gently.

Tyler's strange story about a witch in the hallway had been especially disturbing, but Lily didn't need to hear that. He'd been sure that he'd seen such a creature, yet the nurse had been adamant about not seeing anyone come down the hall dressed in a Halloween costume. She'd suggested that perhaps he'd hallucinated or had a vivid dream, given the powerful antibiotics he was receiving.

A possibility, but he'd seemed truly frightened, and had clung to Erin's hand even in his sleep.

Erin gave Lily an encouraging smile. "Tell me the *best* part about staying with Haley and her mom."

"That *Connor* came after school yesterday," Drew said. "He even stayed for supper."

Jane had mentioned that he'd stopped by, and she'd rhapsodized about what a nice, nice man he was. But Erin hadn't realized that he'd stayed so long. She tried to hide her surprise as she shepherded the kids to her car. "Really."

"He helped me with my homework, and watched TV with us for a while, and talked to Mrs. Adams," Lily added. "He's nice."

"I'm glad you like him, honey." Erin waited until they were buckled in, then slowly drove toward the school as her thoughts spun through what the future might bring.

Whatever hopes and dreams she might have had about Connor before, the cold glint in his eyes yesterday had made their relationship very clear. And now the years ahead stretched out like a minefield of awkward situations, because they would be forever bound together through Lily.

Erin's heart wrenched at the thought of seeing him with another woman and starting a family of his own. How on earth would she handle that?

She dredged up a smile. "Did he, um, say he'd come back to see you again soon?"

"He just said that we'd get to see him a lot, and he *promised*." At school, Lily hopped out of the car with her backpack, then stood at Erin's window. "Haley said the D…DN-something…is going to shoot some wolves, because people say they're killing dogs."

"That's the DNR—Department of Natural Resources, Lily."

Her face filled with sadness. "I miss Scout, but I don't want anyone shooting the wolves, either, do you?"

Erin reached out and cupped Lily's cheek with her hand. "No, honey, I don't like to think about shooting anything. Now, you have a good day, okay?"

Lily nodded somberly as she turned and started up the sidewalk to the door.

Drew slumped in the backseat and didn't move.

"Drew?" Erin eyed him in the rearview mirror. "Is something wrong?"

He scowled. "Nothing that matters."

"It does, if it upsets you. When we get home, you and I can have a good long talk—"

But he jerked on the handle, stepped out and slammed the door, following Lily into the building. And he never looked back.

DISHEARTENED, Erin sped through her morning shower and change of clothes at home, pausing in the kitchen just long enough to grab a piece of peanut butter toast.

She bumped the stack of yesterday's mail as she wiped the crumbs from the counter. The return address edge of a business envelope shifted from between the pages of a sales flyer. The *Green Bay Courier.* How had she missed seeing it last night?

With trembling fingers she ripped it open and spread the photocopies across the counter, then drew in a sharp breath. Three articles. Three small headlines that had probably appeared on inner pages of the paper.

Landers Death Investigated
Hospital Reviews Peterson Case
Local Hospital Cases Mount

She skimmed each story rapidly, then numbly sank into a kitchen chair and read every word. In all three articles, Dr. Connor Reynolds was listed as the physician in question.

She shook the envelope and shuffled through the pages for follow-up stories, but only the initial articles were included.

What had happened later? Had he been reprimanded? Charged? It wasn't possible. Surely the accusations had been proved false. Groaning in frustration, Erin stuffed the pages back into the envelope, grabbed her cell phone and tried Patty one more time.

A sleepy voice answered on the second ring. "'Lo?"

"Oh, Patty—I'm so glad I got you. This is Erin Lang, and I've been trying to reach you since Monday!"

The voice yawned. "Just got home…late last night. Flight delay. Whatsup?"

Erin gripped the phone tighter. "You still work as a nurse in Green Bay, right? At General?"

"Um…yeah. Part-time, anyway…" Her voice faded to a mumble.

"Patty! This is *important.* I work at a small-town hospital now, and I'm trying to follow up on a phone call I received. The caller said that a Dr. Connor Reynolds was repeatedly brought before the hospital review board while practicing there."

"That's true."

"And now I've been sent some newspaper articles on him—but they don't give the results. I'm calling the hospital and newspaper again today, but I really want to hear the inside story first."

Apparently that woke her up, because Patty snorted in obvious disgust. "Reynolds was never found guilty of any negligence. He was the victim of unrelenting harassment from the hospital review board. Case after case—reviewed, dismissed. The papers never picked up *that* part of the story."

"Why?"

"Guess it wasn't such intriguing news. Maybe it

hit some little two-inch column somewhere, but I never saw it. I always thought Reynolds should have sued for harassment."

"Did you work with him at all?"

Patty gave another deep yawn. "Sorry. I remember seeing him in the hallways a few times, and he seemed like a nice guy. A friend of mine works on the medical floor. She said the patients liked him a lot and that he seemed to be a very intelligent, caring man. The nurses all admired him because he treated them with respect."

"So why was he singled out, then?"

"Politics, I s'pose." Patty gave a short laugh. "I heard rumors that the chief of staff had it in for him. And the weird thing is, the guy left the hospital within *weeks* of Reynolds's moving away. We all wondered if maybe Ralston was quietly fired by the board for unprofessional conduct or something."

Shock slammed through Erin like a speeding train. "Ralston? *Victor* Ralston?"

"Yeah. You know him? Wait—" After a moment's pause, Patty came back on the line. "The baby's awake, and I've got to go. Let me know if you need anything else. Good to hear from you!"

Reeling numb, Erin stood at the kitchen counter as the enormity of the situation hit her.

The review committee had been headed up by the one man who should have given Connor the benefit of the doubt. Instead, he'd apparently used his power to avenge his daughter's death.

And for that injustice, Stephanie's father deserved to pay.

THE MOMENT ERIN UNLOCKED the door and stepped into her office at the hospital, the devastation blindsided her.

"Oh, my God," she whispered.

Cabinet drawers were pulled out, files and loose papers strewn on the floor. Books had been yanked from the shelves and thrown. Desk drawers hung askew. One window was open, its miniblinds rustling in the chilly, fitful breeze.

She swallowed hard as she flipped on the lights and scanned the room before stepping inside. Nauseated by the violation of her personal territory, she gingerly stepped through the mess to her desk.

The stack of patient charts on her desk was *gone*.

Erin spun around and searched the floor, the far corners of the room, the wastebasket. Not so much as a single folder was left. And her briefcase—tossed under her desk—had been emptied, as well.

She closed her eyes tightly to ward off the images of whoever may have done this. Of what might have happened if she'd been here last night when the perpetrator broke in.

Her fingers shaking, she dialed Security, then sank into her chair.

Joe Barker appeared at her door seconds later. She'd seen the security guard, burly, dark and in his

midforties, calmly sauntering through the parking
lots and down the halls at all hours of the day. His
unruffled demeanor faded as he walked in to stand
in the center of the room.

"When were you in here last?"

"Between ten and ten-thirty last night. I locked
the door like always. The window was closed. And
believe me, it didn't look like this."

"When you came in this morning, was the door
locked?"

"Yes…yes, it was."

"Maintenance and housekeeping would have a
key," Joe said. "Anyone else?"

Erin chewed her lower lip for a moment, considering all of the staff at the hospital—people she'd
met and wanted to trust. "I haven't given a copy to
anyone, and no one should have been in here last
night, anyway. I worked very late, and it isn't
cleaned on Tuesday and Thursday nights."

He knelt at the lock on the door and studied it
without touching anything, then he straightened.
"Do you have a list of what's missing?"

"I don't even know where to begin. My computer
and printer are here. My radio." She turned around
slowly, cataloging the wreckage, then peered into the
open top drawer of her desk without touching it. "I
think a digital camera is missing, and maybe some
cash. My Coach briefcase would have been worth a
lot to someone on eBay, but it was left behind. Unless they're hidden under all the rubble, I believe

some *documents* are gone, though. Patient files. Employee records and schedules. They have no monetary value, but given the federal laws on privacy, those missing medical files are extremely serious business." She leveled a weary look at him. "I want the police called."

He nodded curtly. "My thought exactly."

Erin moved to the window to close it against the cold—then caught herself, and used a piece of paper to shove it down. She leaned her forehead against the cold glass while Joe speed-dialed the local police department on his cell phone.

So much work…so much time. And now, every bit of the evidence she'd gathered was gone—and some of it was irreplaceable. At the rising sound of people gathering at her door, she turned and saw five or six administrative employees and nurses staring openmouthed at the destruction.

"Please—just go on back to work. It's nothing," she urged.

Madge, the office manager, bustled forward and shooed them all down the hall, then stepped in herself. "Do you need some help in here?"

Joe nodded. "The police will be here any minute. We'll need to know who worked last night, and who came in for first shift. They'll want to question anyone who might have seen or heard anything suspicious. Surely this couldn't have happened without quite a bit of noise."

"Got it." Madge walked in and gave Erin a quick

hug. "Don't worry, dear. We'll have this place back in shape in no time."

"It's not the mess. It's who would have done this, and why. It's as much vandalism as it is theft. Who could be so angry?"

Madge patted her arm. "The police do fingerprints. Right?"

"It only helps if they match prints on file."

Disconcerted, Madge faltered. "Well. I'm sure they'll figure it out."

She hurried back into the hallway. Minutes later a deputy rapped on the door and stepped inside. Tall, lean and sandy haired, he looked more like the boy next door than a man with a badge and a revolver, but he swiftly assessed the scene and then ushered Erin to one of the chairs. He wrote copious notes as she repeated everything she'd said to Joe.

"My biggest concern is the missing patient files. There were a good two-dozen closed files in here, and they're gone—along with a lot of employee records," she said in summary. "Given the risk of identity theft, plus privacy issues, I am very concerned."

The deputy looked at her, his pen poised above his report form. "Can you think of anyone who might have had an interest in these particular files? Who might have known they were in here?"

At a movement by the door, she looked over the man's shoulder and saw Connor standing in the doorway, his face etched with worry.

Remembering her phone message to him last night, she felt his gaze burn into hers. The air crackled between them. Expectant. Tense. As if the weight of the universe balanced on the next breath she took. His expression hardened, but she had no doubts about him—she knew in her heart he was innocent.

She turned back to the deputy. "I can think of *reasons* someone might want them, but no—I can't think of a single person who would have done it. No one at all."

But by the time she spoke the words, Connor had disappeared.

THE MORNING PASSED in a blur. Employees were called in and trooped past her office to the conference room, where they were questioned by the deputy. Another officer came in and dusted for prints, though she could tell from his expression that he figured it wouldn't come to much. Remembering some thefts from her garage back in Wausau that were never solved, she knew he was probably right.

By noon, most of the commotion was over, and Madge had helped Erin put the room back in order. "What else can I do for you, dear? You still look awfully pale."

The office looked neat as it ever had. The tabletops shone. The gray carpeting was spotless. There might never have been an intruder, except for the unease that crawled down Erin's spine whenever she glanced at the window that had been opened, or at the empty briefcase by the desk.

"I guess I'm all set," she said reluctantly. "I haven't had a break yet, so I think I'll go try to catch Jill while she's doing her noon rounds, and visit Tyler for a few minutes, then I'll get back to work. Just one thing—"

Madge laughed. "A week's vacation somewhere else?"

"Actually, a couple of things. I haven't heard how the final push for signatures is coming, have you? Today is the last day."

"They've got until 5:00 p.m. to file at the court-house. Last I heard, they still had volunteers can-vassing the outlying areas, with just a half-dozen signatures to go."

"Good." Erin bit her lower lip. "On another note, I want every lock in this building changed—starting with important areas. The pharmacy. The surgical departments. Every administrative office. Let Main-tenance know that these need to be done immedi-ately. Heaven knows how many copies of our current keys are floating around here."

"Got it."

"Also, I need more information now that those em-ployee records and shift schedules have disappeared. I want a hard copy of any such records from our com-puter files. A list of employee names, hire and fire dates, master scheduling forms, payroll records…any-thing."

Madge pursed her lips. "I'll see what I can find."

"Did the deputy say anything to you when he

left? He walked by a few minutes ago while I was on the phone."

"Just that he'd get back to us. He didn't look very enthused, though." She snorted in disgust. "He probably would have been more interested if there'd been a corpse on your floor. But files? Not high on his list."

The irony of her words sent an uneasy shiver down Erin's spine. If there'd been a series of randomly spaced murders within the hospital, those files might have held proof…evidence that would be much harder to gather a second time.

And if the perpetrator now knew of her interest in the case, he might have a chance to disappear.

TYLER GLUMLY WATCHED the Halloween cartoon special on TV, then rolled his head toward the IV stand next to his bed. Dr. Jill had said he could go home tomorrow morning.

Which was cool—except tonight was Halloween, and he'd been looking forward to the school party and the chance to go trick-or-treating for *weeks*.

When the other kids in school had talked about buying their costumes at Wal-Mart, he'd opened his big mouth and said he'd never ever had a real, store-bought costume. They'd looked at him as if he'd come from a different planet.

Every other kid in town was going from house to house right now, with their flashlights and big bags of candy, while he was lying in this stupid bed. Erin had brought him a big bag of treats, and Connor had stopped by with an orange stuffed cat plus a giant sugar cookie decorated like a pumpkin…but it wasn't the same.

Tyler looked up at the clock and watched the second hand tick, tick, tick slowly around the big white face. Erin had taken Drew and Lily out for pizza tonight, and he was pretty sure they were getting to go trick-or-treating for a while, though she hadn't exactly said.

And now it was a whole 'nother hour until she'd be back, because she had to go out to the cabin and check on the mail and phone messages there.

A nurse—the nice young one who giggled a lot—came bustling in the door with a small tray. "Almost time for lights-out, buddy."

She set the tray on his bedside table and quickly checked his lungs, temp and pulse. "Man, you are in great shape, kid. You'll be ready for the football team in no time."

"Everybody thinks Dr. Jill will let me go home tomorrow."

"Well, then I hope that everyone is right. She left orders for us to disconnect the IV at midnight, after your antibiotic. We'll leave a hep-lock in, so we can still give you an IV antibiotic in the morning, but you don't have to be connected to all this stuff in between time. Good deal?"

"*Yes!*" he said fervently, pumping his arm.

She laughed. "I'm leaving at eleven, so the next

nurse will be in to take care of it." She winked, turned off his lights and disappeared out into the hallway, leaving his door open a few inches. "Your mom called to say that she's been held up at home, and she'll be here by eleven or so. But try to fall asleep before then, okay? Tomorrow will be a big day."

Your mom. Tyler nestled down in the covers and wondered what Erin would think if he ever slipped up and called her that. He almost had, once, because it just seemed so right. She hugged him and said she loved him all the time, and she did all the nice things that moms did on TV. Things he'd only imagined, before coming to live with her.

He stared at the clock, trying to keep his eyes open so he could see her when she came. But his eyes felt *so* heavy, and the pillow so soft…

He drifted into the meadow, where Scout ran full speed after a ball and brought it back, time after time. And Connor was there, tipping his head back with that big laugh that made a guy feel good all over just to hear it.

The door squeaked.

He burrowed into his covers. Deeper into his dreams…but then he heard the sound again and he sat up eagerly. "Erin!"

But the shape was bent over and wide, and not like Erin's at all. The new nurse? The hair at the back of his neck prickled as the figure straightened a little and stared at him, then started across the room.

He fumbled for the call button clipped to his bed rail, but the clip released and sent it clattering to the floor.

"No need for that, boy," the figure whispered. "That little nurse is taking a break, and there's no one here but me."

CHAPTER TWENTY-TWO

EXHAUSTED, ERIN PULLED on a set of navy sweats, ran a comb through her hair and checked the small overnight case she'd packed for one more night at the hospital.

Following a long day at work, she'd taken Drew and Lily to supper, where at least a dozen people had come forward to congratulate her on the successful addition of the tax levy to the November ballot.

Afterward, Erin had ushered the kids around town for some trick-or-treating. Despite Drew's declaration that it was "kid stuff" and that he wouldn't do it, he'd finally consented to join Lily.

At the first house, he'd followed behind her and had stayed well away from the elderly couple standing on their porch with a basket of goodies. At the last second, he'd tentatively stepped forward. Erin chuckled to herself, remembering the boyish grin on his face as he'd finally allowed himself to have fun. After that, it had been all she could do to finally rein the two of them in and take them back to the Adams house.

The only sad part had been the fact that Tyler couldn't be with them. "Next year, buddy," she vowed as she took a last look around her kitchen.

Next year, maybe things would be easier all around. The kids would be settled in better by then. Tyler would be well. Whatever was going on at the hospital would be long-since solved—and that alone would be a tremendous relief.

Who would have had the motive to break into her office, and the means? Who but someone close enough to know the day-to-day operations. Her schedule. And who had a lot to hide…

And then everything fell into place.

The person who had zeroed in on her office last night had *known* Erin was hunting for evidence. And a person who knew the hospital that well would also know Tyler was a patient…a perfect victim for the ultimate revenge.

Erin started to dial the hospital. *After nine o'clock, the receptionist was gone and all calls were routed to the nurses' stations. If there was an accomplice…*

Ending the call, she dialed Connor as she raced for her car. *Please, please be there…*

"Erin." He answered on the second ring, his voice frosty.

"Please! Meet me at the hospital. I think Tyler's in trouble. Hurry!" She jerked her van into a fast three-point turn, then rocketed down the narrow lane to the highway. At the stop sign she squealed the vehicle into the turn and punched 911 with one eye on the road.

The cell phone flickered. Died. *No—not now!*

Flooring the accelerator, she flicked on the bright headlights and prayed that her premonition was wrong.

CONNOR SLAMMED ON HIS brakes at the E.R. entrance and rushed into the hospital building.

The lone ward clerk in the E.R. looked up at him in surprise. "There's been no admits down here," she said, her face filled with confusion. "What—"

He shook his head and kept going, around the corner and through the E.R. to the closed double doors leading into the hospital wing. The moment he stepped through the doors he saw Erin rushing down the hall from the other end.

He held up a hand as they met outside Tyler's door. He carefully, slowly pushed it open.

From a figure hunched next to the bed, hidden in the shadows, came an odd crooning sound. "You understand, don't you? It has to be…. She wasn't going to leave this alone. And people need to learn their lessons."

A high, keening sound rose from the bed. "No! Please…"

Connor signaled Erin with a sharp jerk of his chin and flew into the room at the trespasser, grasping her from behind and pulling her away. A small glass vial shattered against the tiles. A syringe rolled across the floor.

Erin flipped on the light switch as she raced inside, threw herself at Tyler's bed and shoved it to safety against the far wall.

She enfolded the child in a swift, hard embrace, then held him at arm's length, her heart battering against her ribs and her hands shaking. "Are you okay? Did she do anything to you?"

His eyes wide and frightened, his face ghost-white with shock, he stared toward the opposite corner of the room, where Connor had pinned the intruder against the wall.

The woman struggled hard for another moment, then turned limp in Connor's arms. And then she started chanting a singsong litany of words that no longer made any sense at all.

ERIN SAT IN THE LOBBY of the hospital with Tyler on her lap, firmly tucked in the shelter of her arms. She was unable to bear the thought of putting the sleeping child back in bed. *So close—another few minutes and it would have been too late. What would I have ever done without him?*

She dropped a kiss on his silky hair, her eyes on the detective who stood talking to Connor across the room.

Hospital staff members hovered at a distance as several deputies and a detective roamed the hospital wing. Two of them had long since taken Mrs. Banks into custody, though she would soon be transferred to a locked psych ward in Green Bay.

Connor shook the deputy's hand, then crossed the lobby and pulled up a chair next to Erin, his face grim. "Apparently she usually injected succinylcholine, a common paralytic drug found in most anesthesia work areas."

"But that wasn't mentioned in the autopsy reports."

"It metabolizes so quickly that it doesn't show up on postmortem labs. This time, because the surgical area and main pharmacy locks were changed, she couldn't get at her supply."

"H-how could she have managed it? They're supposed to use requisitions. Keep exact records on inventory!"

"Maybe a bottle turned up missing, maybe she altered records. I'm sure the police will be talking to the pharmacist here."

Erin held Tyler closer and shuddered. "H-how did she plan… What did she have…"

"She had a key for the unit refrigerator. She'd drawn up a dose of insulin over five times the lethal level, and was apparently planning to inject it into Tyler's IV line."

"A *child*. What sort of monster could think of harming a child? If we hadn't gotten here when we did…" Unable to form the words, Erin rested her cheek against Tyler's head and swallowed hard, willing her tears away.

Connor rested his large, warm hand on her shoulder. "The detective tried to talk to her, but she was pretty incoherent. She was quoting biblical passages and rattling off something about the devil's voice in her head, telling her that Hadley was evil and she needed to wreak revenge because he didn't save her husband."

"But Tyler…"

"The police think she knew you were closing in on her with your investigation. This might have been retaliation, or a warning. When they get her calmed down, they'll probably learn more."

"Thank you…for coming. For believing in me enough to make the trip here. If you hadn't arrived, I might not have been able to stop her. I owe you everything."

"No," he said slowly, rising to his feet and stepping away. "You don't owe me anything at all."

ERIN BROUGHT TYLER HOME Saturday morning. He slept most of the day, but by Sunday afternoon his color looked brighter. He had little to say about his ordeal, though he kept Erin in sight every waking moment.

The relief over his safe return home was immeasurable, but her emptiness grew when she saw Connor's Tahoe turn up the drive and pull to a stop in front of the cabin. He'd come to see Lily, no doubt, but Erin's traitorous heart tripped over itself the moment he got out of the vehicle.

From the front windows of the cabin, she watched him walk to the back of his SUV and pull out a good-size box, then carry it up onto the porch. The kids must have seen him, too, because all three rushed to the front door to let him in.

He looked over their heads at Erin. "I suppose I should have talked to you first, but things have been a little hectic over the past few days. I figured you wouldn't mind."

He held open the door. "Come on outside, everyone, I have someone I want you to see."

The box on the porch jiggled, then a familiar, furry face appeared over the upraised flaps.

"Scout!" Drew's joyous shout rang out as the younger two kids squealed and rushed forward, but Connor held them all back. "He's not quite ready to play yet. On Wednesday, some hikers found him a couple miles from here with quite a few lacerations and torn ligaments."

"So it *must* have been a wolf that hurt Scout." Drew's ear-to-ear smile dimmed, and his voice hardened. "I hope those DNR guys shoot every one of them."

"Actually, Scout's injuries aren't at all typical of a wolf, and the DNR found large *dog* prints where someone's Boston terrier disappeared. Now the county animal control officer is looking for a dog—or possibly a pack of them in the area."

"Will Scout be okay?" Tyler asked.

"He'd lost a lot of blood and was very weak, so the hikers took him to a vet in town. No one remembered seeing your advertisements, though. I happened to call yesterday, and discovered that he was there."

Erin looked at him in surprise. "*Happened* to call?"

He cleared his throat. "Well...now and then I've been checking the local vet offices, just in case Scout showed up."

Knowing Connor, he'd probably been calling all of them every day, and scouring the countryside for the puppy in his spare time.

Lily rushed up to Connor and gave him a hug around the waist. "Thank you!"

He ran his fingers across her blond hair, then dropped his hands to her shoulders and hugged her back, his eyes troubled and a muscle ticking at the side of his jaw. "I'm just glad to see you happy, Lily." He raised his head and met Erin's gaze. "That's all I want for you."

Erin stilled. *All?*

"We need to talk, Erin," he said in a low voice.

Tension coiled inside her, tighter with every word he spoke. She closed her eyes briefly, not wanting to face what was coming next, then forced herself to stand taller. "Of course. Now?"

"Maybe right after work tomorrow, while the kids are with Haley."

A night to dwell on what he might say. "I'd rather get this over with, if you don't mind. The kids will be fine here if you want to walk over to the stream. It would be a little more private there."

He nodded curtly.

She walked beside him across the meadow, at a loss for anything to say until they reached the bank of the creek. She dusted off her favorite smooth rock and sat. "I—I'm sorry. For everything."

"Sorry? You were just doing your job." He leaned against a nearby maple, his thumbs jammed in his front pockets and one foot braced against the trunk.

"I…never should have doubted you. After I got an anonymous call about you, I worried even more about covering every base, making absolutely sure. I should have listened to my heart."

His gaze sharpened. "A *call?*"

"Looking back, I'm pretty sure it was Stephanie's dad. I've only seen him a couple times in my life, though, so I wouldn't recognize his voice."

"I figured there would be some repercussions after Wayne showed up in town." Connor tipped his head against the tree and looked up at the canopy of crimson-and-gold leaves overhead. "I'm not sure if he came to find me or it was accidental, but he blames me for some failings in his career, and he's never let it go. He probably slithered back to Green Bay, tracked Victor down at his golf club and told him where I was."

Erin shook her head slowly. "That's crazy."

"Yes, it is."

"You could get a lawyer and sue them both for defamation of character. You could have done that long ago."

"Until now, I didn't care. No one could make me feel more guilt than I already had, so I just walked away."

"And now?" Erin took a deep breath.

He swallowed hard, then pushed away from the tree and settled onto a boulder near her. "Now, Ed says he's on his way back to the States, and he wants an answer about the practice."

"You always did plan to move on," Erin whispered.

"There was no reason to stay, because nothing really mattered."

She felt a faint ember of hope. "And then?"

"I remembered how much I cared for you years ago, even when I had no right." A smile tipped up one corner of his mouth. "But then life got a little more complicated."

Erin's heart sank. "Lily."

"I barely know her, yet I love her so much. I want her to have everything she's ever missed." His voice dropped. "You gave my daughter a loving home, and that's a debt I can never repay."

So what you feel for me is just gratitude...nothing more. Overwhelmed by a sense of loss, Erin summoned up her brightest smile. "M-maybe we can work on shared custody, so we can both be part of her life."

His gaze burned her. "No, not that."

Afraid to speak, she watched emotions play across his face. Grief. Loneliness. Longing. No matter how much this hurt her, she knew he deserved more than a lifetime of sharing his only child. "Connor—"

"You think I care about you because of her, but that's not true. I love you, Erin. I just need to know if there's a chance that someday you could feel the same."

He brushed a kiss against her mouth, then angled in for a deeper kiss that made her shiver.

He finally pulled away, and she was able to catch her breath. "Forever, Connor. Always and forever."

Then he kissed her again.

SUDDENLY A PARENT

FAMILY AT LAST
by K.N. Casper

Harlequin Superromance #1292

Adoption is a life-altering commitment.
Especially when you're single. And your new
son doesn't speak your language. But when
Jarrod hires Soviet-born linguist Nina Lockhart
to teach Sasha English, he has no idea
how complicated his life is about to become.

*Available in August 2005
wherever Harlequin books are sold.*

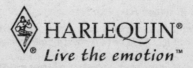

HARLEQUIN®
Live the emotion™

HARLEQUIN *Super*ROMANCE®

HOMETOWN
★ U.S.A. ★

Dear Cordelia
by Pamela Ford
Harlequin Superromance #1291

"Dear Cordelia" is Liza Dunnigan's ticket out
of the food section. If she can score an interview
with the reclusive columnist, she'll land an
investigative reporter job and change her boring,
predictable life. She just has to get past
Cordelia's publicist, Jack Graham, hiding
her true intentions to get what she needs.
But Jack is hiding something, too....

Available in August 2005
wherever Harlequin books are sold.

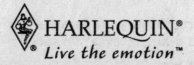

HARLEQUIN®
® *Live the emotion*™

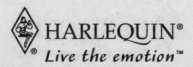